The Clares were a hell of a family. But who dispatched them to the Great Beyond?

Clovis Clare: He was The Family Disgrace, an insouciant Oxford dropout with ten part-time jobs, no money—and everything to gain as the sole heir to the family estate . . .

Easter Lennox: A journalist who tried to keep her distance, even in affairs of the heart, she suddenly found herself covering up for Clovis. Was he capable of murder? Was she?

Angie (Mrs. Lionel) Clare: The tarty, newly-minted widow was all too willing to bury her separation and collect her just desserts at Lionel's grave . . .

Dr. Edwin Clare: Pompous and spiteful, the neurologist shed no tears. But would he kill to possess the heirloom necklace he so clearly prized above his late son and ex-wife?

Mrs. Mallard: Edwin's stern housekeeper protected her beloved employer with devoted ferocity. But once betrayed, to what lengths would she go to seek revenge?

"The scene's set early with a nifty little murder. The writing's crisp and well-paced and the outcome is worth waiting for, but the real strength of this work is the Decidedly Odd characters. *GRAVE RESPONSIBILITY* is a fun read."
                                        —*Sunday News* (Manchester, NH)

Books by Susannah Stacey

Body of Opinion
Goodbye, Nanny Gray
Grave Responsibility
A Knife at the Opera

Published by POCKET BOOKS

GRAVE RESPONSIBILITY

A Superintendent Bone Mystery

SUSANNAH STACEY

POCKET BOOKS

New York   London   Toronto   Sydney   Tokyo   Singapore

Originally published in Great Britain by Barrie & Jenkins, Ltd.

POCKET BOOKS, a division of Simon & Schuster Inc. .
1230 Avenue of the Americas, New York, NY 10020

ISBN: 0-671-77827-7

First Pocket Books printing June 1992

10 9 8 7 6 5 4 3 2 1

POCKET and colophon are registered trademarks of
Simon & Schuster Inc.

Cover art by Mark Hess

Printed in the U.S.A.

To Brigid Brophy
with affection and admiration

GRAVE
RESPONSIBILITY

1

 *T*he white car sat in the carwash while the blue whirling dervishes advanced and spun against its sides in monster frenzy. The ritual over, the car emerged rinsed and shining into the weak sunlight.

The garage attendant was, in fact, off duty, for his relief sat already at the till. Complaining to himself in an undertone, he busied himself setting out the display of plastic chairs which the recent heavy shower had made him stack up. There was no call for him to do this, but he'd had a busy morning and he needed a grudge. He did not see the man bent to the white car's door, taking hold of the handle and looking in, but when the man ran into him the next moment he dropped a chair. The attendant had an impression of anorak and cloth cap. He cursed and was turning to shout at him when a loud noise made him swivel the other way and stare.

The car that had left the carwash had driven straight ahead into the low wall opposite the exit, and the driver's door, opening on the impact, had allowed the driver to fall half out of his seat onto the ground. The car, so immaculate on the outside, now needed cleaning on the inside; a bright red curtain seemed to be painted on the windscreen and more of the same red was collecting rapidly under the driver on the tarmac and spurting in a fountain of scarlet on the inside of the half-open door. The attendant stood without moving, and vomit rose in his throat. After a moment of time, while the fountain wavered, faltered and sank, the attendant broke into a run.

"Isn't Dr. Clare coming, Dr. Morrison? Is he away?"

"He's not here at the moment, Mrs. Paley. Dr. da Sintra is doing his round."

"Will he be back this afternoon? Is he ill?"

"I'm sorry; I can't say. I'm sure he'll be back soon." That sounded the wrong note; she felt stupid. "Dr. da Sintra will be here in a moment."

Michelle Morrison, house officer at the Austin Clinic, was finding it difficult to make the right answers. She pulled the trolley with the ward notes on it aside to let Dr. da Sintra pass, and began to trundle it in his wake. She hoped she wouldn't mix up the notes today or forget anything—exhaustion was becoming a habit. As to where Dr. Clare was, no one knew. His secretary had said, flinging her hair about, "I can't tell you so it's no use asking. All his appointments have had to be canceled. He's just gone off with his brother and he's not come back. I know nothing about it." If it was possible to flounce sitting down, she had done it.

Michelle had left her, wondering if he'd had a quarrel with the secretary—she'd made it plain enough they were going out together—or whether a big family row was going on. That might account for all that had happened lately. Dr. Clare never missed, he wasn't the kind to get sick. He despised illness and the patients knew it. Some of them were made nervous and some aggressive. When Mr. Grant, who was fighting a bitter rearguard action with leukemia, challenged Dr. Clare over his treatment a week ago, Michelle had actually felt her hands go clammy on the folder she was carrying. Dr. Clare had been patient—it was like standing next to a volcano holding its lid on. He smelt always of soap and aftershave and talc and his freshly laundered white coat.

Everything had to be specklessly clean for him and she often wondered what had brought him into a profession where he must deal with the degrading aspects of disease and death. He touched patients as little as possible. Dr. da Sintra actually patted hands. You could see Mrs. Merivale wasn't used to it.

She had nearly broken down this morning when Mr. Hackett's family had come in. The ward sister had handed over his spectacles, the dreadful little packet of his false teeth, his book. Dr. Clare had warned her to say very little, but that was very hard. She might be getting accustomed to the awful business of facing relatives at these times, but this was worse than the usual situation. She did not know how she could get through the day.

Where *on earth* could Dr. Clare have got to?

Easter Lennox, paying off her taxi in the mews, saw her own car near her door and knew Clovis was back, but she did not expect to see pants and socks hanging on a kitchen chair before the open oven. She surveyed them, one dark eyebrow raised, and called out, "Did Lionel throw you in a duckpond?"

A grunt answered her, the don't-bother-me absent grunt of someone interrupted. The living-room was lit by a happy ray of sunlight on a florist's wicker basket where orange flowers blazed, and on Clovis's very similar hair. He wore jeans and her cotton kimono, and had curled himself into a corner of the sofa. He did not look up from the hard-back marbled exercise book he was reading.

"I said, did your brother throw you in a duckpond?"

He raised his head. She thought *what's happened?* He gave his wide quick smile but it got nowhere near his eyes. "Hi, gorgeous."

"How'd you get wet?"

As she asked, she knew it for an error. Clovis was paranoid about questions; childhood hangup, for sure. He surprised her by replying.

"Rain. Caught in a cloudburst. I dried out your car. More or less. Used your hairdryer."

"Oh, *thanks*. I suppose Lionel was uptight as ever!" She went into her room to change, from black silk suit into black pants and loose black teeshirt. Clovis said vaguely, "Yeah, in one of his states."

So they'd quarrelled. She pushed her cloud of dark hair about a bit, decided it would do, and touched up with eye-pencil. She was complacent about her looks: an oval face, mouth small, eyes large, dark and emphasized, perhaps too much distance between eyes and mouth, a nose of character that saved her from prettiness and made her elegant. She was glad to have realized that in her teens.

Clovis's trainers were on the bathroom floor, wet. She picked them up, went to Clovis and dropped them on his lap.

"Slob."

"Oh. Sorry." The voice was still taut, abnormal. He put the shoes on the floor and went back to reading. Reading was, she knew by now, one of his escape routes.

"You said there were *dozens* of those notebooks, your mother's diaries!"

"I said there were a dozen. Or more. My mother picked this out, just the one. I'm understanding more about her."

The voice was pitched high. Lionel must really have put him through it—but how? They met rarely and Clovis never seemed that impressed with his brother.

"What are you understanding?" she hazarded.

"Why she walked out on us—perhaps."

Easter sat down by him. "You still mad at her?"

"No. I never was mad at her. Sore. Sore in the English sense like a sore place. Lionel and I grew up with it."

"If I was her, I'd be pleased to have you get in touch."

He considered this. "If she hadn't been, I don't think I'd have got inside the front door; and Kay would have made sure I didn't come again if she'd not liked my coming." He gave a sudden sharp sigh. "Families . . . Oh God. That Lionel could look so like her and be so different. He's . . ." Clovis fell silent.

Easter pushed her fingers through his hair, that was warm next his head, cool on the back of her hand. He said abruptly, "I've never been surprised she ran out on Dad. Can't stand the old prat myself." He turned his attention back to the manuscript book.

"I'm getting something to eat," she said, rising. "You?"

"No thanks." He was absorbed in reading.

She put the pizza in the microwave and sat at the counter with a portion of it. The tomato sauce bottle wouldn't open. After wrestling with it until her hands felt bruised, she called, "Hey, Rambo. Come and shoot the top off this for me."

Clovis came readily enough, took the bottle, tapped the cap on the counter, and twisted it off.

"My hero." She inverted the bottle and shook.

He perched beside her, took his mother's book from under his arm and found his place. Easter glanced at the small, convoluted but racing hand, wondering what a graphologist would make of it.

The bottle wasn't producing any sauce. "Damn tomato—" She put the cap half on and shook it furiously.

Gouts of sauce hit the glass front of the cabinet, spread out and ran down. Clovis looked up, shot from his place, pelted across the room retching and threw up in the bathroom.

Easter totally barred the role of ministering angel. Her mother had taken a lot of trouble finding the right nurses for her father, spent a lot of time reading to him, talking with him, but wouldn't do a snib more than brow-soothing herself, and Easter was right there with her. The sounds from the bathroom made her gag.

She ran a glass of water for him, mopped the sauce from the doors and the counter top and wondered. So it looked like blood? Had he been watching video nasties? Did he just have a thing, hitherto unsuspected, about blood?

He came back in, propped himself weakly on the sofa-back and said, "Sorry." He glanced at the clean doors of the cabinet.

"Water?" She hefted the glass and put it down.

"Mm-hm. In a minute."

She wanted to ask *What gave?* but that question might be too direct. Some time within the next six months he might explain. He came across now and took the water-glass. He was pale, but better. Then he froze. He was staring at a very small red splash on the manuscript page.

"I'll clean it," she said. "That's too bad. I'm sorry."

"No. I'll clean it." He took it from her and went to the sink, where he carefully cleaned the page with kitchen tissues. Then he emptied the water-glass and poured himself a double gin, added a meager dollop of juice, and drank. Then he sat at the counter and as she finished her pizza he told her in a bright voice, rather fast, a couple of anecdotes about his job last year as a tour courier.

What the hell had Lionel done to poor Clovis? Here was the most laid-back, insouciant man she'd ever met, a man she'd hitched up with because he took everything lightly, now twanging with nerves: throwing up; and making counterfeit of his usual manner.

Clovis leaned his arms along the counter and traced the marble swirls of the diary's cover with one forefinger.

"My mother hasn't said why she left, and Dad's always gone critical if she was mentioned. It's odd finding things . . . and I've found out about myself too. There's this house: Summerdown. My great-great-grandfather had it built. Then he left it to his son, who left it to my mother. She and Kay were in Italy, and they came back as soon as they heard that." He hugged his arms to himself. "Families. I don't understand families . . . I don't know why Father *let* her go. She—you've no idea how fantastic she is. She's so funny; makes things up

. . . and though she's not strong she's so full of life. No, God, that sounds like one of these bubbly twee characters, like someone always bouncing around. I wish you could meet her; but she doesn't like meeting people . . . When I talk to her, or Kay talks, she listens as if she were listening with all of her. Her hair's my color only paler. And she's pretty. Kay's very like her, but only the way a brother is; got the same round forehead; he's got the same *look* more than anything, a sort of happiness. He takes care of her. Once I asked something about Dad and she got up and went straight out of the room. Kay said *I ought to have warned you* and he ran after her. Actually I wonder if Dad hit her. He used to hit Lionel and me. I used to think I'd go deaf."

Easter thought: Clovis is deaf in one sense. He doesn't hear what he doesn't like. I'm suddenly getting a whole lot on Clovis that explains the way he is, and I wonder what triggered it off.

"Did Lionel get in touch with them too?"

"Lionel never wanted to know." He had tensed up all over again. He looked down and his voice was muffled. "He always was the good boy of the family. Dad very nearly approved of Lionel."

Since Clovis was opening up for the very first time in their acquaintance, she wanted to ask more, although a year had taught her that a direct personal question always cued a change of subject, a joke, or a smokescreen of fantasy. She knew she was risking that when she asked, "Did you know she was living in Italy?"

"When I was just a kid, must have been about nine, I asked Dad if she was dead. He said with all the usual parade—drawing himself up to his full height of four foot nine—"

"*Surely* he isn't—"

"—four foot ten then. He said, *She is dead to me!*" Clovis picked out the syllables with prissy emphasis. "It wasn't his fault that she hadn't died. Kay told me Dad drove her into a nervous breakdown. I gave her the second set of baby blues within two years and Dad was threatening her with a mental home if she didn't pull

7

herself together. He wouldn't let her keep the nurse because he said she must face up to things; the nurse was leaving at the end of the week, and Kay said to Miranda, *Come to Italy*. He'd lived there before. He told her Edwin would have to see that the babies were looked after; he'd have to keep the nurse on, and she was very good; but he himself only wanted to save Miranda's reason. He told me Dad refused to understand her; he behaved as if she'd never been orphaned, never been separated from the twin who was all she'd got and half her life; never been brought up by thick-skinned strangers who told her Kay was dead."

"Told her that her brother was dead? Why?"

"So she'd stop pining for him." Clovis had become absorbed in the story, and now he shivered, went back to moodily tracing the pattern on the book and said, "I have to go to Summerdown, to see her. Will you need your car again today? Can I borrow?"

"Hold your hands out. No, right out. Arms' length."

She looked at his hands and said, "I'm not lending you my car, buster. You'd better believe it. I've more sense of civic responsibility *and* I like the car. I'll drive you there. I've a whole heap of research material to get through and I'll sit in the car and read. I don't care how long. You have a tremor in those hands that could pile you up on the street furniture before you were out of town, and you just had a very respectable drink."

"But I'm . . ."

"Clovis. I don't *make* offers I don't mean."

He hesitated, then, "I do have to see Miranda. If you're sure—yes, okay, fine." He flung up shaky hands in surrender. "You're sure. I'm grateful."

From the garden, the house might have reminded someone of the palace of the Sleeping Beauty. Plants rose to peer through the windows, across one of the doors there was a strong lacing of bramble, every wall was under siege. Birds, as if aware they had more freedom here than elsewhere, racketed cheerfully in the branches of the many trees. A forest of saplings had grown up in what had been the back lawn, nettles flourished above old croquet hoops lost in the long grass. To the noise of the birds that afternoon was added another, a curious monotone wailing. It emanated from a figure that wandered through the garden, bent and striking his thighs with clenched fists at every step. Brought to a stop by an arch that had imprisoned itself in a knot of clematis he stood, still moaning, his hands gripping his shoulders. A blackbird, which had hopped ahead of him up the overgrown path, settled again to forage.

2

Inspector Locker came into Superintendent Robert Bone's office, his mouth pursed and his large form drawn in on itself as if he were cold.

"Ah, Steve. Not having a nice day."

"No, sir. Not very nice. This suicide over at Cransley service station. I just got to the Gents in time. Don't think I'll eat for a week."

"Sit down, Steve. Coffee or tea be any use?"

"No, thanks." Steve sagged in the chair, then pulled himself upright. "A Dr. Lionel Clare, when we could get at his identification. He worked at the Austin Clinic. But you'll get the report."

"Heave it off your chest, man." Bone thought Locker needed to talk. To an extent, putting words to things removed them from their immediacy.

"Well, sir, here's the Polaroids. They're not pretty."

Bone could not but agree that few people look their best with a half-severed neck. Lionel Clare's face, even in such circumstances, showed a refinement, a marble symmetry; Bone couldn't see this man as a riotous medical student. The light brown hair was clotted and the face splashed with blood that must have rained back on him.

"The whole of the inside of the car. Like a fountain

10

it'd been. Carotid artery, Dr. Addy said. He was the doctor we could get hold of. He said he hadn't seen anything like it since the War. The carotid artery and half the windpipe. Addy said, 'He knew what he was doing; the stroke avoided the larynx, and he used a lancet; he's most likely a doctor.' When we could get at his pockets we found he was. It was a shambles. Flies came for miles. The proprietor of the Cransley arrived and he wanted everything cleared *prestissimo,* he was losing business. There were some kids leaning out of a window next door that could see over the screens and we had to fix an awning. I told myself you don't join the Force for a quiet life, but I could've done with one a bit less rowdy right then. The car was the worst.

"We have an account by one of the attendants, name of Ron Dace. He was going off duty, just putting in time tidying the forecourt display—garden furniture—and a man ran into him, coming from the carwash exit. He shouted at him, then he heard the collision as the dead man's car hit the wall. So far, this runaway man doesn't seem to be of importance except as a witness; unless the labs and Dr. Foster tell us different, it's suicide all right. Addy said Dr. Clare seems to've killed himself just as his car came clear of the wash. It was in first gear and got carried on to hit the wall, which threw him forward, jerked the car door open and he toppled half out."

"This absconding witness: what did he do? Run off down the road?"

"Got in a car. Ron Dace heard it drive off but he didn't register at the time. Nor did another witness, traveler called Mitchell who was sitting in *his* car lighting a cigarette after filling up. He recalled having seen this small car parked rather crookedly by the street wall of the forecourt, but that was all. The running witness seems to be an oddity, nothing more. Of course he may link up later. Nobody got his car number, they were all focusing on the white Rover that'd hit the wall. But the man could have seen it happen. We're trying to trace him but there's not much to go on."

Locker had relaxed somewhat. He sat back in the chair and looked at the Super. When he'd first met him, the austere expression had daunted Locker. Now he scarcely noticed it. All that he saw now in the spare pale face he took for granted was the nasty scar on the forehead, partly concealed by the blond hair; souvenir of an attack during an arrest.

"I don't like this witness who runs off," Bone said. "You could do with finding him. What about motive for Dr. Clare's suicide? Suppose this person was important to that. Could he be a threat to him, for instance?"

"At the Austin Clinic, they're not up in his private life to any extent. He doesn't live with his wife. He's extremely meticulous and lately he's been harassed by overwork. He's too conscientious, Dr. Austin says—he has a room at the Clinic and was there last night, and he'd told the duty doctor, a Dr. Morrison, to wake him if this Mr. Hackett's condition changed; so she did that and he prescribed something; but the man died a few hours later, and it seems Dr. Clare took it particularly hard. Dr. Austin didn't see why, but Clare was particularly silent and tense about it. Then there's his secretary, who's weeping non-stop. She says Clare broke off their affair two days ago. Dr. Morrison and Dr. da Sintra, who's in charge of the other wing of the Clinic, say Clare hadn't been himself for three days now; da Sintra's contemptuous about the secretary—there was no 'affaire' he said, just a bit of how's-your-father, and Dr. Clare didn't seem to *like* her in the least. His brother was at the Clinic this morning by appointment. He may be able to give us a line."

"The brother's a patient?"

"I think not . . . Yes, it's the secretary says Clare had asked the brother to come. Clare was apparently clearing out his desk and winding things up; they found notes about all his patients. He meant to top himself all right. Though why he should clean his car first . . ."

"You say the Clinic staff emphasized how meticulous he was. For *meticulous* read *fussy*. A man who would scrub his coffin before getting in."

"To commit suicide." He stood up and was on the point of saying more when a knock sounded and WPC Donalds put her head round the door.

"Excuse me, sir. It's Mrs. Lionel Clare asking to see someone about her husband. Shall I take her to your room, Inspector?"

Any answer Locker might have made was rendered redundant by the abrupt appearance of Mrs. Lionel Clare herself. The policewoman was pushed aside by a harvest of plump plastic bags and, with something of the air of a pantomime fairy making an entrance, a woman posed herself in the doorway, free hand on out-thrust hip, surveying them and impervious to Donalds's protests.

She was more thin than slender, not quite as young as her tight, short red dress proclaimed; blond hair streaked with highlights, teased out in an aureole of frizz, gave the face a hint of the clown. She looked at them with eyes small, dark and shrewd. Her mouth was wide and matched the dress. Her legs, visible to the tops of the thighs, looked all the longer and thinner for black tights and high-heeled shoes. She had the air of a woman who, whatever clothes she had on, would at very little encouragement be prepared to take them off.

"Police! Have I a few questions to ask *you!* Just why is the first I hear about my husband being dead is over the phone from his secretary? I thought you were supposed to *call* with the news." She flung aside Donalds's hand on her arm, as the worried woman strove to get her out of the room, and advanced to stand before Locker while eyeing Bone across the desk as though fancying him more. Locker answered her, as Bone waved poor Donalds out.

"I'm sorry, Mrs. Clare, that the officers were unable to contact you. We sent them to the address in Dr. Clare's file at the Clinic."

"Well, I wasn't in, was I?" Bone supposed the police ought, in her scenario, to have toured the streets searching for her. He sustained her eyes' bodysearch with blank politeness. "I was out, shopping." She circled with the hand that held the clutch of plastic bags, purple and lime green and black, stamped with the names, in white and gold, of the shops where she had been distributing her custom. "—and then my card buzzes at Longley's and I'm stuck!" She put out her tongue, inviting them to sympathize with the cute child. "So I have to leave *mountains* of clothes I really need at the shop, and they have the nerve to keep my card as well. So I hurry out to a phone booth, thinking my dear husband'll have to deal with this—"

"Mrs. Clare. Excuse me, but aren't you separated from your husband? The Clinic—"

"Oh, that!" A wave banished such facts, and she sat down in the chair Locker had just vacated. "Lio and I were only taking a rest. He couldn't keep away from me." Again the tongue gave an exclamation point to this remark, and she dumped her purchases and made an elaborate pretense of stretching four inches of skirt where it wouldn't go, while looking at Bone to see how this affected him. Disappointed, she returned to the subject. "And then I hear he's dead! Ellie was in hysterics, silly cow, and saying the police were *swarming* all over the Clinic asking questions."

She rolled her eyes at Bone as if the police might have done far better had they swarmed over her. He reflected how singularly unmoved by this death she seemed to be, but he was also visited by the random thought that a reason for her husband's suicide was not far to seek.

"So now I'm here you'd better tell me. Did he drive his car at someone who hadn't cleaned their fingernails?"

Now might have been the time for Locker to have offered her the chair she had taken. Even this woman might be affected by the grotesque horror of her husband's death. Locker's voice became gravely official. "I'm sorry to have to tell you this, Mrs. Clare, but the circumstances point to suicide."

She stared at Locker, then at Bone as though expecting him to contradict.

"*Suicide?* Why?"

Bone at last spoke. "We hope you can help us there,

14

Mrs. Clare. Was he, do you know, worried about anything?''

"Lionel? Was there anything in the wide world he *wasn't* worried about? You couldn't do a *thing* he didn't get worked up about; but not enough to kill himself. I mean, more likely to kill someone else, he could get so rabid. It just made me laugh." She laughed now, at the memory, in pure amusement. "When he threw things at *me* I just threw them back. You can't put *me* down."

Bone supposed that if her former claim were true, and Lionel could indeed not keep away from her, it was an attraction on a level that he probably resented all the time—had very likely regretted the moment he married her if not before. Angie Clare did not strike him as a woman who would relinquish a man who could support her shopping habit. The anger she spoke of might well, at the last, have turned against himself.

"How did he do it? Ellie squawked something about 'found dead in his car.' Did he take pills? Was he driving?"

Locker pursed his mouth and clearly came to the decision that Angie Clare was no tender violet.

"He cut his throat, Mrs. Clare. In a service station."

She was, amazingly, speechless. It lasted for quite twelve seconds.

"God, how *grim*. Where? At a petrol pump or what?"

"In the carwash."

"That's Lionel. Everything spotless for him and only he was allowed to mess it up." She rose, shimmying her skirt down half an inch, and began to mass the plastic bags together. "I don't envy you that clean-up." If she saw anything in Locker's expression at this she ignored it, and went on: "Poor old Lio. He hadn't much of a chance with that family. Nutters, the lot of them. Father an absolute bastard, mother said to be completely round the twist, brother a no-hoper, Lio himself a sex-mad touch-me-not . . ."

"Have you this brother's address, Mrs. Clare?"

"No, and I shouldn't think even Lio had. A new job and a new pad every week. I mean." She shrugged, raised her eyebrows, stuck out her tongue and flourished her shopping. "I'm off to get a drink. After all that I really need one. Don't know how you can cope with not being supposed to drink at your work." She teetered skillfully to the door on her high heels, the dress enhancing every movement of her back, and paused to wave at them with her free hand, saying, "Let me know if there's anything I can do, right? If Lio's left me what he should have, I intend to be a *very* merry widow."

After the door closed, Locker sank into his chair and regarded Bone. There was silence for a bit.

"I should have got in some more questions, sir. She sort of took over."

Bone straightened the edges of the folders on his desk, a habit of his when chaos threatened. "I think, Steve, she told us quite a bit as it was."

"Unbelievable, isn't she, sir? Didn't seem to care in the least about the poor man. Found myself wishing she could've seen what I saw."

"Might not have made the slightest impression on such a heart of tin . . . Tell you what: she'd have found his wallet faster than you did."

Locker cracked an appalled laugh, choked it, and got to his feet again. "What I don't see is how Dr. Clare, if he was so fussy, went for a piece like that."

Bone adjusted the folders again, and thought. "Opposites attract? Each man hates the thing he loves? You and I, Steve, don't deal much with the rational in people. We come up against the animal under the skin. Or its results."

Locker made another face at the memory. He turned to go and then paused, asking diffidently, "You doing all right on your own, sir?"

"Oh yes. Mrs. Ames sees to the catering and the housework. I miss young Charlotte more than I thought I would but she's having a good time. She rang on Saturday; more to ask after her cat than after me."

"Surely she—"

"She knows I can look after myself; or Mrs. Ames

will. And I'm dining out as often as not. At Sam Pearsall's last night."

"From the look of Mr. Pearsall, the food should be good."

"Very good indeed."

It was tomorrow evening Bone was thinking of with warm anticipation: dinner with Grizel Shaw over at Adlingsden. It made a particular bright light in the week. At the moment, Charlotte's absence helped the situation, letting Grizel be a free agent, not so much a teacher at Charlotte's school, and Bone himself wasn't only a pupil's parent but something he hadn't felt himself to be for a long time, a free and interested male.

He had tracked down Cha's school photograph in her room, undone the scroll and found Grizel in the front row among the staff; and just like a detective he had looked at her through a lens. The face jumped out, thus magnified: the short blonde hair, brilliant eyes rayed with lashes, mouth amused. . . . Orthodox Arabs and Jews were right to refuse photography, he thought, for it looks so lively, that face, one could believe part of the soul was there.

On the drive to Summerdown, Easter had time for thought. What *was* it with Clovis? She liked achievers. She liked moneyed, capable men. Then, doing an article on escort agencies, she'd drawn Clovis: a man with ten part-time jobs and no money. He was flat-sitting and pet-minding for a friend holidaying in Barbados, driving a van for a flower shop, gardening, decorating. It wasn't only that he was conscientious about the dog-walking and was a competent escort. It wasn't only the charm. Clovis had, in his curious way, a strength: he had decided what he wanted to do, and what he would not do. He must have resisted pressure, and he had settled for a life with very little luxury and no complaint ever passed his lips. He could make small things fun. He accepted events, but she had found that she couldn't push him around. When Jeremy erupted from Barbados, claiming flat and dog, Easter had said Clovis could move in with her. He'd arrived with a holdall and a sleep-ingbag and impenetrable good nature.

They drove in comparative silence. He navigated for her, but for the most part sat tense, his face drawn. A crisis had occurred he was not about to tell her of.

They reached country lanes, narrow and meandering, that led to a scattered village, and on until a downhill turn brought them to brick pillars with no gate between them.

"Pull up right inside here. There isn't a way down to the house for a car."

She could see that. A growth of briars and saplings blocked the drive, pierced by a narrow footpath that disappeared downhill among them.

"Hand me the folder off the back seat."

Clovis put the folder beside her, gave a pathetic little half-smile, paused, caught her eye and didn't say *You're sure you don't mind?* or *Will you be all right?* He said, "I'll tell Miranda you're here. She might say I could come and get you."

"Okay. I won't hold my breath."

That made him grin. He set off. Once his footsteps had retreated, there was no sound but distant birds. The engine ticked. She listened to the quiet of the sleeping wood, picked up her folder and started work. She heard Clovis calling out, somewhere beyond the trees, and then a hammering, then silence.

She'd read half a page when footsteps came crashing up the path and Clovis appeared, his eyes huge with alarm, panting "Easter!" Infected by him, she swung herself out of the car before she thought.

"There's no answer. It's all locked and they don't answer."

"Couldn't they be out?"

"She doesn't *go* out, only in the garden. Something's wrong. Oh God."

"Would they answer if they were there?"

"Yes. They'd let me in. Oh God. Come down with me, Easter. Please."

"Sure I will." She locked the car and followed him

down the path, stepping over briars and roots, her booted feet snapping twigs and crunching last year's leaves. They came out in a wide and well-kept gravel courtyard in front of the house. She halted, awed.

"You didn't say it was a mansion."

All the windows were muffled with curtains or inner shutters. A stone porch in the center swallowed up Clovis and she heard, far off in the house, a bell jangle and jangle. She heard Clovis call, "Kay? It's Clovis." He came out, distraught. "I can see Kay's bike in the lobby. I went all round the gardens just now. He must be there." He backed away to look up at the house front. He was biting his lips.

She would have liked to make some placebo of a remark. He had to be over-reacting. Yet the house, there with its blank windows like closed eyes, kept her dumb.

He set off round the side of the house, and she followed. They passed a paved kitchen yard, round to the back where a patch of grass had been mown like a terrace before the long south face of the house. Gabled windows were curtained, the lower ones all shuttered. A square tower, with a wooden-railed balcony and a slated roof, rose in the angle with the kitchen wing.

"There's a window open," she said, pointing to one of the gables. Clovis said nothing, but ran at the garden porch; he climbed with frantic skill but could not surmount the overhang of the porch roof. After a few minutes he let himself down and dropped the last few feet to the grass. He tried the garden door again.

"Have to break in."

"You sure, Clovis? Maybe if we threw dirt at the windows?"

He tightened his mouth. "You don't know."

"Okay. Let's break in. Where's best?"

The conservatory's range of tall windows were not shuttered, only grilled up to eight feet or so. She and Clovis upended a garden bench against the wall and she steadied it for him to climb. He peered through the upper glass panes and pulled off a shoe to use as a hammer. It didn't break the glass. Easter found a good-sized ornamental rock on the edge of what had been a flower bed, and held it up to him.

The glass shattered, some of it falling outside at her feet, and Clovis hammered the rest out. It made small noises on the tiles inside. He got out of his denim jacket and laid it over the edge, and with caution climbed in. She watched him let himself down and come to the door. It was evidently locked as well as bolted, and he had to force the lock, prising it open with a long planting trowel. He was dirty and sweating when he let her in, and breathing hard, but he did not wait. He set off at a run among the tubs and the raised beds and garden chairs, and she ran after.

"Kay? Miranda?" His voice was shrill.

Once in the house itself they were in all but darkness. He turned along a passage into the hall, where gray light filtered from the front door. She saw an oak table with a great pottery bowl on it, and a carved chest with indistinguishable objects. Clovis knew what was there. He picked up a torch and flashed the light about. He said again, "Kay? Mother?" and his voice shook. She could smell damp, and pot-pourri; kerosene, and the old smoke of wood fires.

"Wait here." His torch went with him into the darkness at the back of the house. She listened to silence and found she was hyperventilating. Relaxing her neck and shoulders, making herself take easy breaths, she saw the torchlight come through a room near the porch. Clovis knew his way, and crossed the hall to look into rooms that side. All the time instinct made her skin crawl, and quickened her breathing.

The torch came toward her. Clovis took her hand. His was clammy. She all but said *You're scaring me*.

"Well. Upstairs, then."

"It really is impossible they should be outside some place?"

"Really impossible." He was drawing her after him toward the back of the hall and the stairs.

"Did you look to see if the bike had a flat? Suppose he had to go out on foot?"

"Miranda would have answered by now." His hand's grip, nervous, urgent, brought her hurrying up shallow treads, carpeted where she had almost expected derelict boards. He let go of her hand at the top, and went on toward the front of the house. She caught his muttering *Oh God Oh God Oh God*. She saw light, once the torch was gone, from a room to the left along a passage, and set off for it, reached the door and pushed it wider, and stopped.

Four tall thick white candles dazzled her. Those either side of the bedhead shone on the woman's red-gold hair spread out all around her head on the pillow. The other two burned on the chest at the bed-foot; their light caught the eyes of the man in the wing chair at the bedside but the eyes, opaque, gazed at nothing. His mouth had fallen open. There was a thick smell of candles and of blood. The man's shirt from ribs to belt was a terrible darkness, blackish red.

She had seen photographs and movies of horrors, and had been horrified. It wasn't like that. She was seized with the sick thought that the man would rise and advance toward her, or that a terrible voice would come from that gaping mouth.

Clovis came running. She turned, with some idea of preventing or warning him, but he was there, pushing in front of her. He stood, and began to tremble, making a small noise in his throat. She too felt cold. The smell nauseated her.

This was Clovis's mother. Easter took hold of him, a hand either side on his ribs. She could feel his heart thudding.

"Oh God." The tremor shook him.

"Let me get by you. I'll make sure." She could manage it; but he went in and it was she who followed. They found the man's hand laying on the woman's. His was rigid, hers soft and cold.

Clovis strode from her side, round the bed. He put the torch, still shining, down by the candle that side; he lifted the woman's arm and dragged the coverlet back.

He and Easter stared at the wreck of the flowered dress and its ripped stain from groin to waist. Slowly Clovis lowered the coverlet, laid it flat and put her arm carefully down.

"I'm sorry," he said—whispered. "Oh God, Miranda, I'm sorry."

3

He drew breath. "I suppose we have to do something, tell people, arrange a funeral. I don't know." His voice was higher than usual but toneless, a sleepwalker's.

"A doctor."

"*A doctor?*"

"In the States you can't have a funeral until the doctor signs for cause of death. I would think it's the same here." What, in the name of reason, could the cause be?

"Oh. I wish they could stay here, be buried in the garden. Not be pawed over by doctors . . ."

Once more she took his hand, the strong shape inert in hers. "Clovis. Two people don't just die. Not two people, this way."

"They were twins," he said, as if this were a valid reason. But at once he shook his head. "I know; but you see that she died and he couldn't stand it."

Easter agreed. She was reining her impatience, trying to go at his pace. She was unable to think. This dark house, these bizarre strangers, this awful discovery, were too much for thought.

The woman looked young, very young to be Clovis's mother. Lying on one's back smooths out the slack skin. Perhaps death does more. Easter didn't know. This was

23

the first she had seen. It was the man she could not look
at, because his eyes were open.

"Well," Clovis said, as if deciding; but he did nothing. He half-turned, the candle behind his head providing a red-gold aureole. "One ought to be able to say
goodbye. I mean, it's Kay, it's Miranda. It's so . . . Oh
God.I was so afraid . . ." Suddenly he pulled her toward
the door. "All right. All right. Let's start the infernal
machinery."

They had got downstairs before she stopped thinking
he meant the car.

He took the front door key off a hook, laid the torch
on the table, and wrestled a moment with the door lock.
In dreary silence they set off up the drive. She could
not find any words to say. Were there any you could
possibly say to someone at a time like this? How had
his mother died? And his uncle, who must have laid her
there and lit the candles, how had he died? What had
come upon the quiet pair of them, living here shut away,
alone, self-sufficient and, as Clovis had told her, happy
together? She thought: the pity of it.

They found a telephone where Clovis had remembered, at a crossroads in the scattered village; the phone
worked, which surprised Clovis.

"I don't know what I'm calling," he said. "Should
we knock at a door and see if there's a doctor in the
village?"

"I think you should dial Emergency," she said.

"But an ambulance is no good."

She was standing close to him in the booth. It seemed
the best thing to get an arm round him. "No. Honey,
look, it has to be the police."

He was silent and she could not see his expression.
At last he said in that colorless voice, "You call them."

They waited in silence, in the car by the phone booth,
and she spoke to the police who arrived; she drove back
to Summerdown. She and Clovis stopped at the head of
the stairs and she pointed to the bedroom door. The two
young uniformed men came back after a minute or two,
their businesslike official voices muted. Downstairs, one

stood in the porch writing in his notebook, the other was outside with his radio. Clovis and Easter sat on the club fender in front of the hall fireplace, side by side, each with an arm round the other. When the radio man came in, she caught the words, "Babes in the Wood," and, "The Inspector's going to love this."

Love it or not, Inspector Garron gave no sign. He was a big man with small eyes behind glasses, a fat nose spread over his face a bit as though someone had punched it, and a small mouth under a dark gray moustache. His skin too was grayish. With and after him came more men. Shutters were opened; someone called Prince was announced, but it turned out to be a brisk young woman with a fingerprint outfit. "Prints" rolled their fingers scientifically, reciting a formula about eliminating and identifying and the destruction of their prints as soon as this had been done. Clovis looked at her as if she were talking gibberish, and Easter doubted if he took anything in. Then Garron came downstairs and swept Clovis off into the billiard room. Easter was banished to a pleasant little study-library on the other side of the hall. She wondered why, until she heard the to-and-fro of official feet, the official voices.

Easter, marooned there, looked round for a bit at the books—classics, local history, a shelf of Westerns and romances whose covers dated them as products of the thirties—at the brown velvet curtains from ceiling to floor, at the papers on the desk. It was a room in which someone worked. She could not connect the woman on the bed with a picture of her bent over these papers, and supposed they must belong to the man, Clovis's uncle, Kay. There was a pair of demi-lune spectacles, the kind with a straight edge at the top you can peer over, lying on an open letter on the desk with thin gold arms upright like the legs of a dead insect. It was the objects people had found useful in life that had such pathos after their death.

A box file, with one folder open across it, lay there, the heading of the letters in it being the same as the one under the spectacles: Earl B. Whitewick, with addresses

in New York and Boston; the latest two had the typed
address of a London hotel as well: the Connaught, Car-
los Place. Easter, to stop herself thinking, read them.
The top letter on the file said that the writer understood
how his visit had come at a bad time, but that he hoped
he might prevail upon Kay yet to allow him the privilege
of access to the house. He would repeat that he had no
wish to photograph the owners. He would not dream of
requesting what was so clearly an imposition. His interest was solely in the photographing of his grandfather's
unique architectural work in the house, to complement
the original drawings.

Easter bent to see the letter on the blotter. Earl B.
Whitewick was finding it hard to see what Kay's objec-
tions could be. He would very much dislike to have to
state in his book that access had been refused. Kay
would certainly see that such a statement must be poor
publicity for himself and for his country—it was not in
the British tradition. Earl B. had experienced such hospi-
tality and helpfulness at every one of the other houses
his grandfather had constructed in Britain. Kay must
understand that Whitewick's *life's work* (twice under-
scored) was here concerned. It was the definitive book
on Philip Whitewick's life and achievement. He was
sure Kay must see . . .

But, thought Easter, you didn't know that Kay would
not see. Anyone who got in here would get in over—

She stopped and turned away. She was only trying to
avoid thinking of Clovis.

She was worried about him. He was in shock, he
hadn't even got as far as the defensive-jokes state. He'd
once hinted that he'd been in some sort of trouble with
the police. He would be in trouble now, as direct questions, his least favorite thing, were certain to be on the
agenda.

She saw now that one bookcase, full of imposing
leather book spines, was a fake. She teased at the edge
of it and tried to find how it opened; a particularly worn
book-back, when touched, made the door click and
open. Well, why not? she thought. Natural cussedness

was the reason her father had given for most of the things she had done as a child, and it was the best reason she knew for doing anything.

Gray daylight, seeping from some unshuttered window not visible from here, showed a passage carpeted in red and flanked with small mahogany chairs with tapestry seats. It must have been some house, in its prime, with servants hurrying along here in answer to bells, with everything from buckets of coals to plates of cucumber sandwiches. How had Clovis's mother and uncle fended for themselves in this great warren?

The first door off the corridor made her pause a moment before she turned its handle. She must really get rid of the absurd idea flitting about like a bat in her mind, that the other rooms in this strange house must also have bodies in them.

Here, the shutters had louvers that let in a modicum of light. She saw a great fireplace, brick with copper surround that gleamed softly. Who had cleaned it? Copper had to be polished and this had been. Although she hadn't reckoned Miranda on housework, for some reason, the whole place was reasonably well kept. Two settles faced one another in the inglenook's shadow, making a little room all on its own. She imagined the fire in that hearth lit, and sitting in one of those high-backed sofas; blissful. Easter was now not at all surprised that Clovis's relatives had holed up in this house. She stepped forward, turned cold and choked on a scream.

There were people in the inglenook, sitting looking at her.

She stood there, the loud galloping of her pulse in her ears making her deaf, staring to catch their first movement. Nothing moved. Her head cleared and her heart slowed its hammering as her eyes became accustomed to the dimness. The woman sitting there wore a black satin hat with an osprey plume above one eye pinned with a diamanté brooch. She smiled haughtily. The man opposite was in morning coat, his topper beside him, gazing at Easter with the same disdainful affront familiar from a thousand shop windows.

Dummy! Easter thought. So who's the dummy now? What on earth were they doing here, dressed like that, comfortably ensconced in the corner?

Easter's parents had been enthusiastic visitors to Britain, and on her only previous trip here, as a little girl, they had taken her to a weird country house—in Gloucestershire, yes—which the eccentric owner had turned into a museum, filling the attics with antique bicycles and one room with Japanese armor. This he had put on armatures, standing or sitting, silhouetted against the English country scene beyond the windows, hideous in their masked helmets. She had run, then, hearing her parents calling that the figures were not real. Perhaps Clovis's mother and uncle too had thought to turn their house into a museum.

They could hardly have looked to end up as chief exhibits.

She did not much want to stay here, and thought also that the police might soon be through with Clovis and come seeking her. She gave the couple in the inglenook a polite but placatory wave.

Architecture was one of Bone's interests, and he knew about Summerdown, one of Philip Whitewick's best. The owners had refused his architectural group's request to visit. Hearing the report of a discovery of bodies at the house, he was guiltily amused to find he thought of the opportunity first, the deceased second. Garron would not thank him for his presence, and the case offered probably no more than the death of two elderly recluses, very likely of natural causes. Hadn't they had a son killed in the War? They must be very ancient. He could remember hearing about them when he was still on the beat. Could it be the same couple?

He drove there in evening sunlight. There were cars already in the bay at the top of the drive, and WPC Donalds there told him there was no vehicular access. Bone, wondering at the jargon that became almost a normal way of expression in the Force, set off down the narrow footpath. Inside the gates, a small Renault and the ambulance were parked.

He heard Donalds announcing him on the radio, and could imagine George Garron's small eyes registering resignation when he was told: *Why doesn't the Super stay at his desk? Can't keep his nose out of our cases.*

You can have the case, Garron, he thought. I'm only here for the house.

Which was worth it. He'd seen a sketch of this façade, but in reality it was warmer, more endearing despite the closed curtains; it had not the look of an architect's design, but a house that had grown piece by piece into this comfortable whole. The brick, timber, tile were used in the local idiom, and its irregular form made it look quite organic.

Garron, burly and sleek, but not looking well, was in the hall to greet him. Evening sunlight filtered through from the back of the house, lying golden along the floors of half-glimpsed rooms.

"I'm not going to breathe down your neck, George. Just put me in the picture and I'll look around; observe."

Garron's face did not betray his feelings, far less did he snort or say, "In a pig's eye" or, "That'll be the day." His tone, however, did express reserve.

"Right, sir. The team's up in the bedroom now. It's possible she was killed in that right-hand room at the back—seems to be the lounge. Stains on the carpet."

"The report didn't say she'd been killed."

"The young woman that called in didn't say. We only found out when we got here. It's a weird set-up, I can tell you."

"Let's hear," Bone said.

"Deceased are Miranda and Kay Shelley, twin brother and sister, been living here between five and six years, it's a family house inherited from grandparents. Discovered by her son, who I'm talking to in the billiard room there, and his girlfriend waiting in the study."

"Carry on, then. I'll have a look upstairs."

The stairs led from the back of the hall, a nice reversal

Whitewick had devised. It meant that the stairs didn't dominate the hall as they did in most houses. The team were still photographing, clinical in their protective gear that kept their alien fibers and dust from the scene. A stranger with a doctor's bag was waiting on one of the little chairs in the passage outside.

"Mind you get the sword under the bed," a voice directed. Bone stood in the door and looked.

What was this, a lying-in-state? He was reminded of a Victorian picture he had seen when he was very small of—was it Ophelia lying drowned, her hair spread out on the water, or was it from the Morte d'Arthur, a woman lying in a boat . . . The woman on the bed had hair the color of marmalade, and it had been arranged carefully over the pillow and over her shoulders; her hands were folded on her breast and a white bedspread had been drawn down, back from her body. Her dress, nearly to her ankles, was of some flimsy stuff, sprigged with little rust-red flowers. The big stain up to the waist had dried and crimped; it too was rust-red at the edge.

The man, propped in the tall chair at the side of the bed, had red-brown hair, but there was visible gray in his. His face too had the clay pallor of the dead; the features carried the same elegance, straight-nosed, wide-mouthed, the lines of age showing more on his face because she lay back, the disguise of the years not showing. He wore dark trousers, and a white shirt on which the stain of red was far more shocking than on her dress.

Bone, startled, was aware of having to close his mouth as he watched. Murder came in all shapes and sizes. He had seen some odd things in his time, grotesque and disgusting, for that matter, but he had seen few things more bizarre and—yes, touching. There was dignity and respect in the curious tableau before him, no huddled horror here but death with proper rites paid to it, a couple tenderly united. There had been candles burning in tribute. In this house, it was singularly appropriate, a scene from another age.

"The candles hadn't been burning long." His eye had automatically compared their height with a new unlit one on the dressing table. A half-remembered rhyme teased him:

> Four candles round my bed,
> Four angels at my head . . .

"No, sir, we'll have to test how long they'd burnt."

An oil lamp stood also on the dressing table. "Had they no electricity here?"

"No, sir. We thought of getting the company to re-connect it for us to work, but the wiring may not be safe. We're getting hold of a generator if we can. I've got Polaroids here of how they were when they were found, sir. Do you want to . . . ?"

"Please." Bone took the colored squares. By flashlight that negated the candles, he saw that the man's hand was holding, or resting on, the woman's; that the bedspread had been laid over her up to the chest, hiding the wound. Bone looked through the other pictures: different angles, details. One hand had lain at her side, then, under her brother's.

Bone gave the photographs back.

Some renegade feeling made him regret the disruption of that quiet tragic scene. For the sake of justice this pair were now being taken from their rest, their bodies subjected to the post-mortem and the morgue.

The doctor was called in; soon the bodies were being carried away. Bone prowled the room, seeing the abandoned sword being lifted from under the bed, a piece of stiff folded paper too.

"Is that a note?"

"No, sir. Seems to be just paper."

The candles were taken down and bagged.

> Four angels round my bed,
> Two angels at my head,
> One to watch and one to pray
> And two to bear my soul away . . .

He hadn't got it right yet. And had the brother killed the sister, set up the scene in remorse, and then killed

himself? Her son downstairs—if her name was still
Shelley like her brother's, presumably the son was born
outside marriage—Bone was absorbed by these speculations as he came to the stairhead. A darkened room
opposite invited his interest; his hand automatically
found the useless light-switch. Thin shafts of sunlight
between curtains gave a faint illumination, and his eyes
adapted.

His breath stopped. The long room was full of people,
here in the dark, utterly silent and still. Sense of likeli-
hood deserted him for one long moment as he waited
for them to make a move.

None did. The common world reasserted itself. He
could even make out, on the edge of a sunset ray, the
impossible good looks of a shop-window display figure.

He made his way to the nearest window, his skin
tingling yet with shock, and lifted a curtain. There
were perhaps a dozen figures, sitting and standing, pop-
ulating the gallery as if some Gorgon had petrified a
company of guests. One woman wore a pleated chiffon
dress that might be a Fortuny, a velvet headband, a
marabou stole. A male figure wore the velvet flares
and madras cotton of hippiedom, his neighbor was
clad in tweeds.

He heard Garron giving directions downstairs. Quietly, Bone closed the curtain and left the room. George
could make his own discoveries. This was his case; far
be it from Bone to spoil his surprises for him.

What could be the purpose of these mannequins? Not
to startle visitors. The letter of polite rebuff which
Bone's architectural group had received made it clear
that they wanted no visitors. It was one for the books.
Did they have visitors, though? The son was here. What
relation were the dead couple to those old Shelleys?
The old lady had been an invalid, Bone remembered
hearing. If the old Shelleys' son had died during the
War then these, from the look of them, could be his
children.

As he went out onto the landing, the bodies were
being taken downstairs, anonymous in the long bags,

to be delivered to the pathologist: Ferdy Foster's work.

For the sake of justice, Bone thought, following them down—and noticing the wall paneling, the enameled tiles, the wallpaper that was no reproduction Morris— for justice we have to remove this pair from their chosen home, from the dignity of their lying in state to the indignities of the post-mortem.

Oh fine, he thought. All I was short of: sentimentality.

He heard from the man at the door that Garron and Sergeant Hooley were still interviewing the young man in the billiard room. Bone went through the door indicated and sat down without fuss on a chair just inside it. Garron had paused and looked round, then seeing that his Super meant only to be auditor, he continued. He bulked in one armchair by the billiard room's empty hearth, Hooley now sat down again behind the table. Here in the front of the house, light was beginning to go and they had lit an oil lamp on the small table beside the young man's chair.

He sat rigidly slumped there: a contradiction in terms, but he looked as though he had been hurled into the chair and was fighting some force of gravity that kept him there. His hands lay spread on the chintz-covered chair arms, his hair flamed in the lamplight.

He was Miranda Shelley's son without doubt. He resembled her in coloring—rather too much at the moment, being wax-pale.

"Your mother and your uncle got on well together, did they, living alone so long?"

"Yes." A straight stare, and the mouth shut again. His breathing was noticeable, the stare hostile.

"Were you Miss Shelley's only child?"

"A brother."

"Were is he?"

"Don't know."

"Did he come here often?"

"Never did." He sighed sharply, or rather, took an inward breath.

"What friends or acquaintances had they in this neighborhood?"

"I don't know that there were any. They said the Italians had been more sociable. Kay could have known local people. He went about. To shops and like that. He didn't say if he knew anyone."

"Did Miss Shelley not go out?"

"Not that I know of."

"Was she an invalid?"

"No."

"Why didn't she go out?"

"Didn't want to."

"Was she afraid to go out?"

"Afraid? Why should she be? I said she didn't want to. She chose not to. She felt like not going out."

"Had she other peculiarities?"

"She was no more *peculiar* than you are."

Garron allowed a pause that said *Oh yeah?* The young man's stare looked, by now, psychotic.

"And you said you'd been here how often?"

"Six or seven times."

"What was it you said made you suspicious this time . . . the silence, you said."

"That's what I said."

"Did you not expect silence and quiet here?"

"It's quiet but it's not silent. I expected them to call out. Or Kay would be in the garden, the kitchen garden."

"All right. Let's go back to yesterday morning. Where were you at that time?"

"You've got the address. That's where I was. I don't know what time I got up—I've no watch. Late, because Easter was working."

"Had she left the flat?"

"No, she was—she's a journo. Journalist. She was working on one of her pieces. Articles for magazines. I suppose I got some coffee. I went out to the shop about ten. Local flower shop, Florabundant, and I was delivering flowers. Went back to the mews around midday or so; Easter came in with groceries and we were together after that.''

"Did you go out?"

"Ate out. King's Head, I think. Usually it's the King's Head. We were out with a shifting crowd there, sort of friends, the crowd, till closing, then back to Easter's.''

"And this morning?"

"About the same. That's what generally happens. Stint with the flowers. Something to eat. Then we talked a bit and then we came down here.''

"Why did you come here today?"

"Wanted to introduce Easter." There was an indefinable change of tone. "I didn't tell her, though.''

"Miss Shelley had been married. Did Mr. Shelley never marry?"

"Unless he did while he was abroad alone; before he came back and traced her. He might not have chosen to tell me. He wasn't talkative." A shrug. "Sometimes he'd hardly speak all the time I was here.''

"Did he dislike you?"

"Dislike me? Why?" He rubbed his face suddenly, almost attacking it. "Of course he didn't dislike me. We were friends. Kay was a really good man.''

Could a really good man, Bone thought, nevertheless have a brainstorm? Attack the sister he'd lived with for years? Living with someone for years could be a formula for explosive. A sword . . . His mind went off on a rogue scenario. Family still provided the nation's greatest number of violent deaths. Miranda Shelley had had a husband, presumably this boy's father. What depths of family relationships were there here that could not yet be known?

Garron said, "Sergeant, I'll talk to the young lady," and Hooley got up to fetch her. To the young man, Garron went on, "We shall be likely to talk to you again when we know more, Mr. Clare.''

Clare? This morning's weird suicide was a Dr. Clare. The photographs Locker had taken of Dr. Clare superimposed themselves on the face of the young man who now came toward Bone, and matched.

Hooley came in and said in a low voice across the billiard table to Garron, "She's not there, sir."

Bone had risen. As Clare passed him he said, "What is your brother's name, Mr. Clare?"

He stopped. If he'd been a horse he'd have reared. He seemed to shudder. He gave a wild glance and said, "Lionel."

You said you don't know your brother's whereabouts." Bone had not the option of saying *He's on a slab at the morgue.* Clare was shivering, as if he anticipated the worst.

"No. No, I don't."

"I'm very sorry to have to tell you about him. He is dead."

Clare could not frame any words, but seemed to be asking a question, the natural one to which Bone gave the answer: "He took his own life, apparently. It happened this morning."

Garron had come close and was listening. He said to Hooley, "See if Jack can't rustle up any strong coffee." Bone put Clare onto one of the chairs, for he looked as if he might drop.

"I'm all right." His voice had ratted on him.

"Sit there a minute." Bone too sat down, his instinct being against standing over Clare like a vulture. The young man did not question the news, he appeared to be too shattered for doubts or further queries. After the discovery he had made upstairs so recently, this might well not have equal power. Bone thought too: *Connections? Is there any way these deaths are connected? Surely they are?* At this point the girl was ushered in.

She came straight to Clare. Bone had an impression of black leather and long legs, black hair crimped and wavy and ringleted, a dry scent, a fierce pale face.

"What the shit have they done to you?" The accent, not strongly, American.

"Nothing. Lionel's dead. This morning."

"This morning?" Her emphasis, Bone was interested to hear, was on the time, not the fact.

"After I saw him, he must have—oh God. I thought it was only his usual over-reacting."

"You saw him this morning?" Garron demanded.

"Yes. I forgot I had. All this," and he gestured vaguely at the ambient air, "all this. You know. He phoned up, said he had to see me. I went to the Clinic. The Austin Clinic, where he works. He was in one of his states."

For someone who didn't know where his brother was, knowing his place of work, where in fact he had a room and had lived for a good deal of his time, Clare was not doing very well on credibility. Bone now wondered if it was only by hindsight that he thought Clare had been lying to Garron. Was that all he had done?

"We'd better have an account of your visit to your brother, I'm afraid," Bone said. "Inspector Locker, who is dealing with the case, will want to talk to you."

Garron said to Hooley, "Transcript to Inspector Locker." Jack Bates came in apologetically with coffee—charming cups on a lacquer tray, with a tin of powdered milk.

While Clare was sipping coffee and giving a timetable of his visit to his brother, the girl held his free hand. Bone listened and watched. Coincidences of this sort he had seen before now. Of course lightning strikes twice, and more, where some steeple or tree offers it a path. Some people, and families, seemed to offer disaster the same temptation.

"—It's hard to take it in. Lionel—well, he upset me. He was in one of his states. Always makes me flippant. I thought that was all it was. And the whole thing was so embarrassing I didn't even want to think it had happened."

Bone said mildly, "Is that it, then? Or while we're at it is there any more you've deep-sixed?" Clare showed the whites of his eyes, in a sidelong glance, and said, "*What* more?" harshly.

"*Any* more."

Clare almost violently shook his head.

"Right, then," Bone said, "Inspector Garron will have a word with Miss—?"

"Easter Lennox," she said.

"Miss Lennox, and then you can go home."

"What's going to happen to my mother and Kay? I mean, about a funeral."

"In due time, Mr. Clare. The coroner will decide."

Clare stood up, steadying himself on the girl's arm. Bone felt pity. The young man was likeable. He was also a dubious quantity, with credibility somewhere in the minus numbers. He went out with Bates, troubled, biting his lip and turning to look at the girl.

Garron was holding his stomach Napoleonically. That ulcer must be on the rampage once more. Bone inwardly commended Garron's equable conduct of the enquiry when he must be in some pain. He would tell him so afterwards.

Garron checked how long she had known Clovis Clare: since October or maybe September last; that she had said he could stay at her flat when his own accommodation closed down on him.

"Clovis has his own room—sometimes." She had a smile between feline and demure: Vivien Leigh as Scarlett O'Hara.

"How did Mr. Clare react to the discovery this afternoon?"

"Why, shock. He couldn't speak or think straight. I went into the room to check for a pulse, but of course there was none. I hadn't thought there would be. I could feel rigor mortis in Mr. Shelley's wrist." She sighed. "You'd think he would have called the doctor or the police when his sister was attacked. She was attacked, wasn't she?"

"The killer may have got blood on his clothes."

She gazed limpidly at Garron. Bone could tell, and perhaps she already could, that Garron rated young Clovis's whole behavior as suspect.

"Do you think Clovis killed his mother?" she said with deliberate articulation, "and brought me along to see him 'discover' it? No, I don't think so. He was really horrified and sick. I do know him. He's in pieces."

"Was he quite normal earlier today?"

"First thing in the morning he was. Then he went to meet his brother and that upset him. I don't know what went on between them. We are not into life-stories."

"Inspector Locker will concern himself with that," Bone said. "He will want to ask his own questions later."

"When you came in here with him," Garron asked, "what exactly took place? What did you each do?"

"After we broke in?"

"I said, 'When you came in here with him,' which is what I meant." Garron's stomach-rat was at work.

She gave an account of Clovis's exploration, of his increasing alarm—"When we went upstairs he was frantic."

Garron mutely checked with Bone that he had nothing to ask for himself, and let her return to the study and her disintegrated boyfriend.

"Clare didn't apparently look for Miss Shelley in the lounge, where she actually seems to have died," Garron said, "so unless he knew she'd been carried upstairs . . ." He broke out, "That bleeding little liar could have done anything."

"Could have. So far, he lacks either motive or opportunity."

"It's up to Forensic, as usual," Garron concluded.

"What's your scenario so far, George?"

"Impulse killing then suicide; family quarrel and suicide; we'll collect all the letters and so on. A lot more'll

40

come to light then. No suicide note's appeared as yet, but, on the face of it, Kay Shelley killed himself."

"Seems to run in the family. You handled that devious lad very well, George; the more so as I can see you're getting gyp from your insides. Any more news from the medics?"

"Keep taking the tablets." Garron's gray face showed an unaccustomed and fleeting gratification at Bone's remark. "That sort, spineless little wets, no use when they're up against it. Middle class, too, or upper, with the poncy accent and his mother owning this great heap of a place." He looked at Bone. "There's your motive, all right. Clare hasn't a cent to call his own; working at odd jobs and sponging off his girlfriend: and a year or so ago he discovers his mother and uncle own this place."

"It's a motive, if they told him he'd inherit."

"But opportunity? His timetable will come in for a bit of scrutiny as soon as we get an a.t.d."

"How approximate a time of death are you looking at? He seems to have been either gainfully employed or with Miss Lennox."

"Seems," Garron said. Bone followed him into the hall and stood there listening to the collecting of papers, the dispatching of Clare and the Lennox girl to her home. He listened to the house as it began to settle back into silence. Garron came downstairs. His normally doughy face was mottled.

"The place is full of shop-window dummies!" he said, his indignation laced with shock. "It's not funny coming on a roomful of those in the dark. Bates might have told me."

"Must be eerie," Bone said.

"And we can't get hold of a generator. The main search will have to wait till tomorrow. We're taking all papers: files of letters, and there seem to be diaries. I don't know why those incompetents can't fix up a power line here for us, but I'm not having paraffin lamps all over the bleeding shop—set the place ablaze in no time."

Bone thought it significant that one of Garron's favorite words should be *bleeding*. "Don't give me any of your bleeding nonsense," was one of his phrases, one to which his stomach had too evidently not listened.

The police had used kitchen shelving as boards across the place where Clovis had broken in. They locked up and left the house. It reverted to silence, or to the quiet that old houses have which is never complete silence. Small creakings and settlings, the movement of cloth in a draught, sound always as if someone were about the place. Still figures stood, too, looking into the dark.

I have often wondered about ghosts at Summerdown. There was a time when I thought I was probably a ghost there myself. Granny used to tell Kay and me ghost stories. I liked them then when we were together but not when I remembered them after Grandad parted us. But I always liked the one, Granny said it was true, about a woman who had lovely dreams about a house right from when she was a girl and always woke up happy after wandering round the rooms and the garden. Granny told us the woman went on holiday with her husband in a part of the country neither of them knew and she suddenly made him stop the car in a lane and pointed over a hedge and said, "That's the house of my dreams!" She insisted on going up the path to knock on the door and the woman who opened it fell back with a hand to her mouth and said, "It's the ghost!"

Now I used to think, even if I never got to Summerdown again in the flesh, people would see me there and just say, "It's the ghost." I wouldn't bother them at all. In fact I don't suppose I'd see them because they wouldn't belong at Summerdown the way I do. I wondered if Granny saw me after we were sent away but if she said she did then I expect people thought she was potty. She was a bit potty before Grandad sent us away.

All the same, I've seen him again.

I thought it was Kay the first time. Going past the morning room window. He didn't move like Kay though he was far too quick as though he didn't want to be seen. And I knew it wasn't Kay. It was twilight and hard to see more than a shape but it looked like a man because it was tall but I think *it had long hair so it might have been a girl, a tall girl. I didn't tell Kay. Suppose it had been a thief or a squatter or someone up to no good, Kay might have gone out there after him and got hurt. He's not very strong. I was always stronger. I could easily kill someone if they got into the house and tried to harm it.*

This time he was in the kitchen courtyard. I'd gone to see if we had any coal left, Kay was working in the study and I didn't want to disturb him and I can certainly carry coal as he well knows and I thought we would have an inglenook fire, I didn't bother with a lamp, it was twilight again and dark inside the house but I know my way in my sleep. I was coming out of the first coal store when I saw him, he was running this time past the scullery window on the other side of the courtyard toward the steps leading to the door opposite the second larder. I watched to see what he would do, I found I was clunching my fists but he seemed to disappear.

Perhaps he is a ghost after all, and I don't mind that.

"I hate leaving the house to them," Clovis said, as they drove away from the police cars in the lane. "Wish we could have simply buried her and Kay in the grounds. Police, all over their house. Intruding where she never let anyone in. As if it mattered how it happened, as if how it happened was any use to any living soul. It did happen, that's what's so . . . that's what's worst of anything possible." He stared ahead at the road in the car's lights and Easter did not know what to say. She concentrated on driving. In the middle of Crawley he burst out, "I didn't know I could hate anyone so much."

If she hadn't been negotiating an unknown crossroads in closing-time traffic, she would have commented that the poor bloody police had their job to do, which was interfering.

"You know they were so happy. That's what I went

there for. Because they were happy. It made the whole place good.''

"If they hadn't been so happy he wouldn't have wanted to die when she did," Easter said.

"What do you believe? That they're together? Do you?"

He had turned toward her. She, who had been answering him only to comfort, surprised herself by thinking she did believe it, and said so.

"I don't believe in much," she said, "but that anyone goes out like a light, one minute there, the next nothing, I don't believe. How can the body be there, still, in that case? How can the spirit go out like a light when the body doesn't? How is consciousness worth so little that it's gone while the body still hangs around? It must still exist.'' Normally she avoided speculations of this kind, and would never voice them if she did, but what could you do when something so spectacularly terrible happened to a friend? She had to venture into metaphysics. "They must be somewhere together," she said, "like before they were born."

It might be he found something comfortable about this, as he fell silent, hunched in on himself, staring ahead but thoughtful. Overhanging trees ghosted past.

When they reached the flat, they did not want to go out for dinner as they generally did. She produced the sausages she had bought for tomorrow's breakfast.

"Seems a long time ago I bought these. I had to think back, was it so long that they wouldn't be okay still, and God! it was this morning. And what to have with them? Can of beans?''

"Not for me. Do we have any bread? Or a drink?''

"Gin do you?'' He was standing, hunched still as if withdrawing from contact with the world, and he turned and got out the gin from the cupboard only too eagerly in response to her invitation. He upended the bottle and took a swig. As he wiped the neck he grimaced, saying "*Eeugh*. Never tried that before. But I think drunk is what I'd like to be."

She put the sausages to grill. Clovis should eat something whether or not he wanted to. She was rendered dumb by the situation. There isn't small-talk for a man who has lost most of his family.

Clovis had brought glasses. He perched on a stool at the kitchen counter and poured drinks.

"D'you know a fairytale I used to have nightmares about? A girl who had to climb a glass mountain. There was this picture of a thing like Ayers Rock in glass. I used to be faced with this in my dreams and the feeling of absolute incapacity in the face of something I was compelled to do . . . but you can't ever convey the quality of badness in a bad dream. Nightmares are powered from the times before you could speak."

When your mother left you, Easter thought. You weren't a year old. I hadn't known that until you told the sergeant. A whole can of worms is opening up. But don't make me feel maternal about you. I'm not the type.

"Did she get up the mountain in the end?" she asked, turning the sausages.

"Yes. *She had diamonds on the soles of her shoes.*" He sang it, and kicked down from the stool, got out the cutlery, and freshened up his drink. She opened a pack of salt biscuits and fed him one, then another, and he opened his mouth with passive obedience. She stroked the backs of her fingers down his cheek.

Clovis got his arms round her and held hard. Responding, she tightened her arms round his ribcage and was shaken by the sudden tremor he gave, and felt his heart's seismic beating.

"Honey," she said. "Stop shivering. I'm sorry. It'll be better."

"I'm all right," he said into her hair. "Just hold me." She held him close, for the blood in his mind.

5

On the way to Edwin Clare's house in Pimlico, Bone found himself thinking about the effect of police work on the minds and bodies of those engaged in it. Here was Garron, carted off to hospital not an hour ago with his ulcer: an ulcer could happen to anyone in almost any walk of life, but Bone felt that Garron could not bring himself to digest the crimes he dealt with. Garron had ideals, felt people had an obligation to behave themselves. Easier, in the end, to be like Locker and comfortably swallow all that came your way, unsurprised even if occasionally disappointed by human mismanagement. Crime itself, after all, sprang from an inability to accept the terms of society. The criminal does not conform but, sometimes literally, strikes out for himself.

How was he himself affected by police work, physically? Smiling in the dusk in the back of the car, he put his hand to the scar on his forehead, still slightly tender to the touch, where his last arrest had made its mark. The car, which had been almost crawling along the street, stopped and the driver turned his head.

"Here's the house, sir."

"Stop along there where there's a space." No need to advertise to the world that the police were again visiting.

The tall thin houses were mostly gray, though one had

been painted a frivolous yellow, another strawberry pink, both colors softened in the summer twilight. The whole row glared disapprovingly at the strangers in the street. It was curious how the perfectly standard façades could assume an expression. It's subjective, Bone thought. I don't like the particular task ahead of me and I'm seeing it in these affronted houses.

Sergeant Hooley rang the bell.

The woman who opened the door had an air of even sharper disapproval than had the houses. Although fully dressed in a wine-colored suit and white blouse with an incongruous pussycat bow under her chin, she managed to give the impression that she had been interrupted on her way to bed, and that their presence at the door was an insufferable incursion into her routine. Her face, pale and thin, was high-nosed. She raised her chin at them in the manner of a shop-assistant too insolent to enquire their business in words. Bone showed his card and asked to speak to Dr. Edwin Clare. He was distinctly surprised to find the door closing in his face.

"Dr. Clare is not to be disturbed. The police have called once already today. There is absolutely no need for a further visit at this time of night. You may come again in the morning if you have any further enquiries."

Hooley foresightedly put his foot in the door, but before either she or Bone could speak, an impatient, precise voice called out from further back in the hall, "Who is that? What is going on? Who *is* that, Mrs. Mallard?"

Mrs. Mallard opened the door wide again and turned to the man who was approaching. Her expression had ludicrously changed; the dog that growls at strangers, or at least snaps, but fawns on the master. Her voice had altered from grit to glue.

"Oh, Dr. Clare! I'm afraid it's the police again. I've just explained that you've already told that Inspector all about what you know of poor Mr. Lionel."

"We're not here about your son, Dr. Clare." Bone held up his card again for the tall, thin man to examine. "I'm sorry, but I must see you. There is something we have to tell you."

Edwin Clare looked irritated rather than apprehensive. He had the face more of an academic than of the specialist Bone knew him to be. It was a face, lined and sensitive, with eyes of faded blue, that belonged in a university library, somewhere protected from the coarse intrusions of the world. Frowning, he gestured them in, Mrs. Mallard making heavy weather of crushing herself against the wall for them to enter. Bone felt that in passing her they had breached the first line of his defenses.

The room he led them into was evidently a study. A desk with papers and folders in tidy piles stood against the wall by the window, big tomes of leather-bound books weighed down the shelves above the desk; the walls themselves were papered in an oppressive dark gray as if to remind visitors that heavy thinking went on in here. Edwin Clare offered them two hardbacked chairs and himself took the swivel one at the desk. Mrs. Mallard had followed them in, and was standing by the door with a look of devout attention as though hoping to hear what news was to be imparted. Her employer waved a hand at her abruptly. "Yes, coffee, please, Mrs. Mallard."

Mrs. Mallard smiled forgivingly at him and withdrew. The door, Bone noticed, did not quite close after her. The room was small enough for him to extend an arm and give the door a push until he heard the lock click, before he addressed the man at the desk again.

"We are here about Miranda Shelley, Dr. Clare. I understand that you and she were at one time married."

"Oh, a long time ago. That's all over and done with, I'm happy to say."

Miranda Shelley was certainly over and done with, Bone thought. Her ex-husband might, or might not, be happy to hear that. At the moment he seemed to have no curiosity as to why she was mentioned. He waited, fiddling with a paperknife, and Bone decided to wait too, aware that Sergeant Hooley was glancing from one to the other, spectator of an invisible match. It was Edwin Clare who lost the first point by throwing down the paperknife.

"No, this is quite absurd. Coming all the way from Kent to pester me with questions like this." He had good eyesight, at least, to have spotted where Bone came from. What, though, did he think Bone's silence was asking him? "I told the sergeant who called this afternoon that I have no idea where she is. We have had no contact with her since she deserted us—her husband and children—thirty-odd years ago. If you want to get in touch with her about my son, though I cannot suppose she would have the slightest interest in the news, you will have to do your own detective work."

The swivel chair protested as he flung himself back. Bone revised his earlier impression of Edwin Clare as a retiring academic. If he belonged in a library, he was the one who, if anyone whispered, would scream "Silence!" at the top of an outraged voice.

"We know where she is, Dr. Clare." We know, in fact, Bone thought, that she is in the hands of Dr. Ferdinand Foster, the Home Office pathologist, but that is not something to blurt out to a man who presumably once loved her, however resentful his tone now.

"The last _I_ heard of her, she was living in some farmhouse in Italy. I fancy she won't want any communications from the police." Edwin Clare picked up the paperknife again and pointed it at Bone. "You have to understand that she _abandoned_ her children—infant children the elder barely one year old—and has never cared if they lived or died. To inform her about my son's death is quite superfluous."

"I'm afraid you don't understand why we are here, Dr. Clare. We have to inform you of your wife's—of Miranda Shelley's death."

Now he did look surprised; or was the little clatter of the paperknife falling on the desk a bit theatrical? The first suspect in a murder is a member of the family, and resentful ex-husbands are in no way disqualified.

"Miranda dead? I'd no idea she was ill."

He was scarcely, by his own admission, on terms that would allow him to receive such news. His expression was now of faint concern.

"The death occurred under suspicious circumstances. There is reason to believe that Miranda Shelley was murdered."

And if her ex-husband did it, he sure as hell hadn't lit any candles for her. Edwin Clare seemed partly indignant, partly titillated at the news. She had obviously had no business, connected with him however tenuously, to have got into anything so disreputable, but at the same time, Clare appeared to think it no more than a rather belated punishment for her behavior in general.

"Who did it? Has he been found? Why didn't that brother of hers protect her? This will certainly ruin *his* life." Edwin Clare spoke with such satisfaction that Bone felt the next piece of news would really make his day.

"Kay Shelley is also dead."

Real astonishment now, if Bone knew anything about it. The man was opening his mouth for another question, leaning forward in his eagerness for the answer, when the door opened and Mrs. Mallard came daintily in with a trolley on which was coffee and a plate of biscuits. Her timing was excellent, and it was too bad that she had not quite interrupted any conversation that would give her clues as to what was going on. In the awkward silence, she arranged the coffee cups with a little parade as if to point out the superiority of the china to anything the police could be used to.

Edwin Clare had let his question die on his lips at the interruption, but either he was too familiar with Mrs. Mallard's presence to continue his discretion, or too anxious to know more. He ignored the coffee cup held out to him and demanded, "Are they *both* murdered?"

The coffee cup jittered in its saucer, Mrs. Mallard uttered a faint shriek like a distant train, and breathed, "*Mur*dered?"

If it was her intention to register herself as emotionally incapable of leaving the room at this juncture, she succeeded. Sergeant Hooley sprang to her aid as she swayed above him and, practical man, saved the coffee before she spilt it. Once the coffee was in his hand she collapsed into his empty chair.

Edwin Clare paid no attention whatever to this little sideshow and repeated his question to Bone.

"*Both* murdered? Miranda *and* Kay?"

"Impossible to say at the moment, Dr. Clare. We have not had the forensic reports as yet." At his side, Mrs. Mallard was orchestrating her hyperventilation so that her gasps did not prevent her hearing every word.

"Horrible, quite horrible." Clare seemed suddenly conscious, perhaps from her example, that he should provide a suitable reaction; suited, that is, to the hypocritical expectations of society. A genuine reaction, betrayed only by a certain elation in the voice, might have him skipping about the room clicking his fingers. Bone was tantalized by the smell of coffee and wished he could help himself. Like Dr. Clare, he was bound by unspoken rules. Sergeant Hooley had the bright idea of plying Mrs. Mallard with the coffee she had nearly spilt; Bone hoped she would recover enough to pour the rest out. Meanwhile, as she prettily thanked Hooley, and sipped, and spread one well-tended but bony hand on the pussycat bow, there was work to be done.

"There are some questions, Dr. Clare, that we have to ask you."

"Oh of course, of course. I do not see that anything I know, or rather knew, of Miranda, could be of the slightest use, but I am perfectly willing to help." The extra bonus of his brother-in-law's death seemed to have put Edwin Clare into an expansive mood. There was a suppressed energy about him now.

"But I would like to put these questions to you in private. If Mrs. Mallard is feeling better?"

Mrs. Mallard bridled but, under Dr. Clare's professional eye, gave a spirited sketch of a woman forced into activity too soon for her health. Sergeant Hooley shut the door after her.

"You say you had not seen your wife since she left you."

"No." There was a fractional pause, and Clare produced a rather unreal smile. "Hardly likely to pop over to Italy for that."

A lot of emphasis was being put on Italy, surely? "Miss Shelley was not living in Italy. She had been living with her brother in the house inherited from their grandparents, Summerdown, in Kent. It was at Summerdown that they were found dead."

"Summerdown! Of course, she was mad about the place. So they got back there, did they? Soon after our marriage, she persuaded me to write to old Mr. Shelley and propose a visit, although she was bitter toward him for having—very sensibly in my opinion—sent the pair of them to different relations to be cared for. I was sorry to have taken the trouble, for I received a very curt letter saying that such a visit would be far too disturbing for his wife, who was in fragile health. Suffering from dementia, I expect. Certainly *his* letter disturbed *Miranda;* though it put her off any idea of going there. She was apt to talk as if her grandfather had sold her into slavery or something, rather than simply arranged for her to live with cousins who, after all, spoilt and made much of her."

Not for the first time that evening, Bone wondered why Miranda Shelley had married Edwin Clare. It couldn't have been for a sympathetic ear.

"Do you know of anyone who might have had a reason to harm your wife?"

"Not *my wife*. I thought it was perfectly clear that she was *not* my wife."

"Do you know, Dr. Clare, of anyone who might—"

"No no no no. I can't think of anyone in particular. But then, she was so impulsive; she could easily have turned anyone against her and thought nothing of it. Totally insensitive."

People who accuse others of being insensitive usually mean that their own interests have not been put first. Bone hoped, suddenly and with passion, that he had not been grossly insensitive toward his own wife. Their life together, though its dozen years now seemed brief to him, had been, he hoped, as harmonious in her view as in his. It was possible to be so ignorant of what another person was feeling, no matter how close you believed you were. *How did Grizel Shaw really see him?*

"And Kay Shelley," he heard himself saying, over the gap that had opened in his mind, "was he a man who had enemies?"

"I had no very kindly feelings toward him myself at one time, I may tell you. Extraordinary fellow. Turned up from nowhere and said nothing about where he'd been or what he'd been doing, and simply wouldn't answer questions. He and Miranda would chatter away to each other about their childhood for hours on end just as though I didn't exist. They were twins, you know, and egged each other on. Made up games together, talked a private language like a couple of children. Very unhealthy. Miranda was reasonably sane until he turned up. I'd always had her moods to cope with, and that absurd nostalgia of hers."

"When did he turn up?"

Dr. Clare had finally roused himself to his duties as host and was pouring and handing out cups, and the biscuits. Mrs. Mallard had brought a fourth cup, presumably in expectation of being asked to join them after all. She must have an ambiguous position, between servant and, almost, hostess.

"Oh, Kay arrived not long after we were married. It had taken him time to trace her, apparently. They'd been separated at the end of the War, when their parents were killed in an air raid, by one of the V.1's, and Kay was sent to Canada, I believe it was. They quite lost touch. It was done on purpose, evidently, and an excellent idea. They were bad for each other."

"Was that why they were separated?"

"No no no no. It was thought that if they had to be brought up apart, and no one was able to take both of them together at the time, then it was better to make a completely fresh start, without communication; very sensible."

Bone was all at once grateful not to be a patient of Dr. Clare's. He did not know what a neurologist did, but he could imagine him pronouncing some very sensible prognosis of imminent death and being offended if it were taken badly.

"In your opinion, was their relationship closer than that of brother and sister?" It had to be asked.

"Incest? I certainly wouldn't put it beyond them. They lived in each other's pockets, bed would have made little difference. But," and he leveled a biscuit at Bone, "I have no evidence of it. I saw nothing, during the couple of years when he was either staying in the house or a constant visitor, to suggest it. But from the moment he appeared, Miranda was lost to me. I see it now." He set down his coffee cup with an angry rattle. "We might have managed well enough without his arrival. I thought children would take her mind off him, make her grow up; but not a bit of it. She was completely incompetent. Became quite hysterical if she had to look after them alone, couldn't buckle down to being a mother at all. Used to cry perpetually and claim she was depressed. I told her it was perfectly normal after childbirth, but she was one of these people convinced that their suffering is unique. As for me, I had married a charming girl, a little fanciful and immature, but I could expect her to become a social asset and a helpmeet, and here she was—her behavior became so unbalanced after Clovis's birth that I did consider having her sectioned."

He said this with definite relish, as if it involved surgery and he was willing to take up the knife.

"It was then that she left with her brother. How he coped with her I can't imagine. He encouraged her in these fugues—flights from reality," he explained, impatiently recalling that he was talking to laymen. "Kay encouraged her. Of course, she was hardly over twenty, little more than a child, I see now; but she refused to grow up. Always absurd fantasies and jokes, always this unrealistic craving to go back to a place where she believed she had been happy."

Did he realize, Bone wondered, what he was saying? If he knew Miranda was not happy with him, his attempts to anchor her with the responsibility of children had a flavor of sadism. He pictured the woman he had seen on that bed, serene in spite of violent death, sitting weeping with all that red-gold hair flowing round her, her husband lecturing her, and two screaming babies in the background. No wonder she went away with the twin brother who shared her nature. Clare broke the back of a biscuit, ate half and brushed away crumbs from his trousers.

"You disliked Kay Shelley?"

"Disliked?" Edwin Clare shot Bone a glance almost vicious. "I hope you're not trying to fit me up as his murderer. Certainly I disliked him."

"And you haven't seen Miranda Shelley or had any communication with her since she left you?"

Dr. Clare hesitated, and flicked more crumbs away. "Oh, communication. I wrote her a letter or two, I suppose."

"When was that? Recently?"

Once again he was angry. "I cannot be expected to remember the exact dates of letters I write! I don't enter things like that in a diary."

No, thought Bone, but your wife kept a diary. Garron found her notebooks. Perhaps she entered "things like that" in it. We shall see.

"Within the last year? The last month?"

Dr. Clare picked up the coffee-pot, looked into it, and set it down. "Oh, well. I might have done."

His inability to be sure whether or not he had written a letter conjured up in Bone's mind the picture of a man sleep-writing; perhaps waking in astonishment as he put an envelope into a post box, gracious I've done it again. Bone finished his cool coffee, saying nothing, and his silence did as he meant it to do, drove Clare into adding something. Something fairly baffling.

"I wanted my necklace back."

The statement quivered with self-pity. Bone stared. A little girl, going to a party and asking for a treasured possession lent to another, could not have sounded more poignant.

"You wanted your necklace back."

"Miranda had it, and I needed it. She had no right to keep it after she left me. I wrote to her asking for it back."

"In Italy?"

Edwin's eyes flickered. "Well, no. I made a mistake about that just now. I did find that she had returned to England a short while ago. I wrote to her asking for it back."

Bone understood well enough that the less you appeared to know of the whereabouts of a murdered woman, the better. Yet he had not apparently known of her murder, either, before he was told. Had that slipped his memory too? Had he recently found her to be living in England, convenient to a long-husbanded anger?

"Could you explain a little more?"

Edwin gave up damaging the cover of a folder with the paperknife and burst into eloquence.

"It belonged to my great-grandmother. A beautiful piece. One of those really ornate pieces of Victorian jewelery—garnets, opals, gold filigree—and always handed down to the eldest son to give to his wife on her wedding day. Of course it should have come to Lionel to give to *his* wife when they married." He paused, as if reminded that this son was dead and his wife hardly the woman he would want to see decorated with this treasured necklace. Bone had a vision of Angie Clare wearing it and sticking her tongue out at her father-in-law; he'd have had even less luck getting it back from her than from Miranda: rather like asking a leech to return blood.

"Miranda loved it at once, she used to say that she was born in October and could wear opals without being unlucky." He paused, and Bone thought of Miranda lying in death. He must look at the list of what she had been wearing at the time; perhaps the luck of the opals had run out. Dr. Clare went on, "I didn't ask for it at the time she left. Indeed I did not believe that she intended to stay away. It was all so much of a shock." His voice quivered again as he remembered it. Bone reflected that being momentarily sorry for someone did not render them likeable.

"You want it now, in particular?" Evidently it had not been thought of when Lionel Clare married; or if thought of, despaired of. Bone had the happy idea that a marriage with Mrs. Mallard was in prospect.

"I am shortly to be married again," Edwin said, drawing himself up, and unaware of the effect of his reply on Bone's inward gravity. "Naturally I wish my wife to have my great-grandmother's necklace."

"Did you get it back?"

"I did *not.*" He stopped short at the beginning of what had promised to be an outburst and seemed to consider what he was going to say. "She did not reply. She never replied to *any* of my letters." The sleep-writing, Bone noted, had been quite vigorous. "And so that was that." He stared defiantly at Bone. "Now that she is dead I hope I shall get some justice from her estate."

This was a grand and mediaeval thought, but if Edwin believed Miranda's heirs and assigns would cough up an antique necklace of, apparently, some value, just because her ex-husband claimed it was his by divine right then he might, as they say, have another and less rosy think coming.

"Did you visit her at Summerdown?"

"Of course not." He seemed offended at the idea. "What was the point? She hadn't replied to my letters."

"But she might not have received them."

"You mean the wretched Kay might have kept them from her? I wouldn't put it past him, he'd do anything to annoy me." He was beginning to add something heated, but perhaps recollected that the man he spoke of was recently dead, and made an effort to moderate the bitterness of his tone. "No. I gave it up. For the present."

He stared at Bone as if with challenge and, given that if he had indeed visited Summerdown both the chief witnesses to any such visit were dead, it would be hard to prove. Bone wondered if Clare knew of his ex-wife's habit of keeping a diary.

"Then thank you, Dr. Clare. That will be all," he could not resist providing an echo, "for the present."

As Bone and Hooley, shown out by Dr. Clare, were standing on the step and the door was closing, a pair of narrow feet and a skirt could be seen hurrying down the stairs from the first floor. Mrs. Mallard arrived with a disappointed look. Was Dr. Clare marrying his house-keeper? Could the antique necklace be for her? She didn't look the sort, Bone reflected as he got into the waiting car, who would give up on a necklace easily.

Nor did she seem quite the mate that Edwin Clare would choose, though there was no accounting for such choices and she herself would be unlikely to see any incongruity in the idea. Why had Miranda Shelley married him, though?

Bone couldn't wait to read the diaries.

6

I've talked to Hooley and I've read it all," Locker said. "Looked at the pictures. It's about the strangest thing I've ever seen."

"As a family, they seem given to bizarrerie," Bone said. "How are you finding Garron's team? Co-operating?"

"Nothing that can't be ironed out. Hooley's all right. A good lad." Locker was sorting notes and photographs, settling into his chair. Bone leant back, ready to work, suppressing the guilty relief he felt at Garron's absence. A tricky case didn't need an antagonistic Inspector whose insides were screwing him up.

"Miranda Shelley," Locker said. "Fifty-two. Divorced. Killed by a sword-thrust upward through abdomen et cetera, stains on carpet in sitting-room suggest the murder took place there; sword had apparently been taken from wall there on pegs. Traces of oil from blade on deceased's clothing and wound. Officer's sword dating from 1911, sharp on both edges at the tip. Dr. Cecil Wadey, local GP—Kay Shelley's doctor—called to the scene on late afternoon of Wednesday the 27th, gave probable time of death as about twenty-four hours previously, from body temperature, absence of rigor and state of wound.

"Her brother Kay Shelley, fifty-two, marital status

59

unknown, died of wound apparently self-inflicted with same weapon. Folded stiff paper found on bedroom floor has his prints, and folding and abrasion consistent with its having been wrapped round blade and held firmly. Wound entering below ribs in upward direction pierced heart. Well, all that is straightforward, and it's not too odd that he should have carried her up to her bed and laid her there—"

"He or somebody else."

"Yes, sir. There is this third party. Haemostasis shows Shelley's body lay on a flat surface for some period after death, areas of congestion consistent with deceased having fallen, and traces of blood, lymph and saliva on bedroom carpet suggesting that was where he lay; but the body was discovered seated in a chair by the bed at some time before rigor set in. Dr. Wadey estimated Kay Shelley's death as taking place early on Wednesday morning."

He stopped and looked up because Bone had stirred.

"Go on." Bone had thought of Kay's hours alone in the house with his dead sister. Presumably alone, since the unknown person had only sat him in the chair and lit candles some hours later. He wondered what Shelley had done in that time.

"Candles on the scene had been burning for approximately two hours, but traces of wax on the holders show there could have been others before them, perhaps in normal use."

Locker took breath and gazed rather despondently at the report. He was leaning an arm along the desk, his heavy shoulders hunched. Raising his eyes to Bone, he went on. "So someone came in and arranged him in the chair. Someone sympathetic from the look of it." He tapped a photograph. "They put his hand on his sister's."

"Could be remorse," Bone said. "It still may be the killer."

"Or just fancifulness," Locker agreed. "There's marks of finger pressure on the candles and holders and on the silver matchbox on the dressing table there's wax smudges. Marks on the candles suggest fabric gloves and—'' Locker found a note—"used white cotton gloves were found in a kitchen drawer with other unworn pairs.''

"The white gloves," Bone said, "are a good touch. The person in gloves may be merely fastidious or, as a *remote* possibility, trying to avoid fingerprints, a process the public must be reasonably aware of by now. I find more interesting the fact that he or she knew where to find gloves. It suggests *un habitué de la maison.*''

"Well, I thought, you don't just go hunting around for gloves, on the off chance. 'Prints' tells me there are other random prints about the house but not recent and too dry. A servant might know where things are in the kitchen—the other things in the drawer were linen napkins and maids' aprons. But there hasn't been a servant there since the old Mr. Shelley died. I talked to the woman who used to come in from the village and she didn't know the half of what was in the place. She said she cleaned what she was told to clean and she left the rest alone. She confirmed where the sword hung, but she wasn't supposed to touch it—or anything else much. As it hung on the wall, it suggests an intruder, perhaps disturbed in prowling, snatching it down —an impulse killing.''

"What a family, though," Bone remarked. "What kind of man gets his car washed thoroughly on the outside and then kills himself inside? I know doctors are the most efficient suicides; they succeed more often than any other group in actually killing themselves, and they're among the highest stressed, and among males between twenty and sixty, suicide is the third commonest form of death. *Still,* Lionel Clare's death is a lulu, whatever its cause. And his uncle, though the cause seems clear, and the weapon was to hand . . . sitting there by his sister . . .''

"Who's going to put on white gloves and set up a sort of religious affair like that? Have we got a repentant murderer, sir? Or one with a twisted sense of humor?''

"There seems to be a party to this that we don't know. Forensic have still a lot of work to do—"

"On those gloves, for a start."

"—for a start; and as usual they don't know when in the foreseeable future they *can* start. Do you know one single solitary department that isn't understaffed?"

"Only thing we've too much of is the Press."

Bone glanced at the clock. "I've got nearly an hour before I have to go and shoot some platitudes at *them*. They at least aren't hampered by any doubts about the relationship between the Shelleys. All that gives them any caution in their way of expressing it is the healthy thought that young Clovis might sue."

"What sort of a name is that—Clovis?"

"I looked it up," said Bone, grinning. "A Merovingian king, away back in the mists of history. Also, hero of a novel called *The Chronicles of Clovis* by a bloke called Saki, earlier this century. From having met Edwin Clare, the father, I imagine it was Miranda who named the boys. How are we doing for suspects?"

"Family," Locker said.

"Naturally."

"Person unknown."

"There's a lot of them about."

A silence supervened.

"Let's look at Kay Shelley first," Bone said resolutely. "People living together on close terms, even the best of friends, have rows every so often." For a moment he saw Petra's flashing glare; she used to go very pale when she was angry. And he had shouted at her. It was unfair that death both took her beyond amends and made his anger somehow culpable. "Suppose Kay Shelley has a brainstorm and kills first her, then himself in remorse."

"That's one. Then there's Dr. Wadey's statement."

"That's a possibility, waiting for Ferdy Foster to pronounce on. How did it go? Kay Shelley consulted Wadey about Miranda."

"About various symptoms and signs, things his sister had mentioned or complained of and things he had noticed about her. He told Wadey she wouldn't visit a doctor. By that time she wasn't leaving the grounds at all, and was mostly living indoors. Wadey said he would make a house call, things being as they were, and Kay Shelley told him he would try to introduce the subject and get his sister to agree; but Shelley called later to tell him that she said if anything was wrong she would be taken to a hospital, which she was quite unable to bear. She wouldn't see Dr. Wadey. So they left it like that, with Wadey understanding that Kay Shelley would keep him informed. That was two months ago, on May 19th according to Wadey's diary. He told Garron that he suspected a mercy killing."

"The objection to this as a mercy killing," Bone said, "is that it wasn't merciful. For that reason alone I am inclined to count Kay out as the perpetrator; while we know what family rows can be, you and I and Tom, Dick and Harry, it doesn't mesh with Kay's general behavior to his sister as seen by Clovis."

"Or with the man the village knew, so far as house-to-house has got yet. He was quite well liked in the village. Only other thing the house-to-house brought up doesn't seem relevant: a man living rough. He was first seen about five or seven months before the Shelleys came back, according to whether you listen to Bill Pargeter, who keeps the hardware and general store, or to his wife, but either way it was thought he was living near Summerdown. Old Mr. Shelley was the grandfather of this pair, and he died of pneumonia—properly attested, nurses in attendance, doctor et cetera. This man was seen in the village now and then for about a year, and then, when the Shelley twins had been there for a bit, no one's sure how long, he wasn't seen about so often. He'd done laboring work; very willing but not bright and very shy, the publican said. He used to help him get the cellar stacked but he wouldn't help in the bar. Used to go around giving a hand on a couple of farms; did garden work. However, in the past year or so he's been seen very seldom, and no one can recall him being around in the last month or so."

"But he had been living rough near Summerdown."

"Yes. Local police say he always had an envelope with a fiver to keep him from being run in as having no visible means of support, he said. They thought him harmless. He was dressed in old clothes, sort of Oxfam stuff, but not ragged and mostly clean. He was quite liked, it seems. I can't work out he has any connection. Mrs. Brass in the Post Office—" Locker ran a finger down his notes—"she warned Mr. Kay about him since he was thought to be living near the house, but Mr. Kay said he'd never seen him . . . You know, this Kay Shelley's an odd character. And he didn't leave any note before he killed himself—if he did."

"Nor did his nephew Lionel Clare."

"Well, sir, my idea there is that he didn't intend to kill himself at the garage but later, maybe in his London flat, but this man who ran away may have triggered him off. He saw him as he came out of the carwash, say, and that did it."

Bone said, "I'll buy that. But why did no one see the car that drove away? Steve, is it just me or do you too find something risible about the term 'carwash' in this macabre context?"

"I got young Shay coming in and saying to me, 'Phone message just come in, bloke's topped himself in a carwash,' and I laughed." Steve rubbed his nose. "I pulled myself up, of course, but there it is."

"I am the pig Alexander, who was incurably frivolous. Let's concentrate on someone serious. Edwin Clare. He, like his son and so many of those we deal with, Stevo, has a way of usefully forgetting important facts until they are proved upon him."

"What did Mr.—no, he's doctor too, isn't he; what did Dr. Clare forget?"

"That he knew where his ex-wife was living."

"So. *He* trots over and kills her?"

"Suppose he found out she was in England again, back from their Tuscan farmhouse; and suppose he'd been brooding over her desertion and got himself into a state of murderous indignation . . . or it may be he wanted his necklace back."

Locker raised a gratifyingly bemused face. "He wanted—?"

"—his necklace back. A valuable Victorian family heirloom. Given to Miranda on their wedding and kept by her. As it is customarily given to the bride of the family, and as he is contemplating remarriage, he wanted it back."

"He kills her for the necklace?"

"Steve, people have been killed for fifteen pence. He's a self-important man. I don't see, looking at him now, why she married him: they appear to have nothing whatever in common. Though there's one thing he told me: when they were first married he tried to do her a real kindness by writing to her grandfather asking if she could visit Summerdown. The old gentleman refused, but the incident shows that Edwin Clare was willing to please her at that time."

"And desertion's hard to swallow. It could turn a man very bitter." Locker was reading the transcript of Hooley's notes. "Dr. Clare says he was never at Summerdown. That may be as truthful as his saying he didn't know she was living there."

"He'd be capable of the murder, I think. As I said, self-important, and capable of spite."

"Then there's Lionel Clare," said Locker wistfully. "I had it all worked out he'd done it and killed himself afterwards in consequence; but let alone lack of motive, when we worked out the time getting to Summerdown and back from the Clinic, he wasn't out of sight of anyone long enough. Night porter, house officer, they account for him."

"So far as family goes, then, we're left with Clovis. He does have a motive: no money and nowhere to live. So far as I can see, of course, he's happy enough living with his girlfriend and getting odd work here and there. Very likely he could have wangled his way into living at Summerdown with his mother if he'd tried, though. As to means, he could have got there in the girlfriend's car, which he borrows, or in a van belonging to the florists he works for; or the girl may have driven him there and be in it with him, because although he has an alibi for the relevant time, she is the witness to it.''

"According to George Garron, the Lennox girl could eat Clovis Clare for *hors d'oeuvres* any day. He reckons her a tough lady.''

"Hors d'oeuvres?'' Bone remembered Cha's words, the first sophisticated joke he had heard her make, which had therefore given an impression beyond its merits: whores' duvets.

"M'm, yes. And young Clovis is also someone likely to have tidied up afterwards. He's been to the house quite a few times, might know where the gloves were. He could be the one who did that part of it, certainly; and another point—at no time did he ask what had happened to his mother—how she died. That could mean he's too shocked to ask, couldn't bear to ask; or already knew.''

"What's he like? George didn't take to him.''

"You're going to have the pleasure of talking to him, Steve, this very morning. You'll find out then. For the present, there are these.'' Bone lifted a small pile of hardback exercise books in different sizes and colors. "Miranda Shelley's diaries.''

He picked one out and opened it.

"I've done a little work on it so far. She didn't keep any regular diary, just wrote when it occurred to her, it seems. There's one definite date: she started when she was fifteen. Her writing at that time was illegible. As time goes by, her writing stays illegible but grows progressively smaller. At least, I'm going on the premise that as she's steadily retreating from the world outside, her writing will retreat too. Her punctuation can't be relied on and she goes back and forward in time, remembering things as if they've just happened. The team's going to have a fine time on the photocopies working anything out.''

"I talked to Wadey about her health, like I said, sir. I asked about social services and why he didn't make more push to see her and insist on her getting treatment. He beat about the bush, but then he said it was a professional judgment for which he might be answerable, but he considered that the distress to the patient would have quite outweighed any chance of treatment's being effective. If she'd been taken from Summerdown it might very likely have affected her reason. He's seen emotionally damaged people who've reached a stable condition become severely depressed and regressing sharply if they're removed to hospital from an environment they know."

Bone thought of the tranquil face on the pillow, and of the watchful brother at her side.

"Someone interfered. And someone, Steve, the same or another, propped up Kay Shelley in the chair after he'd fallen, and someone lit the candles."

7

*This book I bought with some of my 15th birthday
money, it is my book and private and if THEY read it
THEY will know they are vile intruders and I never loved
them. I am talking to you, K, because it is the only way
I can since they tore us up. I know youre unhappy too.
And I did write to you the way we promised, I did I did,
but granpa did not send my letters on, he wrote to me
it was better to make a clean break and I shall never
write to him again and I cant love him as we did. No,
the break was dirty, dirty stinking and full of gangreen
and never stopping hurting, never never stopping.*

So, thought Bone, it may well have been for Edwin
Clare too, when she left him. And what of the children
who grew up rejected, with a series of nannies and
housekeepers and that embittered man? But what had
he done to her to make her do such a thing? Certainly,
she suffered.

*THEY said the most terrible thing of all. They came
to me both of them and said we think it is better for you
to be told that Kay is dead. They went on but I didnt
hear because I screamed and screamed. After that I
was ill. THEY didnt say any more about you being dead*

and I didnt ask them. Even then I felt I wouldn't give THEM the satisfaction. But it was also because I knew you werent dead. I would know if you were because there would be nowhere. Unless perhaps I am dead.

Bone shut the book. While it explained a good deal about Miranda, and why she had run away with Kay, and why they had returned to live their self-sufficient life at Summerdown, it did not tell him what he had to know. He put it by, to be read by the team, and he began to look at the other books to see what he could date as recent. He was troubled, as always, by the sense of intrusion in examining the belongings of the dead, in particular this with its vivid pain. He picked the smallest-written, most hieroglyphic, and set himself to read.

"That really is a helluva house," Easter said. "I didn't have any idea of it as that big. Your mother and uncle . . . I didn't picture you in that league, Clovis. I guess British—English—ways still have me confused. When did you first go there?"

Clovis did occasionally answer a direct question; or perhaps the police had got him in practice. "March it was, last year."

"You must've been amazed."

"Impressed. I was impressed. I hadn't known anything about where they were, but Dad was ill and I went to see *him*, I can be very filial, and Mrs. Mallard was being run off her feet, so I scooped up some letters that were for the post, and—you may say characteristically—I looked at the addresses and saw *Miss M Shelley, Summerdown*, and so on. I wrote to her, but no reply, so one time when I *had* time *and* the van I swanned off there. I thought hey-oop, this is great, this I could live in. Loved it right away." Clovis shoved himself off the sofa and folded down by Easter's feet, glass in hand. "When I arrived, nobody answered the door, so I walked about in that courtyard and thought they must be out, and I sat down on one of those staddle stones to wait. Then after a bit I noticed the front door was open, and this tallish thin man standing just inside watching me. So I got up and went over, and he said *Clovis? You're like your mother. I'm Kay Shelley,* and he stood back and let me in."

Clovis had gone ahead of Kay Shelley into a dark hall, a night-time hall with a paraffin lamp and a fire burning. Kay passed him. "Come and sit down," he said, and perched on the near end of a club fender by the fire. Clovis, parking himself on the padded leather at the far end, was in the light from the lamp, Kay with his back to it, his brownish red hair translucent. Opposite them, the diagonal of the staircase rose into the dark above.

Thus being interviewed in the hall like a prospective employee, Clovis set himself to make a good impression. He smiled, not too assertively, at his uncle.

Kay asked only neutral questions, in a quiet voice, about whether Clovis had found the house easily; about Lionel, about Edwin; Clovis told how the one was separating from his wife Angie, the other contemplating marriage to a widow called Rosemary Beacon.

"And you?"

"I'm the family disgrace. The dropout. Left Oxford because I couldn't bear the people. Plenty of jobs, no settling."

There was a pause, a hesitation, before Kay said casually, "Do you feel bitter that your mother left you?"

"Bitter? Well, no. I mean, at school it was a species of social embarrassment, people saying 'Ask your mother to write a note' and so on. We were always looked after, at home, like anything . . . But I've never felt . . . I mean, more and more I've come to think people have to follow what their own natures are."

It seemed to him that to win acceptance here, he had to be more forthcoming than in general he chose to be.

"I got across Dad by doing my own thing, after all. I don't know the situation she was in, and Dad's not a congenial type. You can imagine he hasn't been free with info about any of it, except for the snide stuff. Anything about me he doesn't like is the Shelley in me." Now he played the final card, the mawkish confession, the shaming truth: "Sometimes I've talked to my mother. Told her what was going on. You know?"

There was a sound on the stairs, a rustle and a footstep. She leaned over the banister into the lamplight, pale pointed face, red-gold swinging hair. She had been hidden, listening.

"Hallo, Clovis," she said.

"—so they took me into the room they mostly lived in, at the back, full of lamplight and with a big fire. There was wine, home-made and very strong. We sat and talked. She was very funny. We laughed a lot. I felt again, I could live here."

He finished his drink and paused again. There were a dozen questions Easter wanted to ask him. The factual account he had given left out his feelings, the essential part; but she knew how anyone stepping into his mind-space could set him on edge, silence him.

"So. I've been there quite a few times since then. Oh God, why did I drink? Makes it worse. Makes one feel so bloody."

"Maybe it's not the gin. Maybe you do feel bloody. What else? A tragedy is *sad,* baby, face it."

Pain was not customary in his face. It drew at his mouth as if he tasted quinine. He put up a hand, and she held it.

She took him to bed because he ought not to be alone; and with the idea of distracting him. They lay, however, held tight and silent in the dark. What was in Clovis's mind, Easter did not like to think. In hers she saw, as though projected on a screen, the woman on the bed, the man in the chair.

She had told the Inspector it was nonsense to think Clovis could have brought her on purpose to witness a "discovery" of the bodies, but what after all did she really know about the man in her arms?

Far too early in the morning the doorbell rang. Easter peered from the window, to see a dark car in the middle of the mews and two men at her door. When she raised the window, they turned their heads up toward her, faces pale in the young daylight, and a quiet voice came up the wall: "Police." A hand lifted a card. She, warning Clovis and putting on her black toweling kaftan, went down the steep narrow stairs to look through the spyhole, to which one of them helpfully held up his warrant card. She knew the face on it.

Superintendent Bone came in followed by a heavy, slightly smiling man, younger and a lot cosier than Inspector Garron. He had light brown untidy hair and an incipient weight problem that gave him no trouble at all on the way up the stairs.

"I suppose it has to be this early," she said. "I mean, hell, Clovis needed sleep after what happened yesterday and I'm not daisy-fresh myself."

"When it's unnatural death, Miss Lennox, we don't stop. This is the latest we could wait this morning." The Superintendent was looking very bleak; the scar and fading bruise on his forehead was the darkest thing about him: fair graying hair, light eyes, pallor, and a beige mac over a gray suit.

"Got off on the wrong foot there, I see," she said drily. "Nobody else made it to bed, right? Sit down, I'll make coffee."

"I'll do it." Clovis had got himself into her Breton sweatshirt and his ancient jeans all over clay and paint, a map of his legs in fade. Rumpled, unshaven and wary, he was not an object prepossessing to the conventional mind.

"It's you the fuzz will want to talk to. You sit." If he wanted to get out of talking with them, it was an effort a child would see through. Still, he sat docilely in the basket chair.

The senior fuzz said distantly, "This is Detective-Inspector Steve Locker. He wanted to get in touch with you yesterday to ask you further about your brother, and he is also working on the case at Summerdown."

"I've heard what you had to say at Summerdown yesterday," Steve Locker said. "I'm sorry to have to bother you at such a time."

Clovis rubbed his face grittily. "Well, Lionel rang me about this time that morning . . . Yesterday? So I did my stint for Florabundant and then I went. Borrowed Easter's car and drove to the Austin." His voice was dull, fatigued.

"Round about what time would that be?" Locker had a comfortable accent Easter guessed to be Kentish. She was beginning to be able to tell North England from Scots and this was new.

Clovis shoved his fingers through his hair. "No idea. But the receptionist would know. Funny, because I remember looking at the clock in the hall there, it's an ugly clock and I remember that but I've no idea what it said. I was bothered about Lionel, I suppose. He'd sounded grim. And he was in one of his states. I always feel—felt—if you touched him, he'd detonate."

"Very tense, was he?"

"Yes. Very."

"How did he show this?"

"I thought he had quit his job. He was handling everything very fast and roughly. Throwing folders down; scribbling notes; scrumpling papers and chucking them in the bin."

Clovis's fingers were working on the chair arms. Easter gave him one of the brown pottery mugs of hot coffee to nurse. The Superintendent took his coffee black but Locker spooned the brown sugar and took cream. "Thank you, Miss Lennox. That's very welcome. Mr. Clare, did Dr. Clare say anything direct about his job?"

"Nothing definite. And I didn't probe. Didn't want to attract one of his tirades. I was on edge just from being there. When he'd done the folders he washed his hands for the usual five minutes. He had a passion for hygiene. Obsession."

He drank coffee, tentative about its heat.

"I've tried to think if he gave a clue. Nothing but abstracts. When he was washing, he said he looked forward, or couldn't wait, to be free of all the filth of this existence. Why he should send for me to tell me he was leaving his job I couldn't fathom. There had to be more

73

to it. He said he'd built his house on sand and one moment had swept it all away. He said he'd been so certain of himself, of the person he was, and it was all changed."

"He didn't say why," Bone observed.

"If he did I lost it in all the talk. And people were coming in and so on."

"You didn't ask what the matter was."

"I told you, I was lying low. You didn't know him. He was already giving me one of his usual sibling lectures about the disaster that was Clovis, and in the middle of it some poor chap came in with a bin-liner he'd asked for, to take the junked paper, and shook it out, and it was all dusty, and Lionel flipped. He shouted right in the poor bugger's face about hospital hygiene and the routine of cleanliness and suppose it had been a ward sister who'd asked for the bin-bag, would he have shaken it out in the middle of a surgical ward . . . God, the man got out of there like he felt lucky to escape with his life . . . Once when Lionel was still living with his wife they asked me to dinner to make up the numbers, and Angie stacked the dishes on the draining board, the way you would before scraping them off for the dishwasher, and I helped stack them and we left them there; and Lionel went in for some ice and there was a shout and the most almighty smashing, and we found he'd swept the whole pile off into the sink and onto the floor. He turned on Angie and said *I've told you and told you, never leave filthy dishes, never*. She yelled right back about the mess he'd made. Big fight. I went back in the other room until the decibels dwindled. When I'm doing my courier work I calm these fights by stepping in and letting them play hit-the-ref; but not with that pair. The only tooth I haven't got was socked out by Lionel when he was fifteen, and he wasn't even his full weight."

"Was Dr. Lionel Clare often violent?"

"Not often enough. Better if he had been. Less uptight."

"Could you form no idea of what Dr. Clare was really brooding about?" the Super asked.

Clovis drank, finishing his coffee. "He said what I told you: the whole basis of his life was gone. And there was a phone call, his boss I think, Dr. Austin. Lionel said to him there was no need for a formal enquiry, he was assuming full responsibility and taking appropriate action. I heard Dr. Austin telling Lio to come and see him, and Lio stopped a moment and said very well, and Dr. Austin said come to lunch in his room. And Lionel put down the phone and said tchuh. So I suppose that was it, some mistake he'd made; but it didn't strike me at the time."

Suddenly he put down the mug on the floor and doubled over with his face in his hands, then sat back sniffing and rubbing his nose and said, "Poor bloody Lionel. Sorry. I suppose being a brother you're nearer than you think you are. When he was alive I thought he was a pompous sort of nutter . . . But I didn't know what it all was, and I thought he was over the top. Everything mattered so much, with him. I tried to tell him life wasn't such a big deal, but for him it was—Oh God, for ever struggling up the steep sides of molehills."

"How did he seem when you parted?"

"Furious. Furious with me for the way I talked. Furious with his job. I suppose now, looking at it, he, perhaps he meant to say goodbye. He didn't make anything plain. No statements of the year."

Easter hoped these strangers couldn't tell, as she could from her knowledge of Clovis, that he was lying.

Bone listened to Locker's comments and report. He said, "Any joy yet on that runaway witness?"

"No answer to the appeal on local radio. Kent and Sussex and Surrey all ran it, and there's a notice at the garage."

"Let's go wild a minute, Steve. Can he have been in Dr. Clare's car?"

"Forensic say no one could have been in the passenger seat; there's no interruption to the blood patterns.

75

As to the back, where someone could have been to cut Clare's throat, they can't say yet—it'll take fiber analysis, which may arrive by Christmas. Sir, did you tell Clovis Clare last night *how* his brother died?"

Bone thought. "No."

"He didn't ask, this morning."

"Possibly because he's more likely to run away from facts than to welcome them; but I take your point."

"Mind, sir, I've nothing to go on but the way Miss Lennox started watching him, and a look on her face. Sceptical, I'd say. It may be he knows why his brother killed himself and won't say; it may be more than that. Suppose him in the back of the car, a right-hand slash from behind?"

"Motive, either Summerdown, or a hatred of a pompous, overbearing brother, or both."

"Right, sir."

Bone found the doctor's impression of the wound among the notes. "Inflicted with some force and probably by a person with some knowledge of anatomy—what was Clovis Clare studying when he dropped out of college?—it severed the jugular vein and carotid artery, partially severed the sterno-mastoid muscle and the trachea." He got up and went round behind the seated Locker, crouched and extended his right arm forward, and gestured at Locker's sturdy neck.

"Well, taking into account the side of the car, which would cramp one's movement and—was he wearing a seat-belt? No, since he fell out of the car when the door jarred open." He stood up. "I'd say a blow like that couldn't be inflicted with any ease in the confines of a car, though we need an expert to tell us. When Ferdy Foster is through with his post-mortems we'll pick his brains on that. As to knowledge of anatomy, a lucky stroke might do as much. In that case, the runaway witness is far from extraneous; he's potentially the murderer and may be young Clare."

"Clare's noticeable, sir. Even if you're running toward a sight like Dr. Clare's car was, you'd take in a man with red hair. It's a funny thing we've only the two witnesses: Ron Dace the attendant, Hugh Mitchell, a motorist sitting in his car. Clare's vehicle hit the end wall and a metal petrol-ad with something of a crump according to Dace and Mitchell. They both looked toward it, but nobody living in the street went to a window.''

"Garage forecourts see a lot of collisions, Steve."

Locker grunted, dissatisfied.

Bone sat back. His work these days seemed to rouse all the interest it had held for him long ago, as if a renaissance in his own life affected everything; yet he was detached from it, observing himself as a policeman almost as Grizel Shaw might observe him. Her presence in his mind vitalized his day.

He found he was soundlessly whistling, a breathy ghost of the "Hymn to Joy."

"Well, Steve. Miranda Shelley's diaries. I find that there's some missing. Pat Fredricks and I were collating last night and we can't account for the stretch of time when they, the Shelleys, first came back to Summerdown although she says she wrote of it; and we've not got the latest. Garron's team collected every item they could see, they went through every book in the house for loose papers and searched the place last night and didn't find it.''

"Perhaps the killer took it."

"Garron thought it likely."

"What's your impression of young Mr. Clare, sir?"

"Likeable but dubious. And I couldn't say why *dubious*. It's an impression."

"Police prejudice," said Locker, grinning as he rose to go.

"That'll be it."

Clovis told his story again at the inquest, listened to by a heavy-eyed coroner in a stuffy room paneled with narrow boards in dirty green. A building site next door started up a pile-driver which eventually halted proceedings.

Bone stood among the small crowd outside while negotiations proceeded with the construction gang next door. He saw Clovis and Easter with Dr. Clare, who was talking to Clovis and barely acknowledging the girl's presence. The gist of his talk seemed to be that he felt the particular unkindness of Fate toward him. He cast a fretful glance at Easter's legs, as if she ought not to possess anything so distracting at this grave time. "Lionel, of all people. There's been some appalling pressure, something that will come out, mark my words. Had you really no idea? Even in your usual state of complete self-absorption you must have noticed that Lionel was at the end of his tether."

Clovis looked away and did not reply.

"Damn it, didn't it strike you?"

"Dr. Clare, the coroner asked that already." Easter's cool transatlantic voice intervened. He looked her up and down, but spoke to Clovis. "Of course, you wouldn't notice. You see nothing but yourself."

At this point they were summoned back into court. Sergeant Shay, whom Locker had briefed for a special task, came to inform him that the garage attendant, Ron Dace, had arrived as Clovis ended his evidence and had listened, looked at him, but betrayed no sign of identifying him or of realizing he was someone he had seen before; Shay had asked him if anyone present resembled the runaway witness and he had looked all round and said "No." It did not look as if Clovis were the one.

Angie Clare, who waved at Bone on her way to the stand, had made a surprising concession to the conventions by appearing in a black dress, but it was just as tight and as short as the red one, and with the black tights and high heels gave her the air of a vampire on an outing, especially when she put on the jacket she had been carrying, red as bright as arterial blood. She gave evidence of her husband's shifts of mood, the extremes of feeling that he could undergo. Still not unduly saddened by widowhood, she stuffed her hands into the jacket pockets and absent-mindedly swung her hips as she talked.

"I mean, twice he came really seriously to discuss

divorce, and both times we ended up in bed." She widened her eyes at the coroner and then, as she took in a certain withdrawal on his part, she added, "I don't actually mean bed, you know; just, well, doing it." She turned to the spectators, gave a slight wriggle and deprecatorily stuck out her tongue. "Sorry, but that's what happened. We were sexually totally compatible. I think Lionel would have liked to be totally cerebral, he couldn't cope with his emotions, he didn't want to recognize he had any, really, and I think I was very good for him in that way. Liberating I mean. All the same, I was really startled at the news"— (Could have fooled me, thought Bone) —"I won't say shattered because I'm trying to be exactly truthful, but startled: because I wouldn't have thought Lionel'd ever kill himself."

The coroner appeared not a little startled himself by this witness. Angie Clare had raised the temperature. Clovis gave his sister-in-law an appreciative look as she passed, Easter Lennox moved abruptly and Clovis winced.

Lionel's secretary made Bone recall his theory about Lionel being drawn to what he didn't like: if he had been having an affair with her as she claimed, then it could only be for the same reason for which he married Angie. She too was dressed in black, but her dress had the unfortunate look, with a low neckline and a trail of frills across the hips, of a party frock adapted to funereal use. She was not thin like Angie, but gave an impression of the same hungry sexuality; it must have drawn Lionel like a wasp to an overripe fruit. Her dark hair stood out round her head, maenad style, in carefully gelled frenzy, and she touched her eyes constantly with a succession of colored tissues ripped from a small box she carried.

"I blame myself," she said, when the coroner asked her what she could tell him of Dr. Clare's state of mind. "We'd quarreled, you know. There'd been a relationship—"

Angie Clare burst into smothered laughter and was admonished by the coroner.

"—and I don't think I was understanding enough. He

was a perfectionist and he had suffered a lot in his life. His marriage—''

Here the coroner interrupted and made her give an account of the quarrel, a rather mediocre little confrontation in Bone's view, hardly a trigger for suicide. She had ended by saying that as Dr. Clare's opinion of her was so low, their relationship had better end, ''but I never thought he'd take it like that, never!''

Angie Clare's loud mutter of ''Cobblers!'' was ignored by the coroner, who assured the tearful witness that blame could not attach to her. She had not been mentioned by Dr. Clare.

''But I shall always know,'' she whispered. Angie Clare made a soppy ''Aaah—aah,'' noise of cod sympathy, and the coroner told her to please be silent.

The next witness was the Clinic's house officer, Dr. Michelle Morrison, a pale young woman trying to be businesslike. She wore a gray shirt-waister that could have been a uniform. She sat with hands twisted tightly together, feet close side by side, and cramped shoulders. Her eyes showed chronic fatigue.

She had had to wake Dr. Clare just after eleven-thirty on the night before he died, because a patient of his on the critical list was exhibiting distress. Dr. Clare had told her by what amount to increase the patient's drug dosage and she had returned to the ward and supervised the change. At four-seven the next morning she had been awakened by her bleeper and gone to the ward, where the patient was in acute distress and did not respond to resuscitation. Dr. Clare was called.

''I've never seen him so upset. He had been making tremendous efforts over this case and he did now; but the patient died at four twenty-three.'' Dr. Morrison's voice failed her for a moment, then she said, ''Dr. Clare was very—he was remarkably disturbed. I felt so much to blame—''

Dr. Austin, the Clinic's head, stirred in his place and muttered audibly, ''No, no!''

''Were you in any way to blame?''

Her head had dropped. Dr. Austin repeated, ''No!''

and the coroner wagged a finger at him. Dr. Morrison shook her head, then added, "No." Bone thought she had probably been asleep on her feet. Housemen—house officers—could spend stretches on duty, as a matter of routine, that even police suffered only spasmodically.

Dr. Austin gave evidence that Dr. Clare had insisted that he ought to have got up when Dr. Morrison came with news about the patient, but he himself was satisfied that all that could be done had been done; that had Dr. Clare gone to the ward, the outcome would have been the same. Dr. Clare's reaction was inexplicable to him.

Further evidence from the Clinic staff showed that Dr. Clare had appeared to be under particular stress for the last three days of his life. Nobody knew any cause.

The predictable verdict of suicide having been given, everyone shuffled out. Bone watched a brief colloquy between Edwin Clare, a pleasant-faced woman who was with him, and his son and Miss Lennox. Dr. Clare took the arm of the pleasant-faced woman at one point, and she leant slightly toward him and agreed with what he said, so that Bone's imagination was regretfully obliged to part with the idea of Edwin's marrying Mrs. Mallard. He wondered how she looked forward to being superseded.

Angie Clare and a tall stranger with gray hair and Mount Rushmore features converged on Edwin, and Clovis got away from his father brusquely, leaving him annoyed although Clovis was saying, "Yes, sure, okay." He brushed off a reporter with a flash of wan charm and was gone.

"You didn't tell that reporter to go boil her bloomers. I thought you would."

"Oh no, I'm a peaceable bloke. You know that. Besides, it'd be sexist."

"Which on the whole you're not."

"I try. God, to think there are two more of these damned inquests to get through."

"You know more about Lionel than you let on."

"Oh?" She felt the freeze, and said, "I'm not asking.

I too can be brave, even to the point of heroism. Are you feeling terrible?"

"I should like to be blind drunk for the next three weeks. Give me to drink mandragora, that I might sleep away this great gap of time until we can start living again. Or until I can. You may not want to know me by then."

Easter pulled up for a pedestrian crossing. An old woman in suede bootees was going painfully with a Zimmer over the stripes. A gray lock-knit petticoat dropped below her coat. Easter, between distaste and pity, looked away. I hope I never get that kind of old, she thought. Miranda didn't get to be old; not any kind of old.

They reached the mews. A car stopped at the end of the mews behind them, then moved off. Police, or some poor journo dreaming up a story. Clovis sat inert.

"Come *on*," she said. "Only two inquests and three funerals to go." She put her feet to the cobblestones.

"I don't think I ever can leave you," Clovis said. "It's your simplicity with inspiring statements."

On the stairs he stopped her, took her face between his hands and looked at her.

"Thanks."

Easter half-shut her eyes. "Pay me later."

Bone tasted the canteen soup and put it aside. He moved the desk lamp and bent over the marble-covered book. He was becoming quicker at deciphering Miranda Shelley's writing.

I used to walk through this house in my mind, when I couldn't sleep or if I needed to be comforted. I would come into the hall and find the fire was lit and Tucker washing her face on the rug. I'd go into the study and find Granpa writing at the desk. I used to wonder what he wrote, and now we know. He had such a lovely childhood why did he never think about ours? But in my mind I couldn't always get Granpa to be there. This made me think I was actually really there, that I couldn't manipulate people, and perhaps I was a ghost for the house and it's the force of the mind.

Or I go into the morning-room along the passages and its sunny and theres breakfast and Granny and Mummy planning the day, and our own plates, yellow with the French children painted on that looked so queer. If Granny hadn't been ill when we went she would have seen we had all our special things. All I got was my clothes, horrible Mrs. Underwood packed them up. I hate hate hated when "Mummy" bought me new clothes.

What terribly infuriated me was when sometimes I imagined what I didn't want to. In the middle of enjoying it all I'd see Mrs. Underwood's awful Gary watching me just the stupid way he did, with his shorts too long and his ugly haircut, staring and wanting to join in, and when we were kind and let him he was too stupid he never understood our games. But we were very evil to him.

Now that we are here and more happy than I ever thought we could be, I look back and think that we did stay loyal. You had the worse time, they beat you and worked you too hard and kept you from school and friends. "Mummy" and "Daddy" were only cruel with stupidity, telling me you were dead, telling me Summerdown would have been sold and pulled down. They meant me to stop grieving, to "live in the present" and stop making a song and dance about what was gone.

She said, "I knew you would be happier when you accepted that poor dear Kay is with Jesus." She thought that, because I never spoke of you or Summerdown again.

Adam and Eve were together when they were sent out of Paradise. They hand in hand with wandering steps and slow through Eden took their solitary way, so they werent solitary. But we aren't now!

If looking back on happiness is the worst part of being miserable, then looking back on misery makes happiness more profound.

8

*E*aster who, when she did visit a church, did so for historical research rather than for its official function, decided that the crematorium chapel chosen for Lionel's funeral service would not rank a star in any hypothetical AA Book of Recommended Ways to Go. It smelled of floor-polish which seemed to have been laid on the liver-colored tiles like triangles of gleaming offal all down the nave, so thickly as to make walking a hazard. It had a sickly artificial lavender smell that went badly with the odor of moldering hymnbooks, and the colors chosen for the windows were picture-book primary, the robe of a sugary Virgin in a blue so shrill it offended like the wrong note of a bugle sounding the Last Post.

The Vicar, a large man whose choleric face reflected the floor tiles, was ill at ease. Perhaps he would have been happier supervising one of the old-fashioned burials of suicides, at the crossroads and with a stake. He hurried through the service in a nasal perfunctory chant, as though convinced God had no intention of listening; he glared occasionally at the congregation as though checking if they were picking their noses or writing graffiti on the pews. Easter was sorry for Edwin Clare, who looked genuinely miserable. He had after all lost his son and the woman he had once loved, on almost the same day. She studied him, covertly, behind her service sheet, trying to see Clovis in him. It was an interesting face, thin, sensitive, intelligent, but the face that had most nearly reminded her of Clovis had been lit by candles and waxen in death.

The secretary who'd given evidence at the inquest was there, in the same black dress but with a black silk blazer covering the décolletage. Her hair still stood carefully on end and she fed herself tissues of pastel shades out of her blazer pocket to dab at her eyes. Easter supposed the used ones must go into the other blazer pocket. The clergyman did not look as if he would care to find funereal equivalents of confetti on the chapel floor. Angie Clare was, rather surprisingly, also present; by her expression as she glanced round, from the desire not to miss a party of any kind. Her contribution to mourning her late husband took the shape of a black tam-o'-shanter in velvet, worn rakishly over one eye and pinned with a diamanté brooch. She waggled her fingers at Clovis, a gesture very conspicuous because as widow she had been placed at the front. Edwin was, as the saying goes, no more than polite to her, which in fact means less than polite. Easter wondered if Angie stood to benefit by Lionel's will, if he'd made one, or if he'd left her out. On her own testimony, she had exasperated him all the more because, against his will, she attracted him.

Clovis stirred by her side and she thought, with sudden compunction, I'm forgetting it's his brother. So hard to tell what he feels but he's certainly had a terrible shock, a series of them.

The organ produced a remarkably dreary moan at this point, *vox humana* soaked in self-pity. The blue plush curtains parted with a polite whirr and the coffin started to slide into the darkness beyond. It was a shame man's efforts to sanitize death had such a grotesque effect; far more dignified and satisfying the way Miranda Shelley had lain, surrounded by candles. Better too to be lowered into the earth and, yes, be eaten by worms than go rollerskating into the oven; it dressed Death not in a shroud with a scythe but more like Charlie Chaplin on the rink. Lionel's secretary was providing an *obbligato* of sobs to the treacle moaning of the organ. At anyone else's funeral, she was sure, Clovis would be bursting with suppressed laughter. She risked a glance at him. The rictus his face wore would do duty for any situation from repressing giggles to having had a weight dropped on his foot. He was standing up to things amazingly well. She hoped that not being very close to his brother, and having, in a sense, only just discovered his mother, made things less harsh for him.

His father did not let them escape this time. Easter had hardly made a habit of funerals but she was aware that mourners were supposed to nosh afterward. Edwin Clare was supported in his invitation by the pleasant Rosemary, whom Easter already liked. She appeared to be in her late forties, comfortably built, in a dark coat and skirt that emphasized rather than concealed her curves; she had a rose-petal skin, beginning to crumple at the corners of eyes and mouth. Her chin, which had started to assemble a support act below, had a fetching dimple. Edwin Clare, holding her arm, had a look both possessive and affectionate that humanized him as he looked at her.

"You must both of you come, we're expecting you."

Had Clovis told her his father was going to marry Rosemary? The "we" suggested that she counted herself already as hostess. Was she living with Edwin? Easter was amused at her own reaction—her generation lived with lovers as a norm, but she felt that for the older generation it amounted to *living in sin* and was a bit reprehensible.

Edwin Clare's house turned out to be a tall thin one not far from the Tate Gallery, with steps up to a porch and endless stairs inside. There was a big L-shaped room taking up, it seemed, the whole first floor, with a bathroom—discreetly offered to Easter by Rosemary—on the mezzanine half-way, tucked into the crook of the stairs. The drawing-room was handsome, decorated in shades of cream and white with cushions of pale green and pink, an effect enjoyably like a Neapolitan ice. Was Rosemary jumping the gun and having the place done over already?—for it all looked very new and feminine; but now another woman arrived on the scene to confuse the issue.

"My housekeeper, Mrs. Mallard." Edwin had now adopted a faintly gallant air, a man among women. Mrs. Mallard had arranged what she called "a collation" in the back of the room beyond folding doors.

"Thank you, Mrs. Mallard, we'll all help ourselves," Rosemary said. Mrs. Mallard gave a little smile and, instead of offering the plates, picked up one of the genteelly thin sandwiches and a plate and glanced expectantly at the teapot. Rosemary, driven to it, poured the tea, but she poured for Easter, Clovis, Edwin and herself, and with a little gesture and a nicely calculated smile, indicated to Mrs. Mallard that she might get on with it. Mrs. Mallard poured her tea rather as a well-bred crow might do.

"Have you known Clovis long?"

Easter took a sandwich and resigned herself to a series of questions meant to satisfy the curiosity of both women; although Mrs. Mallard made no attempt to join the conversation she stood as part of it, wearing an attentive, social smile. Rosemary let Easter know that Clovis had a past littered with girlfriends, that his father was always hoping he'd settle down, that it was better, wasn't it, not to commit yourself until you were *quite* sure or it could lead to such tragedies. "It's so terrible to be disappointed, isn't it?" Rosemary glanced at Edwin, who was standing talking in low tones to Clovis by one of the windows overlooking the street. "He had such a terrible time with his first wife—" had he had a *second?* or was Rosemary counting herself?—"you know, it takes time for a wound like that to heal. And now these awful things happening." She shook her head. "Edwin needs all the support and sympathy we can give him."

"He certainly does." Mrs. Mallard evidently couldn't let that pass; her own contribution of support and sympathy was not to go unrecognized. She avoided Rosemary's glance, which would have toasted bread, and directed her own toward Edwin by the window, her head on one side, the very picture of a doting crow. It was pathetic that she should so evidently be in competition with Rosemary, when it was clear she would not last two minutes as housekeeper once Rosemary was in charge. "He's had *such* a difficult life, and his sons have been no help at all."

Easter crammed back the reply that Lionel's suicide had indeed been a very selfish action. Wasn't it supposed to be an act of anger? With whom had Lionel been so angry?

"Clovis is a dear boy. He's had a very nasty shock," Rosemary said. "I'm glad you are his friend and can help him at this time." She pressed Easter's arm lightly, while Mrs. Mallard stared downward as though doubting that a girl morally capable of such a very short skirt could be a help to anyone. "It's been dreadful for him not to have had a mother when he needed her—"

"And now this *scandal*," supplied Mrs. Mallard, avidly *sotto voce*. "It was always peculiar, brother and sister living with each other like that, but now, getting murdered!" She obviously took this for the height of bad taste even if deserved.

Easter saw again that beautiful, waxen face, candle-lit, the glowing hair spread on the pillow; the man in the chair at her side, with sightless eyes. She could not imagine that man wielding a weapon on his beloved sister. She had seen his wound, or at least seen where it was, and the smell of blood had been heavy on the air, nauseating. Of the sword that had caused Miranda's death there had been no sign.

"*I* don't think that's a subject we should discuss," Rosemary was saying, but Easter was jolted out of her musing by an explosion from across the room: Clovis being shouted at by his father.

"You've no business to say so! Not my property, indeed! I'm not talking about your mother, I'm talking about *my necklace!*"

"Oh dear, that necklace!" Rosemary put her hand to her mouth, like a little girl embarrassed. "I do wish he wouldn't."

Mrs. Mallard was peering round Easter, fascinated, and Clovis broke away from his father and came toward Easter as though looking for rescue. Edwin followed him, the face Easter had liked for being sensitive and intelligent now flushed and distorted with anger. He gripped Clovis by the shoulder as he came up with him, and swung him round against the folding doors.

"Don't you walk away from me like that! You think you can walk away from everything—all obligations, all responsibilities."

Clovis turned and Easter recognized the clown at bay.

"But, Dad, you know me. I've not got any! You're always telling me—no job, no qualifications, no sense, nothing to do, nowhere to live—that's your son."

"Nowhere to live! That's rich, from you now."

Clovis glanced at Easter and shrugged, as if this were a reflection on his shacking up with her. His father smacked a hand violently on the table, causing all the china and plates to dance; Rosemary and Mrs. Mallard both made involuntary movements of salvage.

"You can stand there and grin," and unfortunately, Easter noticed, that was just what Clovis was doing, the final infuriating touch for his father. She thought Edwin was about to hit him, this unsatisfactory son left to him. She stepped idly forward. Edwin went on, however: "You can afford to grin! Sneaking off to see your mother behind my back and trying to get into her good books—"

"Now, hang on." Clovis was both surprised and annoyed. Edwin was shaking off Rosemary's hand, laid placatingly on his sleeve, and Mrs. Mallard was quivering like a pointing gun-dog. This was a funeral tea in some style.

"I will not *hang on*. You've got what you wanted! And perhaps the police had better ask themselves *how!*"

Everyone stared, and the silence seemed to bring Edwin to a sense of what he had said, and of his listeners. The flush slowly died on the thin cheeks and he rather absurdly put his hands up and straightened his tie. Rosemary emptied his teacup into the slop-bowl and poured him more; English panacea for all ills, Easter noted. If only someone had given Medea a nice cup of tea at the right moment . . .

"I'd like to know, Dad, just what you're talking about. After saying what you've said, you ought to tell me."

Edwin drank the tea, in a displacement and time-winning gesture, and when he spoke, it was in a tone almost offhand. "I'm talking about the house, although I can't suppose you don't know. About Summerdown, and that it's yours now."

Clovis's eyes widened. She thought he stopped breathing.

"Well, there," said Mrs. Mallard, as if she saw vice rewarded.

"Mine?" Clovis said.

"I should have thought they'd have told you. I dare say they did. It's never been easy to know when you're playacting. You went there and sucked up to them. It seems you were repaid for dancing attendance on that precious pair. I have it on very good authority that they left you the property—"

"Whose authority? Miranda called on you specially to say?"

"That's enough of your jejune cynicism. It's not required. As it happens, Kay told me himself—by letter, of course I mean—that Miranda had left it to you. A mistake of some proportions, to my mind."

"Surely not, if it's leaving me provided for? The prodigal son doesn't need Dad's fatted calf."

"I consider that you've got this in a very underhand way. You knew I wanted us to have no communication with those two."

"But you communicated. You wrote to her, which is how I found out where they lived. So if you did, why not me?"

Edwin's teacup slopped as he put it down, and he

shook a drop of tea from his hand. Mrs. Mallard was at his elbow with a napkin, which he took absently, dabbed with and handed back to her.

"I dare say you won't take advice about it," Edwin said.

"I dare say I shan't," Clovis agreed readily.

"Well, you can't run it. You've no income. That place would take an income like Lionel's to afford it. You'll have to sell." The thought seemed to please Edwin. He looked at Rosemary and seemed of a sudden to wither as he remembered. "I told him when he was here, not three days before he died, that he ought to invest in property."

"Yes, dear," Rosemary said; and casting about for a change of subject to distract him, said, "You haven't talked to Easter."

After a smile at Rosemary that was meant to convey *thanks a million,* Easter said, "I've been wondering, Dr. Clare, whether you managed to keep up with all the research in your subject. I get to read the superficial stuff they print in the science columns. Do you have time, what with your consultancy, to research yourself?" Had Edwin been American, she could have asked him what he'd published, but British doctors didn't have that compulsion to flail out in print. She thought, as he tried politely to answer her, *Clovis could be sitting on a whole lot of money.* What will it do to him? And did he really not know?

His father, admittedly in a rage, had said the police should concern themselves with this acquisition. She thought, surely they won't. No way—surely?

Clovis was ferreting among the bottles, exclaiming and clinking, as she climbed out of her silk suit and into casual gear. "Bitters. Martini. The plonk's gone vinegar. We, I mean you, have no drink."

"There's a half of brandy in the bathroom."

"Bathroom? I prefer to picture you in the bath drinking champagne . . . I suppose brandy is the journalist's bathtime tipple. Or is it for doing your teeth in?"

"Bathroom cabinet, clever clogs; it's the stuff you must never give in cases of accident. Band-Aid for the brain. Go fetch."

They were sitting opposite one another, legs stretched and toes touching, getting outside the brandy slowly and in a silence that was beginning to be restorative, when the doorbell rang.

"You expecting anyone?"

She said, going in stocking-feet to the window, "All my friends think I'm on vacation."

The man stood facing the door and rang again. She saw no camera, so perhaps he was not a reporter. When he stepped back and looked up at the window she saw it was the garage attendant she knew from the inquest. She went down to see what he wanted.

His freckled face was patchily high-colored, like peppered brawn. Hair oiled to the head wisped grayly behind the ears, and showed comb-marks over the pale scalp. The nose was that of a man who'd punished the bottle and the swell under the tight teeshirt showed that the bottle was getting its revenge. His anorak gleamed with a high polish of grease down the fronts. He moistened his lips and gave her a smile that by contrast made his teeth look almost genuine. She was sorry she'd opened the door.

"Mr. Clare in?"

Easter had a nose for trouble and she caught its reek. She started to close the door when she reconsidered: better know what the trouble is. She stood back.

The man followed her, wiping his hands down the sides of his trousers. If he was sweating, it could make him easier to deal with, or it could make him more dangerous. He took a deep breath. He was working himself up to something.

Clovis sat up. He looked startled. A reminder of the inquest wouldn't be welcome. She certainly wasn't going to offer any of the brandy to this man—what was his name? By now she always got names fast: Ron Dace. Nor was she going to ask him to sit down. She stood looking at him and waiting.

"Mr. Clare?"

"How can I help you?" Clovis was a paragon of politeness. Ron Dace had come here to be helped, and her bet was the help would be financial.

"I work at the filling—"

"I know. I remember you from the inquest."

The man was slightly thrown, slightly annoyed at having a prepared opening spoilt. She bet he'd rehearsed it.

"Well, I come about something I saw. Perhaps you and me should discuss it, like, in private?" He cast her a glance of leering chivalry and she saw Clovis turn serious with a snap.

"I've no secrets from Miss Lennox."

That lie is a snorter, darling Clovis, but nice of you. However, it had given a handle to Ron Dace.

"You got secrets from the police, though, haven't you?" The joke set of teeth appeared again. "That's what I've come about. What I saw that day. The carwash."

Clovis did not look at Easter. "You saw what? Or thought you saw?"

"Ah now, Mr. Clare," a horrible, forgiving smile, "can't get out of it like that. I saw all right. I saw you run from your brother's car. You got in your car and drove off like a bat out of hell. And I saw your brother's car come out all red, like I told the coroner." He lingered on the last phrase with relish while Clovis's face bleached out. She moved out of his path for the bathroom, remembering the effect of the tomato sauce. She remembered more. And so much for the tale of being caught in a rainstorm. He'd washed his clothes.

"Then why didn't you tell the coroner what you thought you saw?" Clovis demanded, quite haughtily.

She admired his evasion, his refusal to commit himself. Ron Dace widened his smile to reveal the full set of porcelain fitments.

"Ah now, I thought it was a secret you wanted keeping. I listened to all you said, and not a word of the garage. So it's a secret we can keep between—" his chivalry included Easter again—"the three of us. Of course I'd need a reason to go on keeping it." The smile shrank and disappeared. "Like, a price."

"What price were you thinking of?"

Easter, who had been fretting at a bit of cuticle, ripped it suddenly and winced at the raw skin left behind. Ron Dace watched Clovis and said, "What do you think it's worth?"

"Oh no," Clovis said. "You came here with ideas of what you could get. What did you think of?"

"How about a hundred, for the present?"

It was like making an incision, with the promise to come back and widen it later. Blackmail didn't stop, it was a growing tumor, voracious. What the hell had Clovis done to be in that carwash? What had he done there? Ron Dace took his flight for guilt, and here was Clovis behaving as though it was.

"Don't be stupid. I haven't a hundred or anything like it. I'm out of work."

Dace took a deliberate look round. Clovis said, "*Oh* no," just as she said, "No." She went on, "This is my place, and I'm telling you to go."

"Oh, no offense to you, dear," he said, putting up soothing hands. "This arrangement is with Mr. Clare. The place is yours; all right, and very nice it is too. But this secret's worth a lot to him. A business arrangement between him and me. I did say, Mr. Clare, as a private discussion would've been better. How about we talk it over somewhere else?"

Easter trod into her shoes and pulled them up over her heels. She went to the door and opened it. She didn't like the look on Clovis's face and she was damned if she could stand this man in her apartment.

"I told you to go."

"Mr. Clare, you'd do well to be reasonable. You know you can lay hands on money." Again he surveyed the room. Clovis began to speak but, whatever he might have said, she did not wait. She took the man's arm and spun him round, got his wrist up behind him and grabbed the seat of his pants and twisted the cloth hard. She said "Out," and frogmarched him to the door. His feet went in spite of himself, he tried to struggle but she jerked at his pants and he shouted. He seized hold of the door-jamb but Clovis, rallying late, twisted his little finger and forced his grip free. She stopped at the stair top and said, "You can walk down or I can throw you."

"All right, all right. No need for rough-house."

She put him on the first stair and let go his pants. He walked on down and she let his arm go. He did not turn at the foot but let himself out and slammed the door. The letter-box opened and Dace shouted, "Mr. Clare, I'll talk to you later!" The flap rattled shut. After a moment a car started up and drove off.

"I'm sorry," Clovis said.

"I think we'd better finish that brandy."

Easter came back and picked up her glass, sat and stretched out her feet. After a minute Clovis resumed his position opposite. The same atmosphere did not assert itself. Clovis had gone back to being wary, and fatigue showed under his eyes.

"To clear the air," Easter said, "and to remove any apprehensions you may have in one direction at least, I will make a statement."

"You don't have to say anything."

"Just you leave the words *in* my mouth, Clovis *old thing*." He tentatively almost smiled at her Anglicism. "It is you who don't have to say anything. Let's get this straight. I don't own you, or you me. You don't owe me, either. I'm not some moony ingénue whining *Don't you trust me?* No, don't talk yet; listen. And listen good. I am not about to demand explanation. I am happy with the way we are together. I think you are."

"Oh yes," said Clovis, his eyes attentive.

"Okay then. You're giving or not giving with your story, and I'm not asking. I'm interested in us. Together. And I sure as hell am interested in Miranda."

He finished his brandy and said, "Fair enough," which she had discovered was English for *I accept all that you say and will go along with it despite reservations.* "That bloody little man will be back. I don't want to talk about it. You're right. But I didn't kill Lionel."

"Never thought you did," Easter said, ignoring some half-suspicions she had entertained for a second or two. "Let's go out and eat."

But why did he temporize with that ratbag? And if he was close enough to Lionel to get blood over his clothes and thus into her car, what the hell *had* he been doing?

9

Grizel Shaw wheeled the trolley cautiously round the corner. The "supermarket" was an expanded village store and an insouciant shove of the trolley might mow down a child or shred a neighbor's tights. The woman she therefore missed was in jeans, however, and a washed-out tee-shirt. She turned a wan face and said, "Sorry," as if her presence were at fault, then gave her attention to the packet soups; their charms for her were obviously minimal. She drooped before them, picked out a couple and turned again. Despite the pallor and the sunken eyes, the unkempt hair, Grizel knew her.

"Isn't it Michelle? Weren't you at Paulton?"

The face gave an automatic vague smile, then came alive. "Mrs. Shaw! Hallo!"

Grizel remembered how glossy the dark hair had always been. Michelle, neat as her work, usually a little anxious, seemed to look across the classroom from the desk she had always chosen. Grizel's trained eye noticed more in the changes than the few years justified. Not only the eye noticed: there was a smell she associated with anorexia.

"Come back to dinner with me," she said. "I'm starved for company." The verb was by association, but luckily Michelle did not find it significant. She demurred, for form's sake perhaps, but Grizel's energy wore her down.

"I think I've seen you once or twice," Michelle said, as she sat at the kitchen table with a gin and orange. "I thought some time when there was time I'd try and get in touch, but . . ." Her sentence ran out of steam. "It's lovely to see you."

"What are you doing these days? I don't get the Paulton magazine any more."

"Oh, you wouldn't know if you did. It's ages since I bothered with their Old Girls' questionnaire. I've got a terrific job, really, I'm house officer at the Austin Clinic." The voice didn't match the words' enthusiasm; it had the monotone of stress.

"Wow," Grizel said, busy at the cooker. "You must be as top-notch as I always said, to get in there."

"I'm not very likely to stay."

"Really? Don't you like it?"

"Oh, it's a very good place to be. They do very good work."

"Is it to do with that poor doctor on the news?"

Michelle turned her glass round. Her head went down further and she struggled with her jeans pocket, found it empty and was trying the other one when Grizel gave her a tissue from the box on the window sill. *Thanks* was probably the word she uttered. After a moment Grizel said, "That was clumsy of me. Of course he would be a colleague of yours. I simply didn't think."

"Oh, please, Mrs. Shaw. No . . . it's all so awful. Dr. Clare was so clever, a brilliant doctor. Dr. Austin said over and over how lucky we were to have him. And he always seemed very cold and detached, but he was so good to me—really kind. I'm not supposed to talk about it, but you aren't the Press or anything and I feel I'll crack up or something . . . we always could talk to you. I suppose we were a pest, but you were never stuffy or judgmental."

Grizel thought of saying *If you're not supposed to tell me, you'd better not,* but she was too concerned for

Michelle to do that. Besides, Grizel admitted to unwilling curiosity.

"Finish your drink."

"It must be stronger than I thought . . . or I suppose it's because I'm a bit tired. And it's so appalling about Dr. Clare. He said he was responsible and he told Dr. Austin he was responsible. But it was me made the mistake. I got the dosage from his—from him and I got it wrong. Nobody's to talk about it because the family—I shouldn't have told even you. One gets so tired. I mean I get so tired I go to sleep while someone's talking to me. Standing up. This isn't even my day off but Dr. Austin made me swap. It's easier to go on working when things go wrong, even terrible things like Dr. Clare, but I expect Dr. Austin was right. He said one needs perspective and that I'd got too close to the work. But you *do,* you see. Oh God! So I made this mistake. Only Dr. Clare said it was his mistake. Oh, it's too complicated. I'm not making sense."

Grizel put fried bread and mushrooms before her and said with authority, "Eat."

The phone rang as Bone was putting plates to soak. He answered curtly, looking at his watch, and as he heard the caller's voice his whole state of mind altered at once, making him laugh.

"I was ready to be cross as hell with some poor sod who's only doing his job—and it's you. I reach for the can of worms and find it's caviar."

Grizel's warm voice, lively with a hint of Scots, said, "A nice distinction that we don't want worms but we'll eat fish eggs. You weren't in bed?"

"If I had been I still would be. There's an extension by the bed."

"So there is."

"How are you?"

"You sound as though you really want to know. That's skill. I'm exhausted, Robert. It's as well you couldn't come last night. I had to listen two hours to Michelle Morrison. She's house-dog at the Austin Clinic."

"I remember."

"An old pupil of mine; she lives down the road. She's in a state and a half because she believes she caused someone's death."

"Surely she ought not to do that. Any mistake was Lionel Clare's. He took responsibility for it completely."

"She says she ought to have spotted it. She's in a low state, let me tell you. The poor girl's only gone along with someone else's mistake, and by her account she'd been on duty solidly for long enough to have made it unlikely she'd have spotted a great white shark if it had cruised past the windows. I met her in the shop buying-in a bundle of packet soups, which is about all she does eat, so at least she got a good meal here. And you? Still reading the diaries?"

"Still feeling like a bloody snooper, too. I should grow up and remember I'm a detective and that my business is with other people's lives and privacy."

She said coolly, "When are you next going to come and invade mine?"

"Oh heavens, woman, don't be so inflammatory. I've the diaries, and PM accounts . . ."

"Bring a diary or so with you tonight. I've twenty GCSE folders to assess these holidays. We'll work and I'll give you supper."

And then. Bone's pulse hit the high eighties.

"That would be agreeable," he said.

"Found something?" Grizel asked, lifting her head from the scripts spread around her on the floor. For a moment he didn't answer because she was looking at him with such serious attention.

"Just caught someone out in a lie."

"Important?"

"May be very much so."

She smiled, and bent her head once more. He said, "Sorry I broke your concentration," and she waved a biro-bearing hand in absolution.

* * *

Edwin came today. I never thought I'd see him here. He doesn't belong at Summerdown. He has no business here.

We were upstairs when we heard this knocking and the bell in the kitchens. Kay, just for company, was looking at books in Granny's bedroom bookcase, he has plans to reorganize all the books in the house when there's time but there's always so much to do. I hated housework for Edwin but anything I do for Summerdown is such joy.

I couldn't believe in the knocking somehow, we never have visitors. When a woman came collecting for something last month we propped up Major Tom at the billiard room window and Kay waved the Major's arm at her. We were laughing so much when she scuttled off that Major Tom fell on the window and bashed his nose. We say he's been in the star wars.

I felt at once that Kay knew about the knocking. He doesn't always tell me if he wants to protect me from things. I leave the post to him, can't be bothered with letters, and Kay doesn't answer if he doesn't want to.

When I put up the window and saw Edwin I felt sick. Physically sick. It reminded me at once of all the bad times, of the babies he wanted me to look after, and his scoldings, and he looked so stupid too standing there with his head back looking up at the window. I wanted to throw something, get Kay to pee over him, anything to make him go away, but Kay said, see what the silly twit wants, then he'll go. With Kay there, Edwin can't frighten me any more. The only thing that did frighten me a little and it was why I did go down to open the door was that he might have come to tell me something about Clovis, I never meant to let the children into my life, when I left it was for good, and for their good too because it was far better for them to be brought up by someone who could be trusted to look after them properly the way Edwin said I never did. I never thought I could feel anything for them until Clovis arrived here and then he just filled a gap I had never known was there; and I wouldn't want anything to happen to him.

It was very odd though when I opened the door to Edwin. A big man with a camera came lolloping over the gravel after him calling out in an American voice something like, "Want to talk" and Kay pushed past me and Edwin—who gaped like a fish—and went and showed him off. I hate people who want to see this house; Kays always managed to keep them away somehow, Summerdown is ours and not a gawking-stock.

I wouldn't let Edwin right in though. He had to sit in the porch and talk. It wasn't about Clovis at all it was about the necklace, and he kept staring at it as if he could seize it or strangle me for it. When we were married he put it round my neck like a royal heirloom. Or it was like a rope now she belongs to me *but the necklace isn't like that, it loved me. It's mine now. I sat wearing it and listened to him being pompous. Typical of Edwin wanting presents back, I wonder what she's like whom he's marrying. I don't care about the necklace in a grabbing sort of way and now I think of it I'd like to give it to Clovis for anyone he marries, he should have it and not Lionel whos never bothered to find out anything about me. If Edwin got it I suppose Lionel as the elder would get it if this Rosemary ever let it go, but Edwin doesn't seem to think women won't queue up to hand over jewelery that's been given to them. He kept shooting glances at me if looks could kill I'd be soaked in blood right now. The very sound of his voice* nyah nyah *tired me. I wonder how I could have once thought he was at all like Kay, but I did think so once when I met him.*

Kay had the brilliant idea as usual; he suggested we should play hunt-the-necklace with Edwin. He said it in our language, that always made Edwin go doolally. He went on, that when Edwin came to hunt we didn't really have to let him do it, we could hide. For a moment I thought of sitting under the table in the morning-room and Granny hunting for us in vain, and I thought, death will be like that sitting with Kay in the dark and waiting.

Of course Edwin was cross at any idea of a game. He would have hit me the way he did before but he was frightened of Kay, I could see and I liked that. Kay had to push him out of the door and when he'd done that, Edwin picked up one of the pots outside with one of Kays hyacinths in it and chucked it against the door. It split like a bomb and made me jump. I'd like to know who was being childish?

So much, Bone thought, for Edwin Clare's pretence of having never been to Summerdown.

Grizel was leaning back on her hands, velvet-trousered legs spread out before her, and stretching her neck. "How's it going?"

"She thinks he would like to kill her; but looking as if you'd like to kill someone is no guarantee you will do it."

"The population would dwindle a bit if it were."

He put the book down, and made a note. His eyes were tired. Miranda's writing was so small, and this episode was told in a more straightforward way than others were, presumably because she was angry and because it had to do with the outside world. Sometimes these later accounts were confused and clouded either by her illness or by hash or painkillers.

"You're tired. I'll get the supper." She stood up and stretched again. As she passed Bone on her way to the kitchen, he expected one of her swift caresses and raised his head, but she had gone. She must be tired too.

Miranda's rejection of Edwin was arbitrary as a child's. She had married him, attracted by some fancied resemblance to Kay; an earlier reference showed her impulsive rush to escape her adoptive parents and her wild regret when, within the year, Kay turned up; they had a riotous twentieth birthday together, her diary giving a picture of the baffled Edwin trying to understand and rationalize their imaginative flights, to control their games and drinking, reduce the sound on the records they played, until Kay led Miranda into the garden and produced a joint: they had smoked and come back peaceable. Edwin had been pleased . . . and now she felt sick when she saw him. He stood for a life she had once again escaped.

Quite evidently she infuriated Edwin; her belief that he would like to kill her was typical Miranda drama—Edwin's fury spent itself on plant pots . . . But someone had killed her.

Remembering the petulant but controlled man he had met, Bone tried to see if he had shown the latent violence in his nature. It was in Lionel's too; what about Clovis? Bone palmed his eyes and, in the darkness, wondered about heredity, deprivation of maternal guidance; of Charlotte and his efforts to be both parents to her, while all the time as a cop he was married to his job.

And he should be keeping his mind on his job now. What about his own life? Where in all this was Grizel, and what right had he to involve her?

There had been plenty of opinions and gossip about the Shelleys in the village nearly a mile away; his visits to Grizel would be known and talked of here. Her house, fronted by a long, high-hedged garden, was on the main road that went through the village, and so he parked his car on the road that went round the green opposite. He knew, from house-to-house enquiries in villages like this in the past, how many neighbors were likely to know these facts, to see his visits as the more clandestine because he did not park outside her house.

"Here you are, Robert."

Grizel was putting a tray among the folders and papers on the floor, handing up a cup of soup.

"I think I'm very dull this evening," he said, as he leant to take it.

"I'm suffering from end of term." She did not look up. "At this time of year all teachers are—d'you remember that charming phrase from *The Beggar's Opera*— 'a glass too low?' It'd be so easy to take to drink; gives me precisely the kick that brings me to normal. Three weeks into holidays and I'll be myself again, but I'm no stimulating company now." She looked up. "Don't blame yourself, Robert. Eat your soup. We're working folk, both of us." She gave a smile, a twenty-watt one by comparison with her usual brilliance. "That's why working people shouldn't marry. They both need a wife."

I was glad to leave Edwin outside and hope he never never returns, we certainly shan't open the door if he ever does. We went upstairs and returned to Clark and Julia; I can really concern myself with that as I cant with Edwin.

Julia and Clark? thought Bone. Who were these friends of a woman who knew nobody? Acquaintances from Italy, perhaps?

I take Julia's part. She suffers very deeply. Clark insists that his unfaithfulness was not betrayal, that he was away from her so long and meant nothing. She feels that it threatened their whole marriage. I said to her, I admit I ought never to have married as I did, it was false, it was my falseness, but you married in good faith, I said. It's Clark who married without belief in marriage vows.
Clark became furious at this, quite magnificently angry. He said I was a vile friend to Julia, a snake at the ear of Eve that poured my leperous distilment into her brain. He would snatch Julia from contagion.
I really admired the way Kay took his part.

Bone leant forward, re-reading. This sudden invasion of the pair of warring spouses had taken him completely by surprise. The Shelleys did know people. There had been no mention of these before. Where did they live? And the man Clark's fury at Miranda, which she seemed almost to enjoy, a "magnificent" anger, might it eventually have become a murderous fury?

Kay took Clark away to the conservatory to cool off. Mrs. Perceval finds the whole business very distasteful,

*and said so. We must not leave Clark out there, though.
It's too damp.*

"Too damp?" said Bone aloud.
"M'm?" Grizel said, reading a script.
Clark's voice is quite unlike Kay's. It's amazing.

Was Clark a relation, then? Why else should his voice
be like Kay's? Neither Edwin nor Clovis had mentioned
a word of this Clark. And Mrs. Perceval?
He remembered, then, a white pasteboard visiting
card on the table before one of the figures in the small
room at Summerdown. The figures had been posed to
look negligently at the card: Perceval Shelley.
"Damn!" he said in a burst of frustration. Grizel ex-
claimed and he turned to her with belated recollection
of her presence. "I'm sorry. I thought a whole line of
investigation had opened up, and it's more of their infernal children's games." He rubbed a hand over his brow
and was reminded that the scar was still tender.
"Poor Robert," she said. She put the last folder on
the pile, drew up her knees and hugged them.
"I told you they had all these dressed-up window dummies at Summerdown. It seems they played dolls with
them, invested them with personalities and acted out
scenes between them. Some of the vague references I
took for daydreams or memories probably refer to
that."
"It's an inventive way of being alone without
loneliness."
"I suppose it is." He looked down at her. The light
was beginning to go; the garden beyond the window had
the stillness of dusk and up on the road a car passed
with lights on. "That's a good remark, Grizel. It's too
damned easy to become a stuffy Super. We've all the
infinite and variegated oddities of humankind before us
and I say 'how infuriating.' "
She put her head on one side and he tried to make
out her expression in the twilight.

"Do I infuriate you?"

"*You?* Why on earth do you say that?"

"I used to infuriate Lewis. Particularly when I was too tired to make love. He thought I should give up teaching if it made me so boring."

"I cannot imagine you ever being boring. I'm just afraid I'll bore you. Police work, you must have noticed, is excluding, absorbing, and exhausting."

Grizel had got up and wandered behind Bone. He was electrically aware of her before her fingers touched his forehead and descended to smooth his eyelids shut. Her wrists smelt of flowers. She bent, and kissed his neck below the ear. Her short hair softly rasped his temple and now he could smell her skin and not her scent. Her voice was a little sardonic as she said, "Can police work take a short personal break?"

He put the book down and possessed himself of her hands. She went on, more gently, "The trouble is, we're both afraid. I've got uncongenial memories of Lewis and you've got your past too, of a different kind." She delicately avoided even mentioning Petra's name and Bone was grateful. Easy enough to tell yourself your dead wife would be glad you'd found happiness in the arms of another woman, and that memory could not inhibit you for ever; it was surprisingly hard to believe it.

"It's guilt. We don't think we ought to be enjoying life."

Grizel kissed his hair, her mouth and breath warm through it on his scalp. "Let's enjoy ourselves. It's *our* lives."

The Shelleys' motto, he thought. Why not?

10

What I need is a shower, I think," Easter said. "It was hot as hell in that bar; you were running sweat."

"I'll race you to it," Clovis said, as she parked the car. "Last one in the shower's a—"

"Anyone slinging clothes on the floor on the way there is disqualified," she said."I run a taut flat, you slob."

There was something odd about the front door she didn't take in, but she turned the key in the lock and walked in on glass. After one moment she raced upstairs and viewed her taut flat.

Drawers and their contents lay on the floor, pictures had been torn down, curtains lay on the sofa soaked in wine; smashed bottles, oil, ketchup, pickles and peanut butter, her clothes and Clovis's, molasses and jelly and milk covered the floor. Liquid soap and make-up dripped from the walls. There was a smell of Lanvin's Arpège and vinegar and urine.

Easter was surprised to find she had screamed; it was a yell of fury more than fright. Clovis at her side said, "Bloody hell," in a whisper.

Take a grip of yourself, girl, she said inwardly. She was shaky, she found as she picked her way across the

floor like an offended cat and lifted the telephone. It had
been smeared with something and she dropped it.

"Clovis—go call the police."

"Hang on a minute."

She was starting a protest when she saw him stride
over the horrible debris and fling open bedroom and bathroom doors. He came back saying, "He's not here still.
Come down and bolt the door after me; unless you'd
rather sit in the car."

She leant on the wall inside the front door, swearing
to herself, tense to the point of shaking, occasionally
stamping her feet on glass, until a flashing blue light
arrived outside. Clovis, he told her as they climbed the
stairs again, had been looking for a phone that worked,
and had hailed a patrol car in the high street.

The police, one large and one slighter, cast unim-
pressed eyes about. One of them had a lapel radio that
burped and babbled.

"Can you say what's missing, madam?"

"I haven't looked. I haven't touched anything."

"Where do you keep money or valuables, madam?
Better have a look. You can't hurt much walking over
this. Just avoid touching any polished or smooth
surfaces."

"I've nothing valuable. Costume jewelry." She
picked her way to her bedroom. There it all was on
the bed where the bastard had emptied it. Ashamed of
themselves, her gewgaws, copper and wire bangles, African beads, huge fake diamonds set in black lacquer,
winked sadly at her. Possessions weren't her bag, she
had thought. Only—she looked at the bedside table and
her heart descended and she clenched her fists.

"One photograph in a silver Art Deco frame," she
said flatly.

Clovis came hurrying. "Shit! Your mother's picture."

"Yes."

The police noted this down, still looking round with
the imperturbable air of those to whom wrecked homes
were professional tedium, and talked into the radio. She
had to describe the frame's size and shape.

"Have you nothing else of value? Right. Our finger-print expert will call tomorrow. They'll telephone to warn you of the time . . ."

"The phone's been vandalized."

This threw them slightly, but only for a moment, then they were in gear: "You can get a firm who'll clean this up. Would you like a visit from the local Victims' Help Association? The fingerprint expert will be carrying a warrant card . . . Have you somewhere to stay tonight?"

"Yes," Clovis said. She thought, sure, we have friends who'll come to the aid of the parties. Clovis was being unexpectedly active in support and she was not ashamed of feeling grateful.

"Perhaps when you get there you'll let us have the telephone number."

"Not on the phone," Clovis said.

"What about making the front door secure, sir?"

"What can happen to the place now?" she demanded.

"All the furniture could go," said the larger police-man cheerfully: "cooker, fittings—even what's left of the telly."

"We can fix the door," said Clovis. She noticed even now he wasn't macho enough to say "I." She gave him a weak, brief smile. It was hurting, an acute ache that was physical, about the photograph. She didn't have an-other one of her mother, who hated to be photographed. Don't take a snap of me, honey, she would say, draped glamorously over something or somebody, I look like death. Which was the reason why, when she did die, in a road accident seventeen months ago, without ever hav-ing had a chance to look like death, this was—had only been—the one photo. Easter had bought the Art Deco frame in an antique shop in the King's Road just a week ago, one of those unlucky finds.

"Perhaps you'll let us know, miss, when you've had a chance to check further." The officer put away his notebook, his radio giving a startled belch as though he had disturbed it, and they made their way downstairs, placating the radio's indigestion with a soothing message.

She broke up a crate in the kitchen that had held junk she meant to sort out and that was now all over the kitchen-area floor, and Clovis held the boards while she nailed, and put her fury into hammer blows. With the efficiency of fury, too, she sorted out the papers she'd been working on, from the debris on the floor; some were illegible with the dregs of Cointreau. She bundled everything together and stood looking round to see what next to salvage.

"Leave it," Clovis said. "It won't run away. I'll help you see to it when we get back."

"Back from where?"

"Summerdown. I own it, remember?"

"*Summerdown!* You're joking. I hope."

"No. I mean it."

She saw he did. "Clovis: your mother?"

"That's why I want to go there. It's—it's a place for the living. She loved it and . . . it's as if—I mean—it should be alive. Lived in. And because I didn't know her enough, and I want to . . . can you see?"

"But the police. They'll be there."

"If we're *in* the house, they won't even know. Didn't you hear the sergeant say they couldn't afford a man on it whole-time—they're depending on patrol-car visits. It'd be safer with us there. Easter, I really want to go, to be there, anyway, apart from this." He gestured at the wreck.

Easter hesitated, then shrugged. Revolted and sickened by the state of the flat, she found her anger didn't power her into being able to tackle cleaning it up. She was conscious of temptation, of the pull of the house itself. Clovis, perceptive as ever, saw her yielding.

"And this time," he said, "we're legitimate."

He held up a key.

It had been far easier than he'd expected, forcing the door at the bottom of the tower. The wood was old, not rotting but in no state to resist the repeated furtive leverage of the stone chisel. It took force. Even through the hide gloves it was tough on his hands. Eventually, though, the lock yawned at the splintered edges and he eased the door open, pulling off its surface the brambles that had reached across it hungrily. This was easier than breaking into that flat had been. There, he'd been afraid someone across the mews would see him, someone would pass, that she would come back . . . but with an old isolated house like this one, who was there to hear? And if they did, it'd take the pigs a good half hour to arrive and get down that lane while he could be out and gone to ground in that forest of a garden. His car was up a side lane out of sight, nowhere near that murderous bitch's little Renault. He'd waited until the bedroom light went out in the front of the house, waited longer in the fucking undergrowth watching, got nettle stings all down the side of his face, driving him wild. After that wait, it'd better be worth while. They owed him. And that Clare bastard saying he'd no money: *treasures in old house. Does son stand to inherit?* And it was his all right, they'd driven straight here. God, the only thing was, to have missed seeing her face when she walked into her flat; but what there was in this house should make up for that, and for her manhandling . . .

As he got his bearings and moved forward, he thought if the pigs weren't so dead slow they'd have got Mr. Clovis Clare—what a poove's name that was!—locked up right now instead of screwing that tart in this spooky old mansion. What sort of bloke is hiding the fact he was the last person to see his brother alive before he cuts his throat and then, bingo, his mother gets carved up by persons unknown and it turns out he's likely to come into her money? And he comes to the house where she copped it.

He trod carefully, his trainers faintly squeaking on the boards. His pencil torch slid its light along the parquet, over the rugs and up the legs of a long table. What was it they called them? A *rectory* table; this'd be the dining-room, then. The light swam along the dark surface over the eddies and ridges of dust and stopped on a silver bowl with dried flowers, brown papery globes of flower heads and lots of grasses. A nice little piece. He tipped the dried flowers out on the table, checked a sneeze as the dust reached him and seeds scattered like mouse droppings. He slid the bowl into his holdall and raised the torch again.

The bag fell to the carpet with a dull thud. A man was sitting in the dark at the head of the table looking at him. Christ, this was it. They'd set him up. The torchlight jittered across the still face, then steadied. The eyes weren't looking at him. Hardly breathing, he stood waiting for the eyes to turn, the man to jump up. He stepped nearer, incredulous, taking a deep breath of relief. The eyes were glass, all right, the too-handsome face plastic; dressed up in a posh dinner suit and bow tie, too. Of course it wasn't the redheaded Clare, nor it wasn't police.

The relief made him lean on the table, fingers splayed, wanting to laugh. Yet he was angry. It was a dirty trick setting this here, like in a horror movie. People that did things of that sort deserved all they got. His heart was still pounding as he swiveled the light toward the other end of the table and, for all he was half expecting it, the beam jumped as she appeared out of the dark all in a Joan Collins evening dress with a feather thing in her hair on a diamond spray. His sudden hope sank instantly, but he went to check it out, picking up his holdall on the way. She wore solid Woolworth carats. The necklace was nothing but garnets, not rubies, and the setting was dull and dark, not gold. The dummy, her satin headband pulled awry by his inspection, stared at her partner with toffee-nosed indifference to being handled.

There wasn't much else in the dining-room: a pair of silver candlesticks, which he wrapped in a linen serviette out of a drawer, joined the bowl. A couple of bonbon dishes with a hallmark . . . the baize-lined drawer that should have had the family silver table-ware was empty. The room hadn't any nice little ornaments, nothing in gold that would really count.

He padded next door, cautious for more of the figures. He found them, too, grouped there, all togged up like out of *Upstairs Downstairs,* more paste diamonds but more Woolworth than any use. The place was a bloody Madame Tussaud's. He turned impatiently, scanning with the pencil beam. Too many display plates on those wooden holders, no use to him. All right if he had the contacts but he wasn't going to turn himself into a walking sideboard on the offchance. The pencil beam roved along the mantelpiece and stopped on a pheasant with arched neck and dull-gleaming plumage, feathers etched in the silver; quite heavy, too, solid stuff. It joined the bowl.

At one point the rattle of windows behind the shutters and a tap of branches on the panes in the rising wind made him start. He was quickly reassured—no noise from upstairs where they were. All the rooms downstairs seemed to be shuttered; he could almost turn the lights on, the way burglars did. He wasn't a burglar, after all, no way. This Clare bloke owed him. He'd as good as said he'd pay up if he had the money and if that black-haired skinny bitch hadn't stopped him. *She* wouldn't be so happy now. Not that he'd found much, but she'd have a lot of clearing up to do. Her jewelery was all beads and wood, might be a bloody African's.

He crossed a passage. The next room he found was smaller, quite poky and unrewardingly filled with books. The desk, with only a blotter on it, was empty of papers. He had come to expect figures, dummies, but there were none, nor any treasures either; over the mantelpiece some arty-crafty stuff was painted on the wood. He looked for a safe, but if such a thing existed it was hidden, perhaps behind books. He wasn't going to haul books out, right beneath their bedroom, to find a safe he very likely couldn't open. He wanted treasures that were lying about. The jewelery was going to be upstairs, most likely. It stood to reason a rich woman had jewels. She'd put the rubbish on the dummies but she'd have the real stuff herself. He retraced his steps to where he'd come in and where there were stairs going up to-

ward the tower. Nice secret place, a tower, might well
have things stashed away there. He climbed, the pencil
beam always on the step above. Here was the bedroom
floor; he was setting off along the passage when he heard
voices and a distant door opened, or shut; he wanted
no trouble, and his shoulder still hurt from how she'd
twisted him round; judo, that was, and bloody dangerous. He'd seen how they killed people in the Chinese
movies. He nipped up the next flight of tower stairs to
wait.

At the turn of the stairs, the light caught an angled
gap in the wall and he risked the full beam of the torch
for a second. This was the job, a door painted to look
like part of the wall, but someone had luckily been dead
stupid enough to leave it a bit open.

He pushed the door. The beam showed a pair of feet
standing there just inside, under a long flowing dress. It
gave him a bad moment all right, but the feet wore
painted shoes. He reached out and touched the plastic,
solid arm. The figure's orange wig was long and tied up
with one of those hippie Indian scarves; took him back
to the sixties and the bloody fool Sharon had made of
herself when all that gear was in and they were going
together. He scanned the room with the torch and, in
spite of himself, started at the sight of another dummy
sitting there on the left-hand window seat, hands on its
knees like it was meditating or doing yoga or whatever
those flower people did. The light briefly caught the glitter of eyeballs, the droopy long wig, the fringed suede
waistcoat and purplish madras-cotton shirt. The nutters
who'd set these dummies around hadn't just done Victorian things. He felt sour at the sixties being museum
times. He'd been a young man in the sixties. It was still
yesterday.

He moved the beam to examine the room. The draught
came from the other window that was wide open and
rattling a bit against its catch. There was going to be a
storm. Let's hope it didn't piss down before he could
reach the car . . . a small desk showed up, between the
windows, and he advanced eagerly. There could be a

check book, credit cards. The desk top was cluttered with little china containers of more dried plants, and on the writing shelf a small jar of different kinds of flowers tipped over as he started in on the drawers. Quick now, find something. This house with its silent figures was spooking him. He turned drawers upside down on the floor and scattered cut-out pictures, postcards, silk flowers, plaster animals, *rubbish!* A folded tissue unwrapped itself. He saw the sparkle in its folds, seized it and shook it out on the desk. Here was something! A glitter of gold and colors, flowers made of real jewels, small but real—rubies, emeralds, sapphires, amethyst, brilliantly shimmering. A little brass horse thudded to the floor as he reached for the necklace, but that was not what made him suddenly turn.

The figure from the window seat had risen. Horror disabled him for one second before he was pushed hard against the wall. He hefted the torch as a weapon, and his wrist was seized, the blow he aimed came down on his own head. He felt the jar of it, and felt his arm turned exactly as she had turned it. He was released, and staggered and felt himself stumble, knew he was falling but not where. The wind was against his back. His leg hit something, so did his shoulder, the world was the wrong way up and the wind all round him as he fell.

I can't really say I've seen the ghost. I'll have to say that the ghost has seen me. I had been in the observatory to water the palm. Kay says it's a miracle it's still alive, being neglected all those years, but I think it kept going on the tears of the house. When I was away I dreamt of the house, nearly every night. No, there were weeks either I didn't dream of it, or didn't remember my dreams if I did. It was like being without water in a desert. Then, for no reason I could ever see, I'd wake and realize I'd been there again. I'd get stuck in one room for ages, the dining room for instance with the Spanish leather on the wall. It's so dark I wish I could move into the morning room and see the lavender bushes from the window seat. But I could never choose, and the dreams werent always happy.

What I saw today was like those dreams, it had that sort of atmosphere, the feeling you can't move, helplessness when you don't even know you need help. I was going into the drawing room from the conservatory. I'd had a feeling I was being watched, I'd even peered about under the vine into the shadows, or behind the plants, those that are left like dead creatures—the vine is really like a great gray dragon now with twisted arms stretched across the glass as though it had died in agony. There was nothing there and I thought: I expect I'm going potty, like Granny. People have always told me I'm mad. Don't bite, Miranda, don't scream, you're mad.

I stopped in the doorway of the drawing room because I saw a face. In the mirror over the mantel opposite the door. I couldn't move. I thought, in a minute I shall wake up and know I've been dreaming I'm in the conservatory again.

Perhaps I blinked. In that second the face had gone and I could move. I didnt go back to see if anyone was there, I went to Kay in the study and sat by him while he wrote. He held out his left hand to me while he was writing and I took it and kept it in mine. If he knew about the ghost he would worry about me. What I dont understand is why he hasnt seen it too. He would expect to share a ghost.

A bird woke Easter to morning light, a bird with an urgent message: *leave it, leave it,* and, after a pause, it or another bird added in disapproving tones, *pity you did it, pity you did it.* Well, now, a fair comment of significance for just about everyone. Who had no regrets? A dumb question; some regretted, some didn't. Some types could justify anything they did and there must be others who never thought twice about even murder. If murder was an assertion of power, you might not regret having shown you had power.

And she—what did she regret? *Pity you did it . . .* as

she yawned, and regarded Clovis's hunched shoulders turned from her, his hair on the pillow not unlike a ginger kitten—what was she doing mixed up in all this? She wasn't in love with Clovis but he was the person who made her laugh the most, and he'd been needing help. Was that a good reason for waking up beside him in this house where his mother had been killed not so long ago? Most people would want out from such a scenario. Could be a Ken Russell movie. *I should run naked through the garden to passionate music by Tchaikovsky, while blood drips down the wall in subliminal shots.* See anyone running slow or fast through this garden. There'd been a sword under the bed. Here, in this house, the sword had been used. This wasn't a historic old place where siege and warfare had made bloodshed a usual thing. Miranda must be the first to die violently here. And what about Kay, that elusive silent figure? If Kay had killed himself, *why* wasn't there a suicide note?

Easter did not suffer from hangovers. She disapproved of them. Nevertheless, when she sat up, the world moved in a way she did not much fancy. Water, she thought. I need a lot of water. Then coffee.

She tried to run a hand through her hair, desisted at the tangles, yawned, regretted what this did to her head, and looked to see if there was any water by the bed. Of course there was not. All her deep philosophical thoughts of a moment ago had vanished before a simple thirst. Clovis was breathing softly, with that pause in which the sleeper seems to review the advisability of continuing. A quick headcount assured her that no dummies inhabited this room as well.

There was a noise downstairs, a tearing, crunching sound. Her mind presented her with the picture of a large dog pulling off flesh, cracking bones, but she dismissed this as irrelevant. The noise continued, with furtive pauses, as though whatever was making it waited to see if anyone heard.

Easter turned to shake Clovis.

"Uueerngh?"

"Shsh. Listen."

"What the—"

"Someone's breaking in."

His expression was of complaint rather than alarm. He too gazed round, disoriented. The large dog downstairs worried its meal again and he sat up, pearly naked. He listened, turned to her and said, "Someone's breaking in."

"Yeah." She thought *I don't need this*.

Clovis held his head briefly between his hands, then slid from bed and found his jeans. The noise downstairs stopped. She too dressed, aware of a lack of oxygen; this was, then, a hangover. She had no headache, and at the thought, tapped the bedhead: knock on wood. Her boots were missing, and she had vague memories of casting them off somewhere downstairs in last night's little party.

The noise downstairs resumed again. Clovis took the poker from the bedroom fire irons and padded out. Together they descended the stairs, watchful, pausing to listen.

"It's the front door," he said, and leant over the banister rail to try to see. The sound stopped, and she heard voices further away.

She and Clovis reached the front door, which was almost open, just as a uniformed figure loomed outside.

"Better put the poker down," she said, swiftly, forgetting for a moment that these police wouldn't be armed. Clovis dumped it on the hall chest beside the electric torch, and opened the door. It was an exceptionally large policeman who immediately filled the frame and said, "Well now, may I ask what you're doing here?"

"I'm the owner," Clovis said; he dug in his pocket and once more produced the key. "I'm Clovis Clare; son of the . . . late owner."

"We weren't informed anybody would be here. You don't mind my asking if you can prove it, sir?" He gave first Clovis, then Easter, a stare of overt disbelief.

"I hope I can. I'm not carrying anything identifying."

"I can prove who I am and vouch for him," Easter

said. She wondered how far the second statement was true, but she was going along with it anyway. "Besides, some of your people know us. Sergeant Hooley and Inspector Garron and Inspector Locker—"

"And Superintendent Bone," Clovis said.

"Then you won't mind if I just radio for verification."

"My guest." Clovis swept a hand.

"My colleague went round the back of the house . . ."

"I'll call him," Easter said. The sooner these people were gone, the sooner she could get at a tall glass of cold water and then breakfast, and get the world to settle down. She could vouch for it that alcohol remained in the system; her eyes were still playing up as she ran through the house to the morning-room, site of their last night's happy, if slightly desperate, mini-debauch. She could see along the back of the kitchen wing a youngish policeman alertly scanning windows, and she flung up the sash and leant out.

"It's okay," she called. "Go round the front and come in. We're allowed to be here—genuine inhabitants. Everything's fine."

He came closer all the same, along the weedgrown flagstones. A strong smell of lavender came up from the bushes under the window and, aware also of some peripheral disturbance, Easter looked down.

Directly below her lay the garage man. He was a curious bleached-out color and very wet. The odd angle of his head made him look like a puppet dropped by its handler. He was certainly and unmistakably dead.

Easter, not given to profanity, said, "Holy shit."

It was beginning to be one of those days in July about which people make jokes: this is the summer, it's all we'll get this year, make the most of it. Bone, already in shirtsleeves, shielded his eyes against the morning sun, unwilling to snap down the Venetian blind. He looked through the day's work on his desk, wishing he had a reason to get out of the station, wondering why he felt restless. The card from Cha that morning had been of Lake Windermere in improbably bright colors.

The only times he had ever seen it, the distances and the fells had been invisible with rain, but here the sky was Med Blue. She wrote that she was having a wonderful time. She and Prue had been on the lake in a boat, watched sheepdog trials, put a tent up all by themselves, cooked dinner for themselves and Prue's parents, and the weather was "perfectly O.K." Cha had, in the past when her damaged leg was hurting her, assured him it was "perfectly O.K." so he visualized them struggling with sopping canvas and spitting barbecues. When you were young, things like that were fun.

Time to reach for the retirement clock and the toupee when you started thinking in that fashion. Some people stay children forever. Look at the Shelleys. Miranda's diary had given him a curious sympathy for a point of view not at all his own, for her outlook which said "Go for what you need and damn the rest." There was a lot to be said for self-centeredness on that scale. Is the world well lost for love? Mark Antony, dying of a stomach wound and a botched suicide, might have had second thoughts. Miranda Shelley, when she closed the doors of Summerdown against the world, against the reality she didn't choose to face, could hardly have expected to pay with her life.

Bone realized why he had thought of Mark Antony. Miranda Shelley, white on Ferdy Foster's operating table, had a wound that seamed her from groin to ribs. Impossible to believe that Kay Shelley, her twin, perhaps her lover, had done that.

He opened the diary once more; he had read nearly all there was here. The later books must be found; there had to be at least one more.

Looking back I'm sorry now, really sorry, about Garys hair. It was wrong. He could not help how he was, but children dont know that. He was naturally loopy. He tried so hard, and he was so ugly in horrible clothes and hair cut so badly. He wanted so awfully to join in and be like us and we were dreadful. I was. I thought of it, and the mouthwash powder was red. I

*thought he would just look silly with red hair and his
beastly cross mother would go for him. He could we
know he would go purple? His hair and his head and
his hands and he got it all over his neck and the towel
and his vest. He looked so funny, he really did, and I
still think so, and we laughed and laughed, and turned
him round, and he was looking at the towel and his
hands so he knew about his hair. So he looked at us.
He just looked at us for ages, do you remember? That
was so queer. He didn't do anything until he hit you
and ran. Then we could hear him crying. He never came
bothering us again. He just used to watch us from a
distance, and now I think that's sad.*

So do I, Bone thought. What could happen to a little
boy treated like that? The consequences of childhood
treatment of Miranda and Kay were clear enough.

A tap on the door and Locker came in. Hot weather
didn't suit a man of his bulk and he was already mopping
his face.

"Thought you should know. The patrol car just reported intruders at Summerdown; cars parked at the
top, and they're investigating."

"Intruders," Bone mused. "Wonder if it's the same
who called on Miranda Shelley."

"You think we should send a backup?"

He thought of the Press prying about, or of more dubious characters finding a way into the place with its price-
less furnishings. Or of thieves who might have killed
Miranda, been scared off and now returned for the
Burne-Jones panels, Whitewick chairs and the embroi-
deries. "Shortage of men or not, we should have left it
to more than a patrol, Steve. Come along. We're going
there." They didn't talk much in the car. A wasp swung
in through the wide open window and Bone made such
a vicious swipe at it that he hurt his hand on the back
of the front seat and made the driver swerve slightly.

"Missed."

"The villains have all the luck, sir."

A suffocating smell of pig manure prevented further

speech. It was far too late, and too hot, to wind up the windows and they drove on in sticky silence until the stench dispersed, Bone thinking about Cha in the refreshing rain of the Lakes. The weather man last night had made cheery remarks about "wet spells in the North." If only some witch would cast a wet spell round here, Locker for one would be grateful. He was fanning himself with a road map and loosening his tie.

When they reached Summerdown the heavy stillness of the trees overhead at last gave shade. The radio came across suddenly with a message just as they were climbing out.

"They've discovered a body, sir," the driver said.

11

"Look at that, sir."

A car rounding the bend in the drive had stopped with its bonnet in the undergrowth.

"That belong to the intruders? Or what about the Renault here? Reckon none of them've left anyhow."

How convenient if it were in fact the ones responsible for the Shelley murder, how delightful to walk in on a neatly handcuffed villain. Come back to light more candles, hold a little service? Bone's vagrant imagination had all but fitted up the scene with a pair of homicidal vicars, when they arrived at Summerdown's porch, Locker mourning a rip in his trouser leg delivered by a bramble.

The door was open. Bone put a hand where no one was likely to have touched, and pushed it back, pointing out the splintering round the lock.

"There's your bit of unlawful entry."

What still surprised him was the fact that whoever murdered Miranda Shelley had *not* broken in. It was curious that a woman who refused to see anyone, who kept even her ex-husband out in the porch, had apparently let someone in. Edwin Clare had yet to explain his claim not to have seen Miranda for all those years; it would be quite in line with Bone's knowledge of human

nature if Dr. Clare had killed, not for himself or for his
children, but for a necklace denied him, a last straw.
He was thinking, in fact, how like Edwin Clare's face
was to a camel's in its expression of sensitive superiority, when Clovis Clare came into the hall from the back
of the house.

"Welcome to the ancestral lobby, Superintendent.
We've had another surprise, less nasty but bad enough.
A dead stranger in the lavender bushes."

"Are you the intruders who were reported, Mr.
Clare?"

"Easter and I. Yes. But that part's perfectly all right.
We've jumped probate, but the place is mine."

Miranda, Bone thought, would have opened the door
to her son. To have moved in here so fast argued against
him; it did not suggest a regard for his mother's death.
And now?

Other people were coming into the hall. Bone recognized Brenn and Harker, who looked rather surprised at
having his message answered so promptly and augustly.
Easter Lennox now, with that cloud of black hair and
those snapping black eyes she'd make a fine Lady Macbeth, and moreover you would see why Macbeth had
fallen for her. She came to stand by Clovis Clare as
though ready to do any hatchet jobs he wasn't up to.
Now up came the tall man with gray hair and Mount
Rushmore features who had been at the inquest. Bone
had temporarily placed him as a lawyer—God knows
they might be going to need one—when Clovis waved
an airy hand.

"Earl Whitewick, from the States. *You* know, Superintendent; Philip Whitewick's grandson."

As it happened, Bone did know. He remarked blandly,
"Ah yes, the architect of Summerdown, Plas Pentygh-
ent in Wales, Brae Top in Scotland and Bliss Castle."

The cornflower-blue eyes behind the gold-rimmed
glasses opened wide. "Why, this is certainly gratifying!
I have come straight from Brae Top. I am over here
researching a book on my grandfather . . ."

"I'm sure you'll excuse me." Bone had all this time

been moving toward Harker, in Locker's wake. He gave Whitewick a smile. "I should like to have a long talk about Philip Whitewick—if I get time." The smile was friendly, unusual for Bone, and Whitewick responded.

"Why of course—"

They all turned their heads at the distant sirens. Bone stopped where he was, and motioned to Harker to go out and escort the reinforcements down. He said to Clovis, "How did you get in? Is that"—he pointed at the door—"your work?"

"No, that was what woke us this morning. Our entrance last night was quite mundane." He produced, with a conjuror's air, a key.

"Your mother gave you a key."

The light eyes regarded Bone for a moment while, quite obviously, their owner explored the suggestion for its possibilities; Clare was always going to say the most expedient thing. This time he probably saw that to own a key to a place where murder had been committed was of adverse use. "No. I took it from the desk when you were interviewing Easter that night. Kay showed it to me months ago. He used to . . ." For the first time Bone saw a look of grief on his face; but then his glance passed Bone and altered entirely. The sardonic grin returned.

In the porch stood Edwin Clare, a reconnoitring camel. Dressed in dark gray pin-stripe, pale blue shirt and burgundy tie, he stood framed against the gravel and the undergrowth beyond, as much at home as a civil servant in a fairytale.

"Dad! What a lovely surprise."

"I was in the neighborhood." The camel turned its head toward Bone, then Whitewick. "There seems to be a disturbance, so I came to see what was going on." It was the governor of an outlying province delivering a rebuke to those who should have been in charge. Bone reflected that it was kind of another suspect to arrive in so auspicious a manner and with so poor an excuse. "In the neighborhood" had better be explained. He was about to pursue this when Clovis, an arm round Easter, came forward.

"Really? Thought you might be back for another pop at the necklace."

"I don't know what you're talking about." The camel was definitely having to cope with the last straw. "*Nothing* to do with it. The necklace has nothing to do with it. I was anxious about the house. It seemed to me very possible there would be those who would take advantage of a house known to be empty, which contains things of value. I saw that the police were here. I hope there has in fact been no break-in?"

"Not since this morning, thanks for asking. And we have an unknown body on the premises, or to be exact, just off them."

"*A body?*"

"Was that your car in the lane opposite, Dr. Clare?"

"No. No. My car is . . . Which lane?"

"There are two cars parked in the lane leading off toward Hencham, almost opposite the drive."

"Oh, *that* lane. Certainly."

"You've been here for some little time, then. Whereabouts have you been?"

Clovis watched the scene with an air of happy mischief. His father had come into the hall, and now waved vaguely at the ambient air. "I was walking around the back."

Steve Locker, who had arrived quietly through the study, now said, "I'm sorry to have missed you, sir." Bone took the clue.

"What did you see round the back, Dr. Clare? It may be important."

Edwin Clare had turned toward Locker, and Bone saw, in secret and simple pleasure, that he had small white flowers on the back of his head and collar, and some marks of damp on the backs of his trouser legs. The small white flowers he recognized as coming from the hebe bush that nestled against the front of the house under the windows of the billiard room. Bone beckoned up Hooley and gave him directions; meanwhile he could hear the team's arrival and the tramp of feet through the undergrowth of the drivepath and round to the back of the house.

Edwin Clare was explaining to Locker that he had not got far. His exploration had been halted by a twisted ankle; and turning again toward Bone he did indeed limp with some pathos.

At this moment Hooley appeared in the porch. He was holding, by a pencil through the hole in its handle, a large screwdriver, and on the chest and shoulder of his uniform were small white flowers.

Clovis Clare made the inference at once. "So that's why you were here; you came calling with a jemmy—I was damn right first time: a pop at the necklace. She wouldn't give it to you so you'd come and get it."

"We were in bed asleep. You woke us." Easter Lennox's voice sounded dauntingly flat with its accent.

"What absolute rubbish!" Dr. Clare stretched his neck, indignant and a little shrill. "I simply came to see that all was well at Summerdown. The place was very much loved by Miranda—"

"You bloody hypocrite!" Clovis let go of Easter and lunged forward, so menacingly that his father backed into the hallstand, jangling a collection of parasols and sticks. "You never gave a shit for Miranda's feelings. Summerdown could have burnt to the ground and you'd have been delighted. You hated the place *because* she loved it!"

Edwin Clare's dignity had got somewhat dented by a stick in the hallstand which, when he stepped back, had managed to insert its crook of tarnished silver into his pocket. As he struggled with this, and made noises indicative of an imminent reply to his son's outburst, Bone was thinking: he came to get the necklace and cared enough about it to take the disreputable step of breaking in. Surely, he would have had time, if he'd killed his ex-wife, to search for it then? Yet he might have killed her in fury during an argument and fled in horror from what he had done, or he might have been scared off by Kay.

Having extracted the stick's handle from his pocket, Edwin Clare did not at once return it to its place, but grasped it belligerently.

"You're being quite absurd. You know nothing at all about your mother. Getting sentimental over a woman who abandoned you—and I hardly feel your sentiments are very real if you can come here and install yourself and bring your mistress—Superintendent, surely this house is not to be squatted in?" He made it sound as if his son were using Summerdown as a lavatory.

"I've every right to be here. You told me yourself that Summerdown is mine, and in that case so is everything in it. The necklace'll look nice round Easter's neck, won't it?"

Even Bone was startled at the reaction to this. A blur resolved itself into Edwin Clare laying into his son with the stick that had been in love with his pocket. A number of things happened then, some a little in advance of others, like Easter Lennox darting in to aim a kick into the mêlée. Whitewick, Locker, Hooley and Bone converged, Bone to seize Clare's arm that wielded the stick; Clare proved remarkably strong, thrusting Bone aside into Hooley. It was a chop from Easter Lennox, delivered with a cry like a demented seagull, that brought all action to an end. Edwin Clare dropped the stick and followed it to the floor.

A remembered, plangent voice said, "Hel-*lo!* Everybody having a good time?" And Bone looked at Angie Clare silhouetted in the doorway.

Dr. Clare, as a neurologist, might be supposed to know more about the state of his nervous system than anyone else, but he seemed disposed to milk the situation. Bone believed that his wish to be accommodated in one of the bedrooms was not unconnected with a desire to explore upstairs, and had him installed on a drawing-room sofa. He showed no aversion to entering the drawing-room, as he might have done had he known where Miranda died; on the other hand, he did not remark on its carpetless state. Perhaps he was too absorbed in his symptoms, and in informing P.C. Benn that he intended to charge Easter with assault. Clovis was having two quite nasty blows, one to the shoulder and the other to the side of his head, attended to in a bathroom by the police doctor; Easter and P.C. Chawley were in attendance. Bone turned to Angie Clare. Now that she had come forward she was seen to be wearing a black stretch skirt, the usual black tights and high heels, and a cadmium-yellow silk bomber jacket.

"Hi," she said, with a widening of eyes that suggested she and Bone shared some disreputable knowledge. "When Ma Mallard said Edwin was down here I didn't look to find a *convention* going on; not to mention another installment of the family war."

"Why did you want to find Dr. Clare?"

Angie made a face. "I didn't, believe me. I wanted to find out about the house. This house, I mean. I mean, if Lionel would have inherited anything then I do too."

"He hadn't altered his will when you separated, then."

"We didn't 'separate'—I told you we were resting from each other. He would come to discuss it and we'd just end up in bed. It was the same when he came to talk money. He was *crazy* about me. We never got to talk because afterwards after his shower he'd simply go. Not a word out of him."

Bone imagined Lionel Clare's silent self-loathing.

"If you believe you stand to inherit, Mrs. Clare, you would do best to apply through your solicitors."

"And they take their whack out of it too. You can't win, can you? But I wanted to see what there was here. It's quite a place." She looked round the hall with assessing eyes.

"There's an investigation in progress, Mrs. Clare."

Angie gave one of her undulations. "Investigation? Has someone else died?"

"Yes," Bone said repressively. She allowed a slight pause for the explanation he didn't give and he strode away to join Locker on his heels on the terrace flags and watch the search of the body. The camera team had withdrawn. Locker put aside a broken frond of lavender engaged in a dental check on Ron Dace's open mouth.

"Nothing connected with this place is straightforward," Locker said. "That door there—" he nodded at the foot of the tower—"was forced; with something far bigger than Dr. Clare was working with, more like a cold chisel, I'd say. But it'd been wedged shut. From the inside, I mean, with a piece of wood, firewood."

Sergeant Hooley suddenly snatched his hand from under the body's neck, exclaiming "Damn nettles!" and reached his other hand inside the jacket, leapt to his feet and swore hideously as a bee lurched out past the crumpled shirt and away into the garden.

"That precious pair deny wedging the door. Clare says he has no idea who the body is, and heard nothing the whole night except the rain. He and Lennox were together the whole night. P.C. Benn says he'd go bail—Hooley, you'd better see what there is in the kitchen, or ask the doc for something; a bee sting isn't the end of the world."

"No, sir," said poor Hooley. "Just it's in the palm of me hand."

"Hop into the house and get it seen to," Bone directed; he felt remorse at his enjoyment of pure theater in the successive stings. The morning, unfortunate for some, had presented him with entertainment in its fashion. "P.C. Benn says he'd go bail to what?"

Locker continued, after unzipping the corpse's jacket and turning back the sides to allow any more wildlife to escape. "That the young woman was genuinely surprised when she saw the body. She'd come to lean out of that window and tell him Harker said he should come back, like, the intruders were accounted for; and she looked down and she said a swear word as if she meant it, and stood there frozen." He took a wallet from the inside pocket and said, "Here we go. Ronald Dace, says his credit card; and here's a business card, Cransley—"

"Cransley garage," Bone said. "Steve, he was at the inquest. Lionel Clare's inquest."

Both of them stood up.

"I think Clovis Clare had better explain a thing or two," Locker said. "I didn't recognize Ron Dace either; a bloke can look very different after a fall and a night in the rain. But how did he get his fall, from a house Clare is living in?"

"Where did he fall from?" Bone asked, looking up.

"That's a bit of a problem. If he'd fallen off that tower balcony there'd be signs but there's nothing up there; you can make out shutters in the cladding below that, if you look. There's a room there, we think, with a door into it from the tower stairs, and we're going to have to break it down; it doesn't have any opening that we can see. Dr. Hines says the injuries, so far as he can trace what's damaged, are consistent with a fall that far into bushes that broke the force of the landing."

He looked down again at Ron Dace, and stopped to pull out a corner of shiny paper from an inside pocket of the spread jacket. It was a crumpled photograph, a slightly grainy blow-up of a woman looking over her arm that rested along a chair-back; a good pose that hid the neck and chin of a woman not young. She was still a beauty, and it did not need the inscription to tell who she was: the long nose, longer than Easter's, the eyes a little closer together. The writing said *Easter, because you insisted. The ugly mug shot. Mom.*

"Steve. The extraordinary obliquity of that pair of rapscallions is being more than marginally tiresome."

"That's not all, sir. Not all they've done."

"Not? Give it mouth. What more iniquities?"

Locker knew from the language that Bone was seriously annoyed. He said, "The seals on Miss Shelley's bedroom door have been broken. We found a branch—like a spray—of artificial cherry on her bed. I've not mentioned it to them yet."

"We'll mention it to them now."

"Yes, sir. I'll just see about a team to do a search of this wilderness of a garden for a crowbar or cold chisel. We've not found it in the house."

An enraged yell in a room upstairs, and an outcry of

voices, sent Bone and Locker in by the damaged tower door and up to the first floor.

In the gallery, Harker was beleaguered. Earl Whitewick, backed against a wall, clasping his camera protectively to his chest. Edwin Clare was making a try, evidently not the first, to get it from him, surging forward against Harker's arm while Angie pulled him away by the shoulder of his jacket.

"I insist. You had no right—"

"—caught you out!" Angie cried gleefully.

"I absolutely *require* you to hand that over—"

"Now then, sir—"

Edwin reached toward the camera. Harker swung round to fend him away, and Angie dragged at the jacket, pulling it from Edwin's shoulders. Still he clawed toward the camera, and struck out ineffectively at Harker. At this, he was pinioned and lifted away from Whitewick, who sidled toward Bone. In this movement Angie had been brushed aside and tottered indignantly. In the background, a silent and obviously mesmerized crew of the figures were audience. A seated female figure nearest to them had been tipped sideways almost off her chair.

"I assure you, sir, I thought you were another of these mannequins."

Angie Clare shrieked laughter. "Just another dummy!"

Bone cut in sharply. "What did you photograph, Mr. Whitewick?"

"Why it seems it was Mr. Clare—"

"Doctor Clare!"

"I beg your pardon. It's too bad of me not to have caught your proper title, Dr. Clare. I took a flash of what I thought to be a group of these very interesting figures, and one of them was Dr. Clare."

"And what was my darling daddy-in-law doing? He was looking at the *other* dummy's necklace, that's what."

"There is no reason why I should not—"

"Then why did you want to grab the camera?" She planted her hands on her hips. "Just let us hear about that!'' She turned to Bone and with a clash of bracelets pointed at Edwin. "He's after that necklace we've all heard about, which if it's anyone's is *mine*."

"Nothing of the sort." Edwin Clare's face became suffused. "Miranda should have returned it to me. It belongs to my family."

"And you told me yourself how sorry you were not to be able to give it to the eldest son's bride; which is me."

"I see I have to remind you that you are not a bride but a widow. The necklace is nothing to do with you."

Bone had been following his custom of learning through listening, but he saw no future in the present bicker.

"I should like everyone downstairs," he said. His tone was such that they all moved to the door. "Mr. Whitewick: one moment."

Dr. Clare and Angie went out, subdued, shepherded by P.C. Harker, with whom Locker would certainly be having a word about their being upstairs at all.

Whitewick, Mount Rushmore now registering unease, waited.

"Some correspondence of yours with Mr. Kay Shelley, Mr. Whitewick, suggests that you've been trying for some time to get into this house."

"But lawfully! I assure you, sir, I am not a man to break into a property."

"Kay Shelley had refused permission, I believe."

"There seemed no way I could convince him to allow me—yet I put it to him how important it was to any definitive work to include such things as decorative detail and furnishings, and I assured him, as you will have seen, that I would avoid any trespass on the sensibilities of the family."

"You said a short time ago that you had come straight from Brae Top."

"Yes, I've been photographing there with the full co-operation of Mr. and Mrs. McLintock—"

"You were at the inquest on Lionel Clare."

"Why, you see, I knew of the connection. I had read

of the tragedy. I supposed that Dr. Clare—I certainly should have recalled his proper title—would have little or no feeling about the place and would be willing to permit photography, but he told his daughter-in-law quite, I may say, forcefully, that he had no part in the house, and that it was none of her business who would inherit it.''

"You came here earlier this year.'' Bone made the statement on a hunch born of Miranda's diaries and the letter Whitewick had written to Kay.

"Why, I—yes, I did try to see if I might not persuade Mr. Shelley more effectively in person. Dr. Clare, though I did not at the time know it was he, had arrived, and he had to stand at the door while Mr. Shelley came to speak to me.''

"Was Miss Shelley there?''

"I believe it would be Miss Shelley whom I could see inside the door. She had all but closed it. I introduced myself very quickly, since I thought that Mr. Shelley had mistaken me for a Press photographer, but he was no less adamant than in his letters. I saw it was no moment to pursue it further.'' Whitewick's voice expressed a plaintive bafflement. "He would not even listen to me, and threatened to call the police.''

A threat emptier than Whitewick could know. A telephone wire was still attached to an insulator on a front gable of the house.

"But something very alarming occurred when I was on my way toward that little track. Something struck my camera. I thought it was a shot; the lens seemed to explode. I felt the impact on my chest. There was no shot—no bullet. For one moment I quite believed in some occult power—some malevolence on Mr. Shelley's part. A bullet would have lodged in the camera.''

"Very disturbing for you,'' Bone said. "I'd like you to come downstairs, Mr. Whitewick, and give details of your recent travels and timetable to Sergeant Harker.''

"Captain, you cannot suppose—''

"If you please.'' Bone indicated the door. As they followed, Locker said, "Captain . . .'' and Bone feinted at him with a fist behind Whitewick's retreating back. As Whitewick started down the stairs, Locker in a lowered voice went on, "Super, what do you reckon on him?"

"What do you?"

"May have got in when the Shelleys had the doors open. It's been summer weather. Say Miss Shelley surprised him and he panicked. Mind you, he'd be a cool customer to turn up like this now."

"The case is suppurating with cool customers. Shortly, Steve, we're going to talk to two of them." Bone had, to an extent, his own truth-radar, powered by long discouraging experience. He still put Clovis Clare's credibility rating well off the lower end of the scale.

They went to inspect the secret door and the top of the tower once more. Bone looked at the delicate branch of nacreous cherry blossom on Miranda's bed before the room was once more, uselessly but for form's sake, sealed. Going downstairs he found Easter and Clovis, with Earl Whitewick who still held his camera at the ready hung on his chest; Harker came in at the front door and reported that Dr. Clare was again lying down and Mrs. Clare had left. Chawley stood close by.

"Well, Superintendent," Earl Whitewick said, showing that he had done more homework on titles, "this morning's fatality is a further blow." He reached out and captured one of Easter Lennox's narrow hands in his expansive pair, clearly glad of the opportunity. "I have been hearing of Miss Lennox's traumatic experience of yesterday."

Of yesterday? Bone thought today's might be considered quite sufficient. He held out the creased photograph and said, "This, I suppose, is yours."

Her face came alight and she stood up and reached for it. "Why yes! It was one of the things—Clovis, see—"

"Oh, that's great. That's really great." He had leant to see, and now hugged her shoulders with one arm. He looked up at Bone. "Where'd you find it?"

"You're quite right. That is the point. It was found in the pocket of the body outside your window."

Both of them stared at him; Easter Lennox was the first to show comprehension.

"That little garage man! Clovis, the one from the inquest. I told you I knew his face. *He* must be the one who burglarized my apartment. He must have heard my address at the inquest, but why he thought I had any money I cannot imagine. I was wearing my wooden beads. Will I be able to have this again?" Bone had drawn the photograph away from her hands, and she had not tried again to touch it. "It really matters very much to me. It's important to me, I mean, because I don't have any other picture of her."

"Did you see the man who broke into your apartment?" Bone asked. She shook her head, the cloud of hair swinging after.

"If he had this, he has to be the one. It's the only connection."

"He'd a nerve to come down here," Clare said. "I suppose he heard about it at the inquest? Or read in the papers? There's been some stupid stuff written about the place, you'd think it was the Taj Mahal or Topkapi."

Perhaps, Bone thought, you came down here for the same reason; there are a good many things here that an inpecunious young man might put on the market.

"There are one or two other questions that we want to go into," he said. Earl Whitewick, who had risen courteously when Easter did, now immediately came forward.

"If there's anything I can do?"

Bone did not think Whitewick's help would be required, but he said, "Very good of you," and turned to Clovis. "There's a room above Miss Shelley's bedroom. The door appears to have a trick lock of some kind. Would you open it, please."

Clovis blankly said, "What room? If it's got a trick door I haven't a clue—it must be Miranda's own room, she said . . ."

"If I may." Whitewick, delighted, came between

them. "If I may! It's most gratifying to be of use; but I have my grandfather's notes on Summerdown and many of his drawings, and I believe I can remember the trick to that door. If not, I have them in the trunk of my car; the drawings and notes, I mean. We could refer to them."

"You're providential," Clovis said. "I hate to open Miranda's private room, but if it's police, then—okay, come on."

Bone stood back, and Whitewick, making drawing gestures with his forefinger as if following a plan in his head, set off toward the tower.

Locker and Hooley were on the stairs there, still pressing at the tongue-and-groove boarding of the wall and door; the door was so well fitted that a cursory glance would not see it was there, and only the fact that, from external measurement by the eye, there had to be a room there, had made Locker find it, where Garron's team had failed.

"I think," Whitewick said, "I *think* it is under here." He bent and began pressing the risers of the stairs just beneath the treads. The second one he tried gave a click and the door sprung slightly ajar.

Locker, with innocent speed, blocked the effort by Whitewick and Clovis Clare to get instantly into the room. "Thank you, sir," he said. "Very grateful for your help."

"Many thanks, Mr. Whitewick," said Bone in his turn. "Now if you and Miss Lennox and Mr. Clare will wait for us downstairs once more, we'll talk to you again presently."

Easter's flat sardonic tone said, "Is it all right if we fix breakfast?"

"I expect P.C. Chawley could do with a coffee too," said Bone, ensuring them surveillance. He was in the doorway of the little room, and Locker's opening of a window and a shutter disclosed the fresh flowers in the little vase on the desk. There were sprigs of lavender and hebe, two winding sprays of honeysuckle with pink and golden flowers and unopened buds, an umbel of ground elder, buttercups and rosebuds, and heads of flowering grasses. It was pretty and showed a catholic choice. It stood on a little rush mat on which had dropped one or two globes of moisture, and in the leaf-axils were drops of rain.

"Clare made out that he didn't know how to get in here," Bone said.

"All the same, it's nice if he's put flowers, I suppose. And the cherry on her bed. It's made of shells and jade, I think. There's more of the same sort of twigs in the gallery in a big Chinese pot. Yes, sir, here's the marks on the sill and the inside of the shutter; scrapes and scratches; and a smear of rubber along the floor. This looks like where he went out of, all right."

"And who would find this place if he wasn't lured here?"

"And who'd wedge the door, sir, and where's the jemmy? So far we've not found a crowbar or a cold chisel in the tools here, either in the house toolbox or in the garden shed. There's not much in either of them anyway."

"We'll take Master Clare in, Locker, and see if we can get some sense out of him. His normal reaction seems to be: if you can't avoid it, joke about it. He's the type who'd come out with something wryly hilarious at Tyburn with the rope round his neck. Mind you, I'd expect him to sidestep murder too; it's unpleasant and it's committing—the ultimate commitment, the last word in confrontation. We are going to have to induce that young man to take a straight look, however distasteful and brief, at reality."

As they turned to leave the room, Bone met the calm gaze of the figure standing by the door. A wig of silky red hair and a long flowered dress gave an eerie resemblance to Miranda herself. What a pity this was a witness who would be for ever mute.

The man they had come to find was demonstrating his innocence by eating a hearty breakfast. Bone wondered which of the three who looked up as he and Locker entered the morning-room had fried the eggs and made the toast and coffee, whose fragrant smell made his nostrils dilate. Easter Lennox was pouring it and Clovis said hospitably, "Have a cup, Superintendent? You look as though you could do with one. You can relax, Dad and my refined sister-in-law have dispersed and the beating of Harpies' wings is no longer to be heard. Take the weight off your mind, sit down and have breakfast with us."

"I can fix you some eggs, Captain." Earl Whitewick half-raised his bulk from his chair, answering part of the question about cookery. Easter offered nothing except a cool stare from those large black eyes, as though she suspected why Bone was standing there.

"Mr. Clare, or Mr. Shelley, I must ask you to accompany us to the station for further enquiry." Bone always disliked his official tone: it sounded like another, pompous person speaking. There was no doubt, however, about its effect. Earl Whitewick sat down with a thud, Easter looked daggers Lady Macbeth would have been proud of, and Clovis murdered a fried egg with his dropped knife.

"Are you arresting me?"

"Why can't you question him here? You can't take him away without a warrant."

"British law, Miss Lennox, permits me to hold Mr. Clare for questioning up to twenty-four hours." The official voice, Bone noticed, had got colder and sharper. Clovis got up, pushing away the egg bleeding its golden life away on the plate.

"Let's get it over with then." He looked drawn. "But you know I've got nothing more to say, don't you?"

As to that, thought Bone, we shall see.

12

*B*one stood before the window in his office, whistling soundlessly, a tune which swam into his mind and which he finally pinned down, when he took notice of it, as the waltz from *The Sleeping Beauty;* its first few bars were very like those of a song his grandfather used to sing, "Sweet Rosie O'Grady." The romantic lilt was far from expressing his feelings. If he wanted to dance he would not choose to try it with Clovis Clare. A bathful of eels would be less elusive.

Thinking of eels made him also consider the pellucid coolness of their element. He felt at this moment thirstier for water than for coffee; the afternoon had improved on the morning's heat and the street outside baked and shimmered. From the main road came angry hooting and revving. On the opposite pavement of this side street, a child walked by, at each slow step tantalizingly dragging her tongue over the icecream in a cornet. Bone pictured Fredricks's reaction if he sent her out for ices, and pondered on the fact that men felt more obliged to crush the child in them than women did—perhaps sport was the expression, for many men, of the still-resident child.

Miranda and Kay Shelley had lived much the life of children, without responsibilities save to each other and to Summerdown; they had played their private games.

And he was no nearer to knowing what the nemesis could have been that finally caught up with them, putting a stop, like some dread grown-up, to the fun they were having.

He sighed sharply, turned on his heel and went back to his desk, taking his hands from his pockets as he went and rubbing their palms on a handkerchief. The finger he pressed on the intercom stuck to the button all the same.

"Has there been word from Inspector Locker?"

"He's just come in, sir."

"Ask him to come and see me."

Locker's face had an unhealthy flush and he availed himself gratefully of the chair indicated by Bone. His efforts to go on a diet had led to such uncharacteristic bad temper that both Cherry Locker and his Superintendent had accepted that if good humor and efficiency went with the weight, it was better that he should run whatever risks his bulk might incur.

"Well, Steve. If I put up a destination board, it'd read *Nowhere*. Clovis Clare and I just got there."

Steve Locker shook his head, and then mopped his brow as though even that small movement made him sweat.

"Didn't think you'd get far with that one. If he'd been my son he'd have come in for a good hiding."

"Well, Dr. Clare tried," Bone pointed out. From that brief onslaught in the hall, he had gathered that Clovis's upbringing had not been without tears. "I'm sorry for that young man. I think he's had a miserable time. No doubt Lionel did, too."

"So one kills his mother and the other kills himself?"

"You make it sound nice and homey, Steve, just like a Greek tragedy." Bone picked up a notebook and fanned himself with it. The electric wall fan had jammed, directing a steady draught at the top of the filing cabinet, and could not be used. "No, Clovis Clare has got his story and he's sticking with it. He saw the late Ron Dace for the first time at the inquest and the next time flat on his back saying it with flowers."

"We found the jemmy."

Bone raised his eyebrows interrogatively.

"A jemmy, at least, a cold chisel chucked into the long grass at the back of the house. Could have fallen from his hand as he fell. It's with Prints now."

Bone increased the breeze from the notebook, wondering if the exertion were worth it.

"What do you reckon on Ron Dace being in on the original murder, sir? Runs away when disturbed by Kay Shelley and comes back later to see what he can get."

"No sign of a break-in at the time of Miranda's murder. And she'd never have opened the door to a stranger." Let alone such an unappetizing stranger as Ron Dace.

Locker shifted and brought the handkerchief into action. "He could've walked in. I mean, the house couldn't have been hermetically sealed all the time." The very idea made him mop his face yet again.

"Motive, she surprised him? She found him looking around for things to nick and he panicked, snatches a sword from the wall and slashes out?" The notebook moved more slowly and was cast down. "But what's the connection with Lionel? Coincidence?"

"Well, sir, I was thinking, if he used the garage a lot and got chatting to Ron Dace, you know, the way one does."

"The way you do, Steve, is not necessarily the way Lionel Clare would do. From all I've gathered he'd as soon have kissed a leper as spoken to a man with a dirty face. But suppose he did give Dace the notion that Summerdown was Treasure Island, why does he commit suicide there? Or don't you think that part's connected?"

Locker leant forward, visibly thinking, and Bone, without knowing he was doing it, smiled at him.

"Sir, could Lionel Clare have gone to Summerdown and seen his mother murdered—that morning, perhaps—and decided it was all his fault for talking about the place and come to the garage to have it out with Ron Dace and then decided to top himself out of guilt anyway and—No, it doesn't work.'' Locker slumped back, discouraged.

"More convoluted things have been known to happen. But, so far as we've heard, Lionel Clare never went to Summerdown, and hated the very thought of his mother. Rejection isn't a very endearing thing.''

"How old was he when she left?'' Locker opened his notes and began searching for the information.

"Round about one. She left not long after Clovis was born and Lionel was almost one year older.''

"Old enough to miss her?'' Locker, fond and fierce father of two small boys himself, was indignant.

"You're suggesting that after nearly thirty years, Lionel trots round to Summerdown, tells his mother what he thinks of her and follows it up with a king-size exclamation mark from that sword hanging too conveniently close by . . . m'm. And we're still faced with those awkward facts: Miranda, according to the PM reports, was killed on the evening of the twenty-sixth and Lionel Clare spent the twenty-sixth at the Austin Clinic and slept there, according to the porter and the house officer, and left only at eleven a.m. on the twenty-seventh to go and get his car cleaned and his throat cut.''

"After an interview with his younger brother. Didn't Clovis Clare leave the Clinic at ten forty-five? According to the receptionist and porter again. Has he told you what he said before, that he went straight to Lennox's place in London?''

Bone pulled the damp knot of his tie further down. "He did *not* inform me that he loitered in the Clinic car park to pursue his brother Lionel to the garage, weasel up on him in the carwash and gibber till he opted for saying goodbye with a lancet.''

Locker knew that frivolity, like elaborate language, betokened a dwindling of his Superintendent's patience, and he phrased his next remark soothingly.

"You're right, sir, the suicide has likely nothing to do with it; the death of that patient was probably the reason, and it's merely a coincidence his mother's murder came then. You've often said yourself there's coincidences everywhere that go unnoticed. Cherry was reading a magazine the other day with really out-of-the-way examples in it; like the parallels between the murders of President Lincoln and President Kennedy.''

"I've heard about that. What were they again?"

Locker looked abashed. "I've forgotten most of them, sir. To do with names, I think."

"We have enough muddle to do with names on this case," said Bone irritably. "Two Dr. Clares for a start, then a Mrs. Clare called Shelley and now a Mr. Clare to be called Shelley. I checked with the Shelleys' lawyers that Summerdown is in fact to come to Clovis, and they tell me—a cheerful young man called Grimston—that it may indeed, on condition he changes his name to Shelley."

"Another smack in the face for her ex, I suppose, sir. How much do you fancy Dr. Clare for her death?"

Bone reached out to the intercom and asked for coffee. His mouth was dry, and a hot drink was reputed to be more cooling than a cold one. "Now you're asking. Give me the scene with Dr. Edwin as murderer, Steve."

Locker cogitated. "Didn't like her for a start, did he? Seems to be the one with the biggest *reason* for doing her in."

"So he waited thirty years or so."

"She only just got back from abroad."

"Some years; more than only just."

"He only recently found out? And he lied about it; about knowing where she was and about going there. Why lie?"

"He's not a fool; or not enough of one to see that it's better never to have been near a woman you hate who's got killed."

"And he wanted his necklace."

Bone smiled. He had not forgotten the pathos of Edwin Clare's simple statement.

P. C. Benn came in with a tray at this point. His shirt was sticking to him and he glanced in reproach at the useless wall fan as he put the tray down.

"Hurts me more than it hurts you," Bone said. "Have another try at getting the electrician, will you?"

"Sir." Benn unloaded his tray and withdrew. Bone watched Locker stir two heaped spoonsful of sugar into his cup, and looked away, unable to bear the thought of how cloying it would be to him. He shook his head at the plate of digestive biscuits Locker held out. His mouth tickled to think of them.

"That necklace. It's too often the small things that make a man really angry—as you know. A man might think he'd got over thirty years of desertion and find it all blown up out of proportion again over the necklace. He's going to marry; that brings it back."

"Bit mean, though, asking for the necklace he's given her."

Bone sipped at his coffee. "Ah, but he sees *her* as the mean one. When she chucked him, she should have chucked the bridal necklace back in case it was needed again." The coffee did remind him, that there were things hotter than his face. He could understand why desert Arabs were so fond of drinking it.

Locker was folding and unfolding his handkerchief, thinking. His coffee was already finished—his mouth of asbestos, Bone had commented on before—and he had consumed one biscuit and perched the remaining half of a second in his saucer. He looked up.

"He wouldn't have had to break in that time. She knew him, after all."

Bone remembered Miranda's account of Edwin's first visit, and her remarks on it in the minute script of her diary. "She might, or might not, have let him in, Steve. But then, doors may have been open. And, Steve, we're still left with this intruder, this untraceable third party Prints says was about. Random prints and not many or very recent. If they were recent, he'd be a candidate for it all too."

"Anything useful in the diary Clovis Clare had?"

"It's an old one, Steve. It's more concerned with why she left her husband. No, it's the last one we want, the latest; the readers have worked out that the one she was probably still writing is missing. The last one that's finished, they date to early this year, they found a reference to Clovis. The last book we've got is in patches quite incomprehensible. It's not just that she's writing quite openly by this time about the games they made up about their imaginary people—those mannequin figures—it's full of Julia and Clark, Mr. and Mrs. Perceval, Loveday and Adam, Lord Gervase and Uncle Tom Cobbleigh; no, it's Major Tom, I beg his pardon . . . no, it's also wandering. Then it'll be lucid for a stretch. She was showing the effects of that tumor."

"It's very pitiful, isn't it, sir?"

"Yes," said Bone. "Let's go and have another try at getting sense from her son. Don't let's forget another thing in his favor: Ron Dace was wearing, on a very warm July night, leather gloves. They were his all right, they were a good fit and when Shay pulled them off they kept the shape of his hands the way old gloves do. He went to Summerdown intending to leave no prints."

"Shay's been talking to Dace's family, sir. You want to hear him now?"

"We'd better. I need some twigs even to build a mare's nest. Let Shay bring me his twigs." Bone was reminded, as Locker sent for Shay, of the pretty branch of cherry on Miranda's bed. Teasing his memory was a poem that Petra used to chant. It must be in her anthology that was now in Cha's room. Cherry blossom bough?

The prosaic form of Sergeant Shay was not one to bewitch the eyes. Bone settled to listen.

Ronald Dace lived with his married sister in Tonbridge, an arrangement not to the liking of her husband. Bob Firkin barely tolerated his brother-in-law and barely concealed his relief at hearing he was dead. Allie Firkin had "lent" money to her brother continually; he gave cigarettes and beer to the children, and Sue, who was thirteen, did not like the way he kissed her. Des, who was eleven, thought his uncle a great guy, really nice. Last night his uncle, calling home briefly for some things from his room, had promised him a present—told him not to bother over his broken skateboard, he should have a new one. He was, he'd said, going to collect from someone who owed him. Des had repeated this clearly when asked, and said Uncle Ron was angry. Bob Firkin wasn't surprised at this. Ron was a man who bore grudges.

He had not mentioned the Clares, or Summerdown, to any of the family; at least, he had talked of Dr. Clare's suicide until his sister made him stop because of the children.

"Someone who owed him," Locker said. "At Summerdown?"

"We're going on the strong presumption that it was Ron Dace who broke into Easter Lennox's flat, that he didn't just get the photo from a mate who'd done it. And according to the local police it was a wrecking job. Was he angry because there hadn't been enough there to make it worth his while? That's what often makes these amateur break-in merchants vicious."

"Dace was spiteful anyway," Shay said. "Old Mrs. Firkin, that used to live with them as well, Bob's mother, she had a cat she really loved. Her son said she lived for that cat. It got poisoned, and Dace called young Des to watch it. When it was dead he told the kid to take it to his granma. That was near two years ago, when the kid was nine. He said he'd felt kind of nasty watching it die. Then some time later Ron said he'd done it, given it poison."

Bone mused on this foul little tale.

"I think we'll have a try at finding out what Dace thought was owed him. If he was going to collect it at Summerdown, Clovis knows why. And if, as I still believe, Dace recognized Clovis as the runaway witness, then it would be totally characteristic of that evasive young person to fly from a reality as disturbing."

Clovis Clare wilted, a neglected plant, in the interview room. A cup and saucer and a sandwich wrapper were on the table; his forearms had made patterns of damp on the plastic top just in front of him. His father's attack showed in an angry graze down one side of his face. He was tired, and he was distressed; but he still denied knowledge of Ron Dace, being present at the petrol station, knowing of the secret room at Summerdown . . . Bone supposed there were limits to the young man's ignorance.

13

*E*aster considered that disingenuousness was a game for others beside Clovis. Detective-Inspector Locker had advised her in what was all but an order to go back to town and her flat, or to friends, or to a hotel; and she had nodded and smiled. She had her own opinion about it. Earl Whitewick promised to convey her to the hotel where he intended to stay, and in Locker's hearing she thanked him. What was far more important to her was her own reaction to seeing Clovis led away and to his distraught glance at her as he went. She was surprised at herself.

By midday she had seen a restored Edwin escorted to his car, cutting her dead in the hall as he went. She supposed he had received a scold from the impressive Detective-Superintendent, as they had been shut into the drawing-room for a while. She'd got her own scold from Locker, who warned her of the danger of felling British citizens with Japanese methods, whether or not in defense of others; it had been a formal and unconvincing little speech, and his eyes kept almost smiling. Easter, demure as a kitten, agreed it was reprehensible, and that she was lucky to escape charges.

She suggested that Dr. Clare was lucky too, at which

the nice Locker bit his lip in a hurry and turned away, to brisk up the searchers in the garden.

She did consider going back to London, but the prospect of her devastated flat discouraged her. She, who always faced things and dealt with them, felt shaken, vulnerable, unequal to it.

Earl Whitewick had, with Bone's permission, been taking Polaroids outside the house. As the main body of the police slowly left, he turned up in the hall where Easter lingered, and suggested that she go to lunch with him.

"You should take a rest from this ambience, Miss Lennox. I don't suggest that your anxiety can be put away, but what about a little healthy distraction?"

It may be that the lingering fuzz thought she was leaving for good when they said goodbye and she went off with Whitewick, but Easter had taken a leaf out of Clovis's book and the front door key, which he had put on its hook on the wall the night before. She slammed the front door with a sound of finality, but there was no way she was going to leave the house for Edwin to get into. She now believed in Clovis's innocence but not at all in his veracity. He did not want to admit, obviously, to breaking the police seals on Miranda's door or to knowing how to enter the secret room; so he had also to deny putting flowers there. He'd had time, during the evening they arrived, to do that; but he hadn't left her side in the night except for the bathroom, where he'd been reasonably audible; she had, for this reason and that, slept soundly, and he'd woken her when he came back to bed, cold as a fish, but that he had gone to a rendezvous with Ron Dace, tossed him from a window, and returned as if from the bathroom, she could not believe. It just wasn't Clovis. And there had been no time, the day before, to arrange a rendezvous with the little creep anyway. She didn't see Clovis saying, "Come to Summerdown," to a klutz like that.

In the car, Earl raised the subject of British law, and their combined ignorance was such that he suggested they stop by the first place they saw with a lawyer's

shingle and enquire what Clovis's legal standing was. In
the small town, as they walked to the inn, they came
on a brass plate with "Vardle and Byne, Solicitors"
and, Earl's reluctance to become involved with anyone
who solicited being overcome by Easter's greater famil-
iarity with English terms, they ventured in. When enquiry showed that a Mr. Grimston would be free in a
few minutes, they sat down and waited. The prospect
of meeting a Dickensian lawyer excited both of them,
but Mr. Grimston was a brisk, slightly portly youngish
man in a smooth linen jacket, who placed a bowl of ice
in front of the electric fan on the shelf and undid his
shirt at the neck behind his tie.

"Clovis *Clare?*" he said, polite enquiry giving way to
alert interest. "Miss Shelley's son? In *police* custody?"
It would have been less surprising to him, she felt, if
it had been giraffe custody. However, he gave a clear
exposition: since Clovis had gone with the police to help
in their enquiries, they could hold him for twenty-four
hours and must then either charge him or let him go,
and as Vardle and Byne had been the Shelleys' lawyers
since the eighteen eighties, he himself would represent
Clovis and his interests if a charge were made. Mrs.
Byne was attending a magistrate's court today, but he
would keep her informed; Mrs. Byne had gone to Summerdown with one of the clerks to attend to the signature of Miss Shelley's Will, not so long ago. An
eccentric but charming lady, Miss Shelley . . . Easter
and Earl issued into the baking street almost dazed, and
Earl remarked that he didn't place a whole lot of confidence in that young man's discretion, however much
law he knew.

A good lunch and some drinks restored Easter's spirits. Over the dessert, Whitewick said, "I hope I shall
have the opportunity of photographing freely at Summerdown before long."

"I would think so." Easter's concern was not, at the
moment, for Whitewick's photographic needs. "When
Clovis gets back."

"I cannot believe that he would not agree to a full

session; Summerdown is worth a book on its own—so untouched."

Easter caught the note almost of anguish in his voice, and thought his grandfather's work was a real obsession with him. "Hey, I'm not saying Clovis won't let you."

"It would be intolerable." The big craggy face twisted. "After all I've been through—after all I've done."

Easter, telling him not to worry, was visited by a small cold unreasonable thought. *What* had he done? Had he seen Miranda as the cause of his interdiction from Summerdown? Had he—she looked at him again and reason asserted itself. No one who had snatched a sword from the wall and slashed open a woman's body could be sitting here laying into Black Forest gateau with a pastry fork so comfortably. Despite all she had read of criminals she could not think so.

Earl took her back to Summerdown and offered, with perhaps more than paternal warmth, to book her a room at his hotel and collect her later in the day; Easter let him understand that she wanted to return to London, and he, relinquishing her hand only after clasping it reassuringly in both of his for some time as he bade her farewell, asked her to keep him in the picture. "I feel a great concern for you two young people."

"Of course I'll let you know what happens. And you must see Summerdown properly, when Clovis is back." Easter added, in a sentiment uncommon with her, "I'm grateful for your help."

Earl lifted his hands in denial, smiled at her kindly, and strode away up the drive. The narrow path had now become well trampled and clearer than it must have been for years.

There was still a police presence. A car with a blue knob on its roof sat beside hers inside the gates. However, she had seen nobody, and did not until, having shut the front door and finding she was in darkness, she took the torch and went through the silent rooms and heard whistling outside at the back. Through the louvres in the closed shutters she watched a policeman patrol across the back of the house and disappear round the kitchen wing toward the front. From well back in the porch, she watched him go off up the drive, but heard no car departing. Well, she thought, if I keep quiet they won't know I'm here, and if they do find out, they can't deport me. I'm Clovis's guest. I'll stay here and look after his house. He'll be back in the morning.

The house was quiet. Because the police had put up the shutters, downstairs was dark. She wandered about upstairs, into bedrooms. As in the room they had chosen last night, there were painted friezes, of entwined flowers, along under the ceilings, and bedsteads with carved or painted medallions. By every bed was a small cupboard, and on it a carafe of china or colored glass, with a tumbler upended over it. Inside the cupboards, she found to her amazed glee, were painted or patterned chamber-pots. She kept well back from the windows in case the policeman on duty came round again, but she looked out over the tangle of garden in the late afternoon sun. The weeping cherry stood in what might once have been the center of the parterre. Beneath the drooping leaves she saw, as she had seen yesterday, what looked like a figure standing there. It was in shadow, but she made out baggy, pale brown trousers and a pale lilac shirt. Upwards of that was hidden by leaves.

As she watched, she heard once more the whistling, and the figure slid away from sight. Police boots thumped along the paving stones below the windows. She heard the stutter of a radio, and an official-sounding voice answering. The tread returned and was gone. Easter went through the house to the front and saw the uniform go away through the trees of the driveway. Then a car started up and drove away.

I'm on my own, she thought.

At the same moment there came to her the idea that Clovis might not necessarily be lying about the tribute of flowers. He might have been exactly as puzzled by them as he said he was. They might have been put there by someone else; and although they seemed to show a feeling for Miranda, the feeling could very well be remorse.

Good grief, she thought, this is classic. The heroine alone. I am going right downstairs and making sure of every door and window. Okay, so the police did it; this is for me.

There were more outer doors than seemed possible. The conservatory had two: one to the garden and another to a boiler and fuel store; both had bolts and she made sure of them. The inner front door shut off the porch, and though it also cut off all light to the hall she closed it and ran the bolts across. The Shelleys believed in security and she was glad of it. The door at the foot of the tower was nailed shut now. The kitchen yard seemed full of outer doors and she went round to the far side first. There were no shutters to these windows, but they all locked; the doors' bolts were rusted home. She went through the kitchen, which in the evening sun was a pleasant room which the staff must have enjoyed. Beyond it, a storeroom with shelves lining the walls, then a junk room with an outer door to the yard. It had no key and no bolts; sockets for bolts on the doorjamb, yes, and screw-holes for bolts, but no more. Well, if they had been taken off they could be, and would be, put back. There was a tool room, and she would be likely to find the very bolts there, and screws and a screwdriver.

As she turned from the door, she realized that it made her scalp prickle to have her back to it. Anyone might have the key. After a moment of thought, she rooted in the drawers of the old kitchen sideboard, and found several things that might do: an old steel for sharpening knives, a cracked wooden scoop with a handle darkened by use, a wooden spoon worn to a sharp edge. She took them through to the end room and found that the steel made a good wedge; she kicked it well under the door, and jammed the scoop alongside for good measure. When it was done she felt safer, but not secure as she had done before. She had that sensation at the back of the neck that you get when you think someone is watching you.

At least everything was locked up. The day was now

turning dimmer, with a gathering thunderous haze. She could tell Superintendent Bone tomorrow about the man in the garden; that someone was haunting the place.

She wished the word *haunting* had not popped up there. It had a dark transparency about it, a breath followed by that long minor sound and the falling, vanishing syllable at the end.

This is hysterical, sister. If you go on like that you will end up scaring yourself. You will scare yourself, as they put it, silly. She marched into the dark hall with her torch, and went to the study. She wished that the Shelleys had a telephone; indeed, a cable and junction box inside the window showed there had once been a telephone here. At least there was water, mains water to the house. She hoped the police had not efficiently turned it off—and ran to try the tap in the butler's pantry. It worked.

This is like a siege, she thought. The evening was growing prematurely dark, with clouds piling across, and an odd light in the wrong quarter. She closed the drapes upstairs. If she was to move around at all, better the police patrol didn't see a light. They'd be getting bugged about intruders at Summerdown.

The memory of Clovis's face as he left between two policemen came back to her; he had that almost bluish pallor peculiar to those with his kind of red hair. The idea he could be guilty still teased her—there was an uneasy gap between what one believed and what, irrationally, one feared . . . that English impersonal "one" she had learnt from Clovis. It was part of his habitual distancing of himself from actual personal statement. How well did she know him? History was full of women who had never had the least idea what their men were up to: killers were married to wives who believed them to be devoted partners and decent citizens. Mrs. Genghis Khan doubtless thought her mate a kindly, well-mannered bloke. Hitler was fond of dogs and gave tea-parties waited on by white-gloved footmen.

I will go to bed early, she thought, with a good book; or two or three good books. I'll take a couple of big candles in case this lamp gives out; I don't know where the kerosene is kept and I couldn't refill this lamp if I did. First, I will look around the house. I am holding the fort here, I am Miranda's chatelaine. Check the fortress. Edwin may come back yet for the necklace, as he'll certainly think the place empty tonight.

She set out on her rounds.

As she passed through the rooms, carrying the lamp which gave a better, less furtive light than the torch, the figures that stood or sat in familiar places had become old friends. She could understand why Miranda and Kay liked them there. They had a life of their own, just as the house had; they were as necessary and as ornamental as the furniture.

The light she carried would be visible from outside in the kitchen wing, but she had not heard any car return and hoped the police weren't hovering once more. The one who'd been called away would presumably check back later. She went through to the far door and held up the lamp to check the wedges.

They were not there.

She stood, the lamp in her hand, staring, confronted with the fact that could not be true. She had kicked them firmly home, the steel and the scoop, so that the door had not moved at all when she pulled at its handle. There was no sign of either steel or spoon nearby.

Part of her mind noticed that her knees felt weak and her head felt cold and that she had taken a deep breath and held it and seemed to have stopped breathing.

Someone was in the house. Whoever had the key to that door had been here when she wedged it, for they couldn't have been moved from outside. Someone didn't want their getaway slowed down by a wedged door. Someone in this house had killed Ron Dace and might well have killed Miranda. She swung round. The light shone through the stone-floored passage to the kitchen, to darkness and shadows where anything or anyone might lurk.

She strained her ears to listen but heard nothing except the banging of her heart. In any case, the intruder must be a silent mover. She had heard nothing all this time.

Her first instinct was to rush from the house to her car and drive away, anywhere. To a police station. To Whitewick's hotel. Her car keys were upstairs in her coat pocket. She tried the yard door but it was locked. The front door was through dark corridors with doors opening either side. If she reached it and escaped into the garden, could she run through those brambles to the road, to the further risk of flagging down a car to hitch a ride . . . she thought of being tripped as she ran, of someone ahead of her. . .

Snap out of it, she told herself. A decision had to be taken; she was perhaps least safe standing by this door which he used, which he must have visited quite recently. Her bedroom had a lock and a key. She had noticed that when she admired the brass doorplate last night. If she could get to her room and turn the key—if it was still there, unlike the wedges—she might manage to wait till daylight; she might halloo any visiting policeman; she might escape by daylight.

To get to her room she must walk through the kitchen, past the butler's pantry, the foot of the tower, taking this turn and that, passing open doorways, lit by the lamp. It was now a long way, though she had walked it in a minute not so long ago.

She hesitated at the tower stairs, but because of yet another irrational feeling, this time about Ron Dace, she walked on to the main stairway. Her whole body was keyed to the moment when the lamp would be dashed from her hand, when she would be seized from behind . . . the torch would have been better; she was too conscious of the lamp's potential danger.

When she came to the staircase her heart was beating so violently that it seemed likely to jump from her mouth and start up the stairs before her. She thought of her judo classes and knew how far she was from any inner balance and calm. I thought I could do that; I was a phony. The lamplight shivered because her hand was shaking, so that the shadows moved. She made herself go on up toward them.

She had just reached the landing, with the gallery doors before her, when one of the shadows did move. A man stepped forward into the periphery of the light, materializing out of the dim vista of figures beyond. She saw a long, pale face framed in long, dark hair, a face with hollowed eyes and open mouth. He did not speak, he hissed. Like a cobra. As he advanced, she set down the lamp on the floor and ran the last two steps to come up from a crouch to hit him in the wind. Her stiff hand seemed to go through him as he shifted in her shadow, and she aimed with her forearm for his throat. Dismayingly, he caught her arm and turned the force of her thrust against her. In that long slow-motion as she fell, she thought, what is the use of knowing judo if other people know it too? There was time to regret what was happening and wonder at its consequences: mind is fast, body slow. Her head glancingly struck the newel post and she lay, dazed and unable to stop the universe from spinning round her. Colors and sounds swam and receded and then her head cleared enough to see, suddenly, flames spring up all round her.

She felt the heat on her skin and tried to twist away from the flames. The kerosene sent a tower of fire toward the ceiling. Not murdered, burnt alive, she thought; oh, and this lovely house. Then the fire went past her, she was being dragged away from the heat into the gallery doorway. There was a scraping shuffle and the man stepped over her, carrying something in a clumsy roll in his arms. He was between her and the flames, and raised his arms making a great shadow, then there was darkness and she heard him stamping, like a strange ritual dance. There was smoke and she coughed like a cat, and her head hurt. He was busy, chasing a runnel of flame that started up. She thought of escape while he trampled in the following darkness, but her body was not getting the messages and her head swam.

A few minutes afterwards—or longer, for she felt herself sliding out of consciousness although aware of pain—he was bending over her again. He had lit a candle on the gallery table. His long hair was touching her as he peered at her face.

"Miss, miss!" Was that the hiss she had heard? "Are you hurt badly? Let me help you." Fingers examined her head and a pencil torch shone on her face and arm for a moment. "That's a nasty burn, that is. You want some water on that. Come in the bathroom."

She was half carried there, and he sat her by the bath on a cork-topped stool, draped her arm over the bath's edge and held the shower head to run brilliantly cold water of a sudden over the pain. It brought her to full consciousness and she struggled, but he held her there. "No, it has to be cold water. You hold it there, miss."

"Sure; of course. Yeah, right." She took the shower head, a big rose on an ungainly metal snake of pipe, and directed it at her arm, swearing through her teeth at the pain.

He lit a candle. This was the bathroom just across from the gallery and Miranda's room. It must be her bathroom. There were bath salts and talc. Doggedly, she held the spray to run over her arm, although the cold hurt now.

"It does hurt, a burn. I know, I was burnt in the War. In the Blitz, when I was a kid. Here, this should go on your head." He put a linen towel to her brow and she had to let him hold it there.

"Lucky it's not more extensive," she said, playing the shower over her arm.

"You moved quick." He bent over her to look at it; his long hair glowed henna red but at the parting, along the top of his head behind the embroidered headband, gray showed. There were lines on the sallow face. Had this man thrown Ron Dace from the window? Was this the murderer she had imagined stalking her through the empty house? Had he hacked Miranda to death with that sword? Here he was, regarding her arm with concern. "What they use on burns now, it's cooking film. I'll get you some."

He was gone. Once he was out of the door she heard

nothing until he was back again, with the long box of film. He wrapped her arm in it.

"That should keep the air out. Thanks," she said.

"You'd do better now laying down. There's the couch in the gallery."

Her legs had no strength, which startled her, but he directed her aimless feet, helping her to lie down, putting the candle on one of the small tables, where it illuminated the smooth features of a figure sitting near it and staring blandly into the dark. There was a horrible smell of scorched cloth and kerosene from the landing.

The man crouched before her, and adjusted the clingfilm on her arm. In doing so, his hand touched hers and darted back, away from the contact. What was he doing here, this faded hippie out of the shadows? He wasn't showing anything but gentle consideration now, but that in no way meant he wasn't a murderer as well.

Just then a blue-white light flickered around the edges of the curtains, so powerful that the whole shape of the gallery, peopled with figures, showed for a micro-second and left its image in the dark. Lightning, she thought; a storm. Ron Dace last night lay under the window in the rain.

"Did you kill that man? Yesterday?"

He drew back. She had never seen anyone wring their hands before. He twisted his hands and pressed them together.

"He fell. I didn't push him. He went through the window just like that—" He swivelled a hand and thrust it out, and Easter thought that if the gesture was meant to illustrate what he'd done, then it looked like a push to *her*. He might well be happier persuading himself it was an accident.

"You know the police have gotten Clovis for it. They're questioning him at the station."

He hung his head, a child caught out, and his mouth trembled. "I saw them go. I thought it could be for that. What could I do, though?"

"You could have told them what really happened. What was he doing up there?"

A weak sparkle came into the eyes raised for a moment to hers, and he said with some strength of indignation, "Stealing. He was stealing. I was there, in Miss Miranda's room. I thought I could meditate there. I like to be near her. He came in with his torch and started messing around in her desk. His dirty fingers touching her things! I jumped up, like, and he went for me with the torch but I turned him by the arm like I did you and he sort of was off balance and I saw him against the window and out he went. It was all in a minute." The candlelight showed his face awed, some sixteenth-century saint with a vision. "I cleared up. He had things in a bag that I put back and I wiped everything clean. I took his bag and the tool away, and fixed the door so no one could get in again. She'd have been so angry at him being in her room touching her things."

"Did she let you go in there? Did you know her well?"

His eyes flicked to hers and away. He said in a voice more hushed, "No one went into that room but her. Even Mr. Kay didn't, though she went into the study when she liked. I put fresh flowers where she used to have them. She used to like flowers." He spoke wistfully. Whether or not he knew Miranda well, it was clear he had adored her. Surely he was not her murderer? Though *each man kills the thing he loves;* a moment of anger or jealousy saw the end of love and life. He could have tidied away the memory of what had happened then as he had tidied away Ron Dace's fall. There might be forming in his mind some tidy reason for doing away with Easter herself. He did not, right now, seem dangerous. He had saved her from the fire. Still, she was far from thinking him safe; there was a chancy, unaccountable feel about him, and she was also fairly sure that he was under ninety cents in the dollar.

"I wish I'd known her," she said. "I only lately got to hear Clovis's mother was still around; and then . . . what happened to her?"

He rose abruptly and she saw the ease with which he

moved. He had parried her attack without trouble. He might not be young but he was limber.

His face had shut down, mulish, the mouth tight. He shook his head.

"Look, you should tell the police about Ron Dace—about the man who fell out of the window. Clovis is Miranda's son. You want to help him, don't you? What would she think if you didn't help him?"

He was backing from her, with an inarticulate sound of protest, half moan and half grunt; he backed out of the candlelight and into the shadows by the door. "No," he said faintly out of the dark, and then she knew, by an absence in the air, that he had gone.

Bone was not best pleased to find a team from South Eastern News at the top of Summerdown drive. They had only just disembarked, and P. C. Benn had come haring up the drive, red-faced from exertion and in shirt-sleeves and wellies. Bone said he had no news, but agreed to say it on camera, and was therefore saying it when Locker arrived, decanted Clovis and took him smartly away down the drive. Bone then talked to the producer and said since there had been a break-in at Summerdown already, outside views of the place might only lead to more such efforts. He couldn't say when the owner would be available to give permission to shoot indoors. He agreed that a mysterious death at the house so soon after two other mysterious deaths was, on the whole, newsworthy. The producer agreed that restricted shots of the outside should be taken, and glanced at W. D. C. Fredricks getting out of her car and disappearing down the narrow pathway.

"Woman involved?" he asked. "A woman in the case?"

"Women on the Force have the same duties as men," Bone told him reprovingly. He was having to expend good humor and charm and he did not feel he had much to spare. Trees were dripping on them after last night's storm, which had kept him awake and enabled him to go over and over his workload and his own worries; the area was suffering from a serial killer known as the Southern Strangler and although nothing had happened in Bone's patch he had to attend a regional conference about it; Garron was being operated on today; the Italian police had sent no information yet about the Shelleys' sojourn there; a postcard from Cha said that she and Prue had met some *dishy!!!* fell-walkers; Inspector Blane was being ostentatiously decent about the cancellation of his holiday because of Garron.

The TV team hung about and Bone followed his own team down the path to the house. At the door Locker warned him: Benn thought the young woman was still inside, as he had heard drains flushing and all the curtains upstairs were closed again. Bone was not surprised.

In fact, "the young woman" had to let them in, as she had bolted the inner door. As she embraced Clovis and stood with her arm round him, pale and tall with the cloud of black hair on her shoulders, Bone thought she looked more than usually like a terrorist. Her hair was in fact scorched at the side, and a bandage on her arm, or at least a swathe of plastic film, completed the piratical air. What had she been up to? At the moment he was more than ever ready to believe that she and not Clovis had tossed Ron Dace out of that window.

As they came in, a voice hailed him from the door. The American, Whitewick, was coming in together with a smooth young man he introduced as Simon Grimston.

"—representing the Shelleys' solicitors," Grimston said.

"I don't think we have any work for you this morning," Bone said. "As you see, we've brought Mr. Clare—"

"Mr. Shelley," Grimston murmured politely.

"Whatever, back here. It's Miss Lennox we want to talk to this morning. Is there somewhere we can all sit down?" It might mean putting one or two of the mannequins off their chairs, he thought. Clovis was holding Easter's bandaged arm as if it were damaged antique china, while they talked together in a murmur and Fredricks, obvious but unobtrusive, listened.

"Come into the morning-room," Clovis said. "There's room there; and I dare say Mrs. Perceval would move out if necessary."

"How have you injured yourself, Miss Lennox?" Bone enquired.

"I nearly burnt the house down last night."

Bone took breath. "I'm remarkably glad you failed. How did you manage it?" Clovis, opening shutters, glanced at her smiling.

"There's no end to my resourcefulness. And I hit my head, so I'd like to sit with my back to the light. I didn't sleep well and the milk was soured this morning so breakfast wasn't attractive enough to eat."

"Let that be my responsibility!" Earl Whitewick, to whom Locker had been intimating that he might wait in another room, now turned quickly round and came across to take Easter's good hand. "Since I am superfluous here, I'll be your commissary. No, no, it will be my pleasure. I shall be back right away. I take it the Captain has no objection?"

Bone, thus designated once more, had no objection, and Whitewick delightedly hurried out. Easter subsided onto the window seat and Clovis leant on the wall near her and watched with concern as she put her hands to her head briefly.

"Miss Lennox, would you rather come down to the station later in the day? WDC Fredricks can bring you along later if you're too ill to talk at the moment."

"No," she said resolutely. "I'm fine. It's no reason not to talk to you, though I don't think I've anything to say."

"Precisely what do you know about Ron Dace?"

She looked, so far as he could tell, politely wondering. Mrs. Perceval Shelley, by the chimney, seemed to regard her with interest but the other figures, still in the dimness by the shuttered southern windows, even had their backs turned. "Know about Ron Dace?" Easter echoed.

"We do have reason to believe you've not been frank about your acquaintance with him."

She put her head back, eyes shut, and Clovis said, "She's not well enough, Super. Anyway, how could she know him?"

"I'm not trying to evade the question," she said. "It's okay, Clovis. But I must take a painkiller. I'll be more able . . . There's a whole drugstore up in the bathroom. I'm sorry, Mr. Bone."

"Miss Fredricks here will give you a hand." Bone could not be sure whether her natural pallor was more pronounced or not. "Where did this burn happen? What part of the house is burnt?"

"Up on the landing."

At this point, a surge of TV people came with PC Benn round the end of the house and advanced toward the site of Ron Dace's death. Bone said, "We'll adjourn upstairs in any case. Mr. Grimston, Mr.—Shelley?"

Clovis, already surging forward to obey the suggestion, did a double take, turning startled eyes on Bone as he went, and stumbling on a corner of the hearthrug. Locker fielded him and shepherded him up the stairs.

The landing floor was scarred, and a long strip of badly scorched rug lay there, rumpled.

Fredricks supervised the taking of a couple of tablets, and as she brought Easter back along the gallery landing she said to Locker in a low tone that a doctor ought to see the burn before long.

"It's superficial," Easter said impatiently. "Looks worse than it is, with all that goo wrapped round. I'm fine." She swung her head up, and the movement made her gasp and take hold of Clovis's shoulder.

"Easter—"

"I'm fine. I never fainted yet."

"Come on. Sit down." He led her into the gallery. Bone, who had been listening while he examined the empty lamp that stood by the banisters, followed and took a wing chair. Fredricks drew the nearby curtains and Bone said, "That will do. Miss Lennox won't need much light."

Clovis had put Easter down on the small couch. She was at first clearly recovering herself; then she looked past Bone at the figures in the gloom at the far end of the room, and said, "Wouldn't you rather find a place clear of these waxworks?"

"Let's just sit tight and look at the truth as soon as you're able. But it's still open to you to come and talk to us later on. You don't seem at all well, and a doctor should look at that arm for you." Behind Bone's shoulder, he was aware, the odd collection of dummies stood or sat, a curious mixture in clothes from bustles to crumpled madras cotton, bonnets to headbands, stiff shirts to fringed jerkins. Fredricks put her back to them and stood at ease, waiting.

"Miss Lennox: we've had additional information this morning from Ron Dace's family; something he said suggests very strongly that he had an actual encounter with you the day before he died."

"That's crazy."

The message from Mrs. Firkin had not been complimentary. Young Des, going up to his uncle's room with him when he came in, had watched him change his shirt and seen a bruise on his shoulder. His question *How'd you get that, Ron?* had been answered, as Bone already knew, by *A dog bit me.* This morning, Mrs. Firkin said that Des had remembered more: *A dog bit me. An American bitch with long black hair.*

Clovis had been about to speak, when she said, "Clovis was with me all day. How could Ron Dace have anything to do with me? It's crazy enough that he turns up here. I'm sorry but I don't have anything to say."

In Bone's mind was the bruise on Edwin Clare's shoulder, the chop that had momentarily disabled his arm. He said, "I suggest that you hit Ron Dace at this encounter, in much the same way that you struck Dr. Clare when he hit his son. You'd do better to tell us exactly what happened."

She had become as still as any mannequin.

"I suggest that he came here by appointment; that you let him in and talked with him, in the tower room, and that he made demands you didn't choose to meet and that you, perhaps using a judo throw, sent him out of the window. That you then faked the break-in and the discovery next morning."

"No," she said. Clovis was ready to speak, and her hand on his and her steady will prevented him. Bone administered himself a severe mental kick for not using the information first on Clovis; however, any moment now he was going to come out with the truth, an act so unaccustomed with him that no wonder it was giving him trouble.

"Superintendent," she said, "if someone is *thrown* from a window, wouldn't they land at some distance? Wouldn't it make a different trajectory from a fall? If a body *falls,* isn't it more likely to go down pretty straight and land underneath where it fell from? Wouldn't you say that the nasty little burglar looked like he'd *fallen?"*

Bone thought that the smell of something fishy here was definitely that of red herring. Locker stirred, on his chair by the door, and said, "Are you saying you *dropped* him from the window?"

"I'm saying nobody *threw* him out. That's a low window, opening outward. He could very easily, in the dark with no more than a torch, have just fallen out."

There was not more than a moment of silence before Locker said, "A torch, Miss Lennox? He hadn't one when he was found. What became of the torch, would you say?"

They were looking past Bone, though, and Locker too looked. He had taken in Clovis's stare of amazement, Easter's resignation. Bone leant round the wing of his chair, to see one of the statuesque figures advancing up the room, walking with stiff hesitation like a badly animated robot, in the moccasins and buckskins, the limp cotton and long hair, of the sixties young.

Bone had once walked into a hanging body in the dark. He had received a baby in a lacy shawl from its bright-eyed, smiling mother and found it was decomposed. He was locked in the same freeze-dried immobility now, and he heard Fredricks's indrawn yelping scream.

"I was there," the figure said hoarsely. "I did it. She's innocent."

Bone overcame his immediate fantasy that they had set up a remote-controlled figurine on which they meant to blame their crime. He must be wholly unnerved to have imagined a thing so far-fetched, but he was not surprised that Fredricks had screamed, and resolved to forget he had heard her.

"It's all right," Easter said. "You mustn't say you did it. Superintendent, this man frightened Ron Dace just the way he did us this minute, and Dace fell out of the window. He told me last night. All he did was fend off a blow with the torch."

"Who are you?" Bone asked sharply, rising.

"Adam."

"Adam?" Clovis spoke, disbelieving. "I thought you were one of the made-up people when Miranda talked about you."

"I did it," the hoarse voice repeated. "I did all of it."

They took Adam in if only to get him away from Easter Lennox, whose protective instincts he seemed to have aroused in no mean way. Bone thought she might well protect *him,* too, given a chance, from ever finding out what happened in that house the night the Shelleys died.

"Adam didn't kill that lousy little creep," she protested, watching him go away, shambling between Locker and Benn.

"I heard what you said," Bone told her. "If it's true, he has nothing to worry about. You still have. Do you want to explain about Ron Dace's bruise?"

She said nothing. Bone, watching Clovis fidget, thought, *It implicates him. Let them stew a little.* What she and Clare are not saying may explain why Ron Dace came to Summerdown, but even she admits that Adam was responsible for his death.

He looked at Clovis who hung back in the porch.
"You can't hide forever," he said, and left them.

Adam proved to be no sort of hand at a story. Bone
wrote, and passed to Locker across the interview-room
table: *We'll get "diminished responsibility" on this one*.

Adam professed to have no name but "Adam" and
nowhere to live. He lived "near Summerdown." Locker
let it go for the moment, moving on to Ron Dace's
death.

Bone watched the lank, awkward figure, wilting under
dyed drooping hair, and heard the rusty voice giving a
tangled account. Basically it was as Easter Lennox had
said. His long, plain face turned from Locker to Bone
and back, anxious, confused, a dog without a bone, a
worm without a turning.

Locker, using a comfortable, matter-of-fact voice to
reassure this nervous creature, asked, "How do you get
into the house, then?" Adam stared at the mesh on the
window and rubbed his nose.

"There's a window doesn't shut."

"Really?" said Locker. "We didn't find it, see, when
we were shutting the house up. We'd better know where
it is. There might be more intruders."

"It's in the kitchen wing. I'll warn Mr. Shelley."

"Do you mean Mr. Clare?"

Adam repeated uncertainly, "Mr. Shelley."

"Where, precisely, is this window?"

"Oh—it's the old lamp room." Adam leant forward
earnestly and Locker nodded, making a note. Adam
glanced with interest at the tape recorder.

Bone said, "What makes you call Mr. Clare 'Mr.
Shelley'?"

"He has to be, when the house is his. And the house
is his now, so he is Mr. Shelley."

"How did you know that?" Bone knew it from Grimston, but he could not recollect that Grimston had mentioned it this morning.

"Mr. Kay told me. He said, *When we are dead . . .*"
Adam stopped and gulped.

"Where were you when they died?" Bone asked gently.

There was a silence, Adam's head bent so that the mouse-gray of his parting showed. His locks were bound with a strip of white cotton printed with Japanese characters. After a moment his body shook and a deep, lugubrious moan emerged. He tried to stifle it but he sat there, holding the sides of his chair, bowed over and sobbing.

Bone repressed a quick urge to lean over the table and pat the bent head as one might pat a distressed dog. There was something very helpless and touchingly vulnerable about this man. If he had killed Ron Dace it must surely have been an accident. On the other hand, if he had also killed Miranda Shelley, that was making him too accidentprone for belief. Did he perhaps have fits, in which he was not responsible for what he was doing? Was this outburst for what he had done or just grief for Miranda Shelley's death? If he got in and out of the house by a window—and Locker's little head-shake had told Bone it wasn't the lamproom window at least—was he the very intruder they were looking for? Bone remembered the diaries' mention of a ghost. If he himself had caught sight of this creature opposite, reflected in a mirror, in the dusk, he might well think he'd seen a visitant from another world. He'd do fair duty as ectoplasm at any séance.

"Adam . . ."

The moaning increased in volume, reminding Bone of a child who doesn't want to hear what is said to it, putting its fingers in its ears and making a noise to drown out the words. He exchanged a glance with Locker, who shrugged.

"Adam. You were fond of Miss Shelley." Bone had raised his voice to penetrate the noise Adam was making, and heard the last words ring out as the moaning stopped and Adam raised his head. The eyes that regarded him were of a blue so pale that the color seemed to have leached away; Bone had the unpleasant fancy that they might one day become transparent, very suitable to a ghost. The track of tears down the face showed that there had been a layer of dirt on it to start with.

"I loved her." The dull voice had no gift of expression but its very dullness held pain and intensity. "I loved her. I would never have let any harm come to her . . . I'd have killed anyone who touched her."

Perhaps, Bone thought, that was meant literally. Had he eavesdropped on some scene of incestuous love and, on an impulse of rage and jealousy, killed both the Shelleys? Yet, according to Ferdy Foster, Kay had committed suicide. *There are no certainties*, Ferdy's gravelly voice had said over the phone, *but this is typical textbook stuff*.

"What about Mr. Shelley—Mr. Kay? Were you fond of him?"

Adam nodded with pathetic eagerness, the greasy hennaed hair nodding with him. "I'd do anything for Mr. Kay. I worked for him. In the garden."

Were they really getting somewhere? He saw Locker make a note of the tape counter's number.

"I dug. I helped with the vegetables." An echo of a smile came, as at a happy time recollected. "Mr. Kay gave me vegetables. He gave me money for food."

"Where did you sleep?"

Adam's gaze wandered and examined the bare wall behind Bone. .

"I don't know."

"Was it in the house? In Summerdown itself?"

Adam considered this helpfully but shook his head. "I don't know."

If he *were* a dog, I think I'd fetch him a smack . . . Patiently, Bone suggested: "In the garden? Did you sleep outdoors?"

"In the garden. I sleep in the garden." A willing affirmation, with more nods.

Bone sighed. Locker tried another tack. "Had you known Miss Shelley and her brother for long?"

Adam's head bowed again and Bone thought they had lost him. The voice, when it came, was very far away, a ghost's voice.

"Forever."

"You'd known them a long time." Even supposing Adam had appeared on the scene, in his nebulous fashion, two years ago when the Shelleys returned from Italy to take up their inheritance at Summerdown, that was hardly a long time. To Adam, of course, time was conceivably a very relative affair. Strange, but somehow to be expected, that weirdos should attract their like. Set up a fantasy world anywhere and there'd be candidates queuing for admission. People watch soap operas but they deliberately believe in them, they join the fantasy, send baby clothes and wedding presents . . . Adam lifted his faded eyes.

"I'd always known them."

In another reincarnation, no doubt. We were chums in Ancient Egypt, shared an asp, a tomb. Perhaps he thought they went back to Bible times like the Book of Genesis. Adam was in the garden there, after all.

"Always!"

The voice went up in a wild shriek and Adam clasped his head. Bone and Locker sat looking at each other and then at him as he started to rock to and fro; and then suddenly Bone's mind did a somersault. It had always irked him that Adam in the Bible was created grown-up, never having been a child. This Adam, this long wet strip of nothing, had been a child once like all mortal men except the first. *Always* meant all your life, from childhood. Bone leant forward and this time his statement had conviction.

"You're Gary Underwood."

Adam had stopped rocking and sat still, looking at Bone with his mouth open. Bone repeated, "You're Gary Underwood. Your mother was housekeeper to old Mrs. Shelley, Miranda Shelley's grandmother. You knew Miranda and Kay when you were all three children at Summerdown together during the War."

"I'm Adam." He sounded frightened now, unsure. A hand came up to twist one of the lank strands of dyed hair. "Adam. *Not* Gary."

"But you were Gary."

The hair was twirled more slowly.

"They made fun of you. When you dyed your hair, it turned purple."

Adam looked down at the strand in his fingers as if to be sure of the color it was now.

"I only wanted to look like them." He was pleading with Bone to understand, evidently unaware of his tacit admission that he was Gary Underwood. "They wouldn't let me play with them."

Poor ghost. How harmless a ghost was he? Miranda had written that Gary threw something at Kay when he was teased, before he ran away. A boy might throw something, a man might seize a weapon that came too readily to hand. Bone recalled a very recent case of his in which a man had killed—twice—because he fancied himself mocked. No one in their right mind would tease a dangerous psychopath, but how dangerous might Gary be? For that matter, could one describe Miranda and Kay as being in their right minds? Edwin Clare had said Miranda had never grown up and made a joke of everything. Had they thought of some further trick to play on Gary, with fatal results?

"You lit the candles for Miranda. And put Kay in the chair."

Adam's mouth opened and the face crumpled round it, as though the drawstrings of a dorothy-bag had been pulled.

"She looked so lovely . . .' The words merged into the familiar wail and he began rocking again. His hands came up to cover his ears, to shut out the world.

Locker switched off the recording; like Bone he recognized that there was no more to be got from Gary Underwood at the moment. The constable who led him back to a cell had to guide him with a hand on one of the arms, as he kept his hands to his ears, and Bone and Locker heard his wail go down the corridor unmitigated in its anguish.

"I think," said Bone, "we'll send Shay and his team to go over the whole garden at Summerdown. We haven't needed to explore that jungle until now, but I don't believe he's been living rough for two years. He's a bit grimy but not browned or weathered. How do you fancy a night out in the cabbages in January, Steve?''

Locker shook his head, following Bone into his office. "People manage, somehow. What about the dossers under the arches?''

"You see him cadging a cardboard box from Kay Shelley, and newspapers from somewhere, and sleeping in the porch? What I'd like to know is how much Miranda knew about him. She mentions an Adam in her diaries but whether it's the real one or a fiction of Kay's—it seems he didn't tell her things he thought would upset her.''

"How much sense are you making of the diaries, sir?''

"Ah, that's a point. The one that might really tell us something, the current one she was writing up to the time she was killed—that's the one we want; I'd hoped it would be in the tower room, her secret room, but it's not. Young Clovis had the one his mother gave him to explain why she'd left him and his brother as babies, I gather; he swears blind he hasn't any more.''

Locker pursed his lips. "That one doesn't know what the truth is.''

"You know, Steve—Pontius Pilate was on to something when he asked what truth is. Everyone's got their own version. Images don't make the same impression on different brains. Look at witnesses. You're lucky if you get two of them to agree on any one thing, was the bag-snatcher tall or short; they want to get it right but they really don't know.''

Locker's look of reserved judgement showed he did not know what this had to do with Clovis Clare's lying.

"It's the world he lives in. He doesn't so much lie, as simply not see the thing he doesn't want to see. What about his mother? She managed to blot out her husband and small children when they got in the way of what she wanted to see. And you're not telling me this Adam-

Gary character knows what the truth is wherever it's at."

Locker went gloomy. "You reckon he's our man?" He turned the tape in his hand. "I'll get Shay down there with everyone we can spare and find where this bloke's been holed up. What do you look to find there, sir?"

"Truth?" Bone said.

Later in the day they talked to Adam again, and by keeping away from the subject of the Shelleys, did manage to establish something about his past. He had traveled, drifting from place to place round the world. He had been jailed more than once, the cause for which he was hazy—"once it was a vag charge." Only once? thought Bone. He must have been without visible means of support often and often. He had worked wherever he could, on ships, harvesting. "I'm strong," he said. Bone noticed that when he was not in distress he could sit very still, and he imagined him among the figures at Summerdown, listening. His unwashed skin had a patina not unlike the gloss of the dummies, but none of their everlasting youth. He had worked for a Japanese family in San Francisco, and had lived in Japan under their patronage; this, from his face, had been a good time. Bone wondered how such things as passports had been coped with, and it seemed to him that the young Gary had been more on the ball than this man was now. Great tracts of time seemed to have been forgotten, although Adam was apparently serious in trying to remember. Bone asked, "Do you do hash a lot?" but Adam had little idea of when or how much, or of time in the general sense. It was useless to ask about Miranda's death, as Adam became too distressed. In the normal way Bone would still have pursued the subject despite compunction because he was a copper with a job to do, but in this case he was obliged to desist, Adam bursting out helplessly into his wailing moan. As he was led away, Locker, snapping the tape into its case, said boot-faced,"We could Sellotape him on top of a squad car and use him for a siren."

This vision pleased Bone so much that it went far to lighten a mood that was tending to the morose.

Sergeant Shay returned from Summerdown in a triumphant glow, his hair and trouser legs wet and his brow scratched, but with such a smile on his reddened face that his superiors automatically smiled too. He put down on the desk before Bone a blue, hardbacked exercise book with a red spine, and a handkerchief with an "M" in flowers on the corner, and then, with an air and a flourish, a glittering handful of brilliance that resolved itself into a necklace, a gold chain studded with small flowers of ruby and emerald, with a series of pendant loops of flowers and a medallion of complicated jewelry in the center.

"That was hung on the wall, sir, with a photo in the middle of it that I take to be Miss Shelley; but I didn't bring it away—I thought it was this we were looking for. You never saw such a place. We missed it, sir. We totally missed it. Benn and I we crawled right through underneath and we didn't see a thing."

"Sergeant—"

"I'm coming to it, sir, really I am. We gave up, and we went back to the house and he made us tea, Mr. Clare did, Miss Lennox being at the doctor's with her arm—" Bone debated whether Easter would necessarily have been the one who got tea had she been there, but he did not disturb Shay's chauvinist assumption—"and we all sat about the dining-room along with some of those waxworks, taking five before we started again, and the American gentleman said 'Have you come across the tree house? Is it still there?' Well, sir, news to me I can tell you; but he had a map that he'd been showing them, that it seems was a photocopy of his grandfather's designs for the house; and Mr. Perceval Shelley, that Mr. Clare said was his great-great-grandfather, he wanted a playhouse for the children, and Mr. Whitewick designed a tree house."

He paused here for the effect on Bone, who was spreading the necklace out and listening, as the cock of his head showed, with acute interest.

"Come on, then, man!" Locker adjured.

"When we went to the spot on the map, it was this huge overgrown yew tree; or a bunch of them; and we forced a way among the trunks, like, and the lower branches, looking more for something on the ground, or for a way through that'd show use. Once we looked *up*, there it was. Not easy to see, what with all the branches, but perched there—well, then, he's been clever. It doesn't look used, the way in. No beaten path to that door. We found how you can reach the door, that's not so high off the ground as all that, and inside, you never saw such a place. Snug! I'd like to live there myself, this time of year anyway. Very small, and the windows looking out on branches so it was dark except toward the house; and it had been mended with laths and tar paper, and there was a Primus in one corner, with tin nailed round the walls there. It was neat as a pin; bit of mat on the floor, bedding rolled up, shelves with jars and tins, plastic water carrier. Bar you had to go about bent over, with it being child height, only six foot under the roof ridge, it was great."

It was unexpected that a place inhabited by Adam should be well-kept and tidy. Bone said, "Hang on a minute," and got on the intercom for the diary to be fetched and photocopied, "Priority, mind;" he could not bear to wait to get his hands on it, but the team must be able to work; he had seen that the writing was progressively less coherent and infinitely less legible. His own flowing but organized signature on the requisition chit reminded him of Grizel's graphology: "cautious but imaginative." He must get her to analyze Miranda's script.

"I reckon the yew trees were meant to be cut out round the windows so it'd not be so dark. Regular bijou residence, that is."

Sergeant Shay was quite envious of Adam's nest.

* * *

He received the diary back with avidity. Adam might have reasons for sequestering it, and those reasons might become clear in the reading. He set himself to decipherment.

This volume at least was not a thick one, and sadly not more than twenty pages had been written, yet it was toward the end, and getting on for evening, when he came on something.

Of course I was expecting him but I told Kay I couldn't stay in the house. I felt so restless and sometimes, and this is very strange to me, I feel I won't be in Summerdown for ever—I can't imagine life without the house so perhaps it will have to be death. I think Kay has the same sense of this, but for once I can't be sure and I don't want to talk about it.

And then suddenly there he was coming down the path toward me, my own image the child from the past— I thought of that poem, by was it Shelley, that I read in school, that made me think of Kay so I cried and Miss Gelshaft was furious—something about a man who met himself in the garden and it meant he was going to die. Well if I wasn't going to die I wouldn't have asked to see him. Because he has to forgive me for what we did to him. I know it was long ago but I know he can't forget it I shall give him his chance to do the right thing.

Bone paused. That was an interesting way of looking at forgiveness, that it offered more of an opportunity to the forgiver than to the forgiven. He had read that some beggars in parts of the East don't solicit alms; they present themselves in their affliction and their poverty, and they do not thank for what they are given since they are doing a favor to the almsgivers, offering them a chance to fulfill the obligation to charity.

My own image. He thought of Adam, the child from the past, sitting with shoulders hunched under the ratty hennaed ringlets, a grotesque parody of Miranda's Pre-Raphaelite hair. How hard he had tried to imitate his idol! At least now he knew how to avoid the effect at which they had once laughed so much; the purple stain would wear away, but not the scar. Some people are born thin-skinned, literally one layer of skin short; Adam's spirit was so vulnerable. Bone narrowed his eyes at the tiny scrawled writing.

I told him I wanted him to release me, make me free of that guilt after all those years but he said he couldn't—he had loved me once more than anything in the world he said but now all that was gone and there was nothing I could do to change it, he seemed almost pleased at having the chance to refuse me something so perhaps that will have to do instead. Kay took him away again and I cried all over again because I was sorry for him and we had messed up his life between us.

It was true, Bone reflected, that Gary Underwood had never managed a career or a relationship, from what he had said. He had drifted from one situation to another, a ghost in search of a place to haunt, until he came again to Summerdown.

Was all this not too much fuss to make over a practical joke played on a child forty years ago? Could Miranda and Kay Shelley be said to have ruined this wretched creature's life? Yet the joke they had played on him was not so important in itself: it stood for their rejection of him, a symbol. She had written of Gary's withdrawal from them after it. He had no longer tried to join in, but watched them from a distance. The Watcher. Miranda had spoken of being watched. How long had Gary-Adam watched the twins after their return; how long had he, in his obsession with her, planned his revenge? If he had, after his meanderings through life, returned to Summerdown and found Miranda and Kay there, his memories and his grudges must all have come to life again. And then Kay had discovered him, employed him; and finally Miranda, sensing death was near, had tried to get his pardon. She, living in the memories of childhood as she did, would appreciate what a wound they had made: *we were evil to him.*

This incident had happened not so far before the end of her life. Perhaps it had revived all that childhood rejection in Adam, had showed him fatally that she remembered the wounding time.

Had he taken this volume away because he thought it might implicate him? Or to read what Miranda said of him, which was so little? How much had he, in those dim-lit rooms, sat still as an image to listen to them unknown?

Bone read on: she wrote how she was *still stupid with the pills, that don't stop the terrible headache but make me ill after. We changed the dresses on four of the people, Kay talks of getting electricity again I wont I won't but he says for the kitchen. He held me all night and this time the pills worked better we talked of Italy.*

Bone sat, his hands either side of the book, when he came to the unfinished final page.

could Miranda have provoked her death? Could he have dared, possibly, to make advances to her at last, and received another, unbearable, rejection?

"Gloomy thoughts, Robert? You're punishing that toast—Whose legs are you breaking?"

"Now there's a question. Funny to think that once, not so many centuries back, we wouldn't have accepted someone's evidence unless we'd tortured them first."

"There's a good number of people who don't tell the truth until they have to."

Bone thought of Clovis. "M'm. But plenty must have lied the moment it hurt. It's no guarantee."

"What makes me sick is all the police in the world now who still use torture as a matter of course. I was brought up to think of the police as the folk you went to when you were in trouble."

Bone considered his toast, frowning. "That's not the way the young see it now; which is a pity—but we've got our share of the high-handed and violent and the corrupt. The kids now don't think they might be facing the Tonton Macoute or the KGB instead, they just quite rightly expect fairness and justice from us."

"Have you come across corruption and injustice, Robert?"

He glanced up. *"And* I've been slow to blow the whistle on it, and not wanted to speak up when there was an enquiry. *Esprit de corps* is a rather dangerous commodity. Are you always this serious at breakfast?"

"You know the proverb, Robert: serious at breakfast, frivolous at dinner." She looked at him wickedly. "When do you have to leave for work?"

"Before I drink this tea. Aren't you lucky to be on holiday? No, but Steve will be wanting to know what's to be done with a bloke we have in custody at the moment."

Grizel sipped her tea, watching him over the rim of the cup. "And can you tell him, Robert?"

He was silent for a moment, thinking how sensitive she was to his doubts and hesitations. She must be perfectly well aware of his constraints and worries about their own relationship. What were hers?

"I don't know what to do any more than Steve does. We have no firm evidence and the man himself is, in my opinion, not all there."

"Not all there makes him sound like a ghost."

"In a way he is. He's been haunting a house and two people he got imprinted on as a child, and even though they're dead he can't stop."

"Am I allowed to ask if that's the couple at that house Summerdown? It was on the South East news yesterday. The brother and sister laid out with candles?"

"You're allowed to ask." Bone smiled, and she put down her cup, laughing. He was amazed how attractive lines round the mouth and eyes could be.

"Old Blabbermouth Bone. Police secrets. Better than secret police. Very well, I'll change the subject. Have you heard from Cha?"

"A postcard yesterday. She and Grue, I gather, are resolutely ignoring the rain and having a wonderful time. Getting the knack of eating sausages before they blow off the fork in a Force Nine gale. I've a feeling she will always treat the phrase *under the weather* with respect from now on. What are you looking at?"

She put out a hand to take his, a light, warm hand. "I'm looking at you, Robert. Because you have a nice face, just like your daughter. You do know Cha is the image of you."

"My God." Bone was on his feet, hardly noticing her hand drop from his or that she was staring. "Must get dressed."

He hurried for the stairs, avoiding Ziggy who liked to head any rush for the door. Bone had already shaved, from a natural wish not to appear too unattractive at breakfast, and it took him only minutes to shower and hurry into clothes—after a clean shirt, the first clothes to hand. The sound of plates being stacked in the kitchen made him know with a shock that he would have forgotten Grizel was in the flat. He reached the kitchen doorway as she did, and they collided.

"You're going?" he asked.

"I could say the same to you."

"I'm sorry. I have to go. You've helped enormously." He kissed her quickly, a little awkwardly, the scent of her skin reminding him of the night. Curious that the husband-like peck on the lips should be more embarrassing than memories of passion. He saw her, as he drew back, smiling. Reflected sunlight turned her skin to gold.

"I love you when you're on the trail, Robert."

"Give a Bone a dog?" He had visions of his new idea straining on a leash, dragging him toward who knows what. It felt as urgent as that. "Shall I see you soon?"

"Ring me when you can. And good luck to the dog."

Blane was at the station, uncomfortably smart in a dark suit and discreet tie, his face pinkly shining as though his razor had taken off the top surface as well as stubble. He was carrying a folder and clipboard and trying not to look as if he had been waiting.

"The car's here, sir."

Bone prevented himself just in time from striking his brow with his palm. Surely only a night with Grizel and the case he was on could have wiped all thought of today's conference from his mind. It was perhaps because the Southern Strangler had not hit in his patch as yet. Blane, who had been dealing with the information on killings this year, that ranged from East Kent to Sussex and Surrey, looked solidly satisfied with the prospect of a day in London, of taking notes and making solemn contributions. Bone, on the other hand, could have barked with frustration or, possibly, put his hands over his ears and made a noise like Gary Underwood.

"I've got to have a word with Steve. Get in the car, Jack; be with you in a moment." He wasn't even in his best suit; Cha would have been very fussed over that if she'd been at home. He could tell by Locker's expression that he didn't look quite the job for New Scotland Yard. He gave Locker his instructions and left in a hurry. He must not be late at such a collection of bigwigs, no matter what he was wearing.

In the car he did what he rarely did with those below him in rank, withdrew into a silence that Blane, after glancing at him once or twice, did not care to penetrate. His thoughts were with Locker and, if he had been given to biting his nails, they would have been down to the quick by London.

Once at the conference he set himself to be distracted from his speculations and impatience, to take notice of the facts and figures given, the videos of police at the place where a victim had been found, the wavering of a camcorder on someone's shoulder catching, here, an overalled row tramping through undergrowth, now, a white face beseeching the sky. He noticed some of the police in the videos smiling and chatting; murder was, after all, a job to them and one in which it did not do to become emotionally involved. The smiles, the chat, even a bit of larking that seemed to be going on, were a defense. Long ago, his own Super had told him off for getting too involved. It was a mark against him. He stopped doodling in jagged lines on his scratch-pad and made himself listen. If this Strangler wasn't caught, it might well be his patch next.

Nevertheless, when cups jangled at the back of the hall and a break came, with groups forming and people hailing old acquaintances, Bone escaped from a threatened chat with a Surrey Super who was joshing him about his scarred brow, and asked the way to a telephone. He hoped Locker had got back from his errand. In fact he was put through at once to Locker, who had that moment returned from the Austin Clinic. Bone had sent him to interview one of the house officers, Dr. Michelle Morrison. Yes, said Locker, it had taken some pressure all right, but he'd got through and Bone was justified.

"You're positive, Steve?"

"Positive, sir. Lionel Clare has no alibi for the night of Miss Shelley's murder."

Bone went back to the conference room trying to contain his high spirits, and drank a cup of tepid coffee with thirsty pleasure. Several people smiled at him, and he was surprised because as far as he knew they were all but strangers; he did not realize that his expression evoked a response. He took up his pen when everyone again took their places, and began an elaborate doodle which, spreading into baroque architecture, attracted Blane's disapproving attention. Defiantly Bone outlined a candle and gave it a flame at the top like an inverted tear.

People were still rustling papers and an announcement was made that there would be a rather longer break for lunch than had been stated on the program, as some fresh information was to be given in the afternoon. Bone thought cynically, someone's forgotten something and they're having to rush it here for the afternoon session; brilliant, he thought. He knew exactly what he was going to do with the extra time.

He was genial to Blane, who, as the session broke up, diffidently said he had engaged to lunch with a Sussex man who shared his passion for computers. "No problem, Jack. I've a piece of official business to see to and I'll take Shay. Understand that I've made a scintillating joke about bits and bytes, and have a good lunch."

He could see that Blane feared he might not be back in time for the afternoon session. He wondered the same himself.

Shay was obviously delighted to be threading the London traffic in a taxi, eating a hot dog along with his Super, and Bone had the impression that he too was not fond of the claustrophobia-inducing atmosphere of conference rooms.

"We are off to see Clovis Clare and the lovely Miss Lennox," Bone told him.

"She scares me, sir." Shay appeared to enjoy the thought.

"She might give Dracula a moment's indigestion. But it is her boyfriend who has some explaining to do." Bone did some explaining himself, of Locker's errand, to bring Shay up to date, watching him take the point and thinking how simple it all seemed when it had worked out. He had seen once on TV a seeing-eye dog, reputed to have psychic powers, which had led his master on command straight—the wrong word in the circumstances—out of the center of Hampton Court maze. Now *that* was the kind of dog Grizel should have wished on him.

Clovis and Easter were, as their dutiful message through the police "presence" at Summerdown had said, clearing out Easter's flat. Clovis, harassed but dogged, was throwing everything irretrievably broken into cardboard cartons, as Easter brought Bone and Shay up the stairs. The window, as wide as it could go, made little difference to a powerful smell. Easter had been strafing the walls with disinfectant, marginally less nauseating than other odors pervading the place. She had spread plastic sheeting over the disemboweled sofa, and ushered them toward it. Her hair was snooded in purple silk, revealing that she had a classic Egyptian profile.

"Thought you were the insurance. They're sending someone round to make an assessment."

"Ron Dace ran amok all right," Bone said. "It's very nasty."

"It's a peculiar thing, though," she remarked. "It's a whole lot easier to face this now he's dead. Some of the offense has gone from it."

Clovis, in an orange teeshirt, sat dispiritedly on his heels among the cartons. He pushed his fingers through his hair leaving shreds of paper and foil and a feather or two, and said, "What's happened, Super? You look as if life's just been good for you."

Bone perched on the sofa arm. "Enough. It may be that you have been hoping we'd reach the right conclusions without the necessary help from you."

Clovis straightened up. "I've given you all the help I can!"

"I concede that you perhaps gave us all the help you felt able to give. Still, you concealed knowledge and you denied truth. You have been a most dedicated nuisance, Mr. Shelley."

Easter moved to stand near Clovis, and watched

them. She had a wet cloth she was absently passing from hand to hand; Bone wondered whether, if he harassed Clovis, he would get the cloth in his face and a swift kick, and he was not alone in so thinking. Shay wandered to a strategic point alongside.

Clovis shoved his hands in his pockets, hunched his shoulders and said, "What have I done?"

"You knew that your brother had been to Summerdown. You know why he killed himself. You went to intercept him at the garage, to talk to him again, but he killed himself as soon as he saw you. Given that it was a horrendous experience for you, denying it wasted a lot of our time. Ron Dace recognized you, and since you didn't mention at the inquest that you'd been there, he saw a chance to make money. He came here, and Miss Lennox saw him off."

There was a pause. They all looked at Clovis, who looked at the floor. After a long moment he took breath, put his head back and crossed his arms, gripping his elbows.

"Yes. Well. Okay. It was so foul I've not been thinking about it since. Lionel didn't tell me what he'd done. He didn't say anything clearly." He added apologetically, "Family failing. You see he didn't tell me what he'd done. When I got to Summerdown next day and they didn't answer, I knew. I couldn't imagine—I didn't think he'd done that. It wasn't until he was driving away from the Clinic that I really got that he meant to kill himself. I was slow. Stupefied . . . I've been looking at it since and wonder why I was so slow. I even asked him *Where do you mean to go?* and he said I was a fool. He said I should do as he was going to do, that people with our taint ought not to pollute society. He talked about tainted blood, he said his whole life was one unspeakable filth and falseness. He said Mrs. Mallard had enlightened him about something even our father had sheltered us from knowing."

He stopped. The rapid monotone slowed down now.

"I didn't ask him anything. I said I was stupefied. He told me our mother hadn't denied it.

"So I knew he'd been to Summerdown again. And then when I'd seen—after—at the garage—"

He took a difficult, shuddering breath. Easter, with no change of countenance, balled the cloth up and wrung its neck.

"I did my best not to think about it. And my best is good. You can ignore things until they—it's a mechanism, like putting them behind a glass wall. Only I thought I must see Miranda. She'd a right to know about Lionel's death if Kay thought she could stand it. So we went down there. And then when we got there I knew what he'd done."

He shook his head violently.

"It's so—as if he had the right! Judging, deciding, I don't understand. But I thought, after that," he looked toward Easter, "if we went and lived there, it would mean the place wasn't spoiled in spite of him."

Easter nodded. Then she turned on her heel and marched to the bathroom, chucking the cloth into a corner on her way. She crouched and fished behind the bath. Bone, wondering what strange rite was in the making, saw her emerge with a bottle of Hennessy. She took off the top and sloshed a good slug into a plastic bathroom cup.

"Come on, Clovis." She held it before him. "You've been telling the truth. For you, major surgery."

He took it without hesitation and drank. Easter went back to the kitchen and returned with a chipped mug, a sugar bowl, and a jampot in the shape of an orange.

"Not for me," Bone said. She poured all the same, and held out the cup, gazing steadily under her brows.

"No party-poopers, Mr. Bone."

He took it and grinned. Shay said, "Only a small 'un, Miss Lennox. I mean it."

"One lump," she said, wetting the lower reaches of the sugar bowl. She drank jam herself, and turned to keep an eye on Clovis. "Mr. Bone. You seem of a sudden very clear on what happened. How come you knew? First it can't be Lionel and then it is."

"Miranda Shelley wrote that her son came to see her.

A child from the past, meeting her in the garden." He didn't say, for Clovis's sake, how it had come to him that morning, Lionel's face as he lay in the mortuary, Miranda's . . . their difference of coloring and of size apart, he was indeed her image. "She had asked him to come, but the meeting was not a happy one. When I knew that, and knew he'd been to Summerdown once at least, I pursued a different line. Enquiry this morning showed he was not at the Clinic when the house officer said he was. And we had three people concerned with him who did not speak, and who would protect him or his memory: Kay left no word, Adam and you would not say."

"Lionel told me, almost. He said, *I did what had to be done*. If you'd charged Adam with killing her, I would have had to say. I would have said it."

"You have to say one thing, at least, more. You say that Mrs. Mallard told your brother this. What precisely was it that he knew?"

Clovis looked down, swilling the last of the brandy in the cup. Then he drank it off. "If I've got a hereditary taint I'll have a vasectomy, not," and he flinched but went on, looking Bone in the eyes, "not cut my throat. I don't know more, but Mrs. Mallard does. If you buzz down to Pimlico now you'll find her bobbing and bleating round my father as she serves him lunch."

Bone stood up, putting his empty mug on the gaping screenless TV. "Yes, I shall do that."

"Is Adam all right?" Easter demanded.

"Yes. That reminds me that we have a couple of things from him that Mr. Shelley might like to have back. There's a key to one of the yard doors, and a very pretty and I'd say quite valuable Victorian necklace."

Clovis and Easter looked at each other. Clovis said, "Poor old Dad," and they began to laugh.

16

The lunchtime traffic crawled along the Embankment in fits and starts, at the mercy of traffic lights and giving Bone time to speculate on what Mrs. Mallard would say. He thanked Heaven that Blane, competent and meticulous, would be able to give him a thorough briefing on the conference if he missed any of it. Meanwhile, he considered Mrs. Mallard. He had already formed an impression of her as a sycophant and an eavesdropper. It did not seem to be stretching it too far to add *mischief-maker* to these accomplishments. He hoped she would be at home. It was not a good idea to alert anyone with a telephone call, the less time people had to prepare their ideas and edit their memories, the better.

As it turned out, Mrs. Mallard was at home, but only just.

After they had rung the bell, and watched the taxi-driver put up his flag and drive away, they had a wait which made Shay put his finger to the bell again. At last the door was opened by a flustered woman whom Bone thought he recognized, the middle-aged English rose who had been on Edwin Clare's arm at the inquest on his son. The rose's petals were crumpled now, even wind-dashed.

"What do you want? I'm sorry, this is a most inconvenient—"

"Police," said Bone, and flipped open the wallet with his card. She stared at it without reaction. From the far end of the narrow hall behind her came a sudden crash, and she jumped.

"May we see Dr. Clare's housekeeper, Mrs. Mallard? We—"

Another crash, and Edwin Clare's unattractive voice raised, expostulating. Without a word, the woman turned and hurried off down the hall. Bone followed at once, leaving Shay to shut the door.

The room at the back turned out to be a kitchen. The scene there was one that would have done excellently as a Victorian picture-that-tells-a-story, the title perhaps *The Housekeeper at Bay*. Edwin Clare, his tie crooked as though someone had seized him by it, was pressed against the wall as they came in, the English rose huddled protectively beside him. Facing them, with her back to the sink and within reach of a pine dresser—disastrously in reach, to go by the fragments of dishes lying at Edwin Clare's feet—was Mrs. Mallard. She acknowledged the police presence by a mere glance in their direction. They were at that moment, Bone felt, useful additions to her audience.

"So you've called the police, have you?" Mrs. Mallard panted, and the sound was as shocking as Queen Victoria throwing a fit. The pussycat bow of her gray silk blouse was undone and the streamers flapped as she lunged for another plate off the dresser. "To turn me out of the place I've made my own!"

Edwin Clare was, not for the first time, having problems with the women in his life. He, like Mrs. Mallard, seemed to think the police had not arrived by chance.

"Get rid of her," he hissed to Bone, edging the rose toward the door and Bone. "Get *rid* of her!"

"Get rid of her! That's my reward for all that I've done, is it?" Mrs. Mallard was holding a dinner plate, white with a blue and gold border, kin to those which had met an end at Dr. Clare's feet. She brandished it at her employer, who shrank, blocked from escape by his supportive fiancée and by the fact that Bone and Shay occupied the doorway. "Get rid of her? I look after you and your family in spite of everything" (in spite of what? wondered Bone) "and this is all my thanks! To be cast aside *like an old glove!*" She dashed the plate rather disappointingly at her own feet.

A pretty *active* old glove all the same, thought Bone. It was perhaps going to be ticklish questioning Mrs. Mallard at the present. Even being in the same room with her was taking on the aspect of one of the more dangerous spectator sports. He remembered the doting looks she had cast at Edwin Clare when he had last seen them. What he was seeing now was what he had imagined Adam's devotion to Miranda had become. Mrs. Mallard might have known her cue.

"I've given my *life-blood* to your family!" An unfortunate phrase, Bone thought; probably reminding everyone present of the late Miranda, Kay and Lionel, who had been more literal in this expenditure. "I would have accepted her as your wife—" the woman clutching Edwin's arm appeared more than a little stunned at this generosity—"but I cannot tolerate being dismissed as though I had meant *nothing* to you, as though I had not been a loyal *friend* to you, discreet and loyal *at all times.*"

Discreet about *what* was a question Bone would have liked to put to her, but she precluded any rational intervention with a staccato "And then this shock!"

Edwin, finding that Bone was not going to intervene or treat this incident as a domestic one and disarm Mrs. Mallard of the dinner service, attempted to do his own soothing here. "Mrs. Mallard, a friend, a friend of *course,* you've always been a valued friend, but I explained that Mrs. Beacon will not be needing a housekeeper after we are married. I did give you notice of this a week ago and you said nothing then."

Mrs. Mallard tried out a light shriek at this, and found it worked very well, forcing Edwin to step back on Shay's foot and evoking a faint echo from Mrs. Beacon.

"Nothing! I said nothing because *my heart was bleeding!* Your son asked me what was wrong, why I was so *white* and I told him. I had been spurned, cast off—" Mrs. Mallard hesitated among her arsenal of clichés to find one that would achieve the maximum effect. The son mentioned must be Lionel, Clovis not being in the habit of visiting his father unless he had to, and *a week ago* would place it the day before Lionel's suicide. He spoke, with the hope of turning the flood of her recriminations to his advantage.

"What did Lionel Clare say, Mrs. Mallard?"

She seemed rather pleased to be asked, and tossed her head almost skittishly at Bone.

"Oh, of course he stood up for his *father,* as he called him! I soon put him right, I can tell you."

"What do you mean?" Edwin said shortly. "What else would he call me?"

Mrs. Mallard snorted. "Oh, I've always admired you for it, bringing up those two as your own, but it was time someone told Lionel the truth." She had clearly enjoyed being the one to do it. "I told him he was the child of Miranda Shelley and that dreadful brother of hers. *The child of incest!*"

So it was out, what Bone had guessed quicker than Clovis seemed to have done, the thing that had driven the fastidious, the neurotic Lionel Clare to murder and to suicide. Mrs. Mallard could be proud of her loyalty and discretion.

Edwin Clare was stuttering with indignation—"Nothing of the sort! Who told you that?"

"You did, Dr. Clare. You told me yourself. You came back from lunch one day not long ago and took me into your confidence"—She simpered in retrospect and, looking down demurely, saw that her bow was undone and began to tie it with fussy precision. "You told me that your wife was lost to you from the moment her brother returned." She held up a finger as he tried to speak, and rode his voice down. "I remember the very words: lost to you, you said. *She was never mine again.* You said you loved her then so much that you would have done

197

anything in the world to keep her and that you fathered the children only for her sake.'' Edwin attempted to interrupt and she shook the raised finger at him. ''Your own words! *I thought she would take the children when she went,* you said, and that if her brother had taken her on he ought to have taken responsibility for them as well. You're not going to deny you said just that, Dr. Clare! I have an excellent memory, as you well know.''

Bone believed her. What she had just said had all the flavor of Edwin's particular pomposity, very likely emphasized at the time by the effects of that lunch he had come back from. At the same time, he saw how ambiguous the words were, how easily misinterpreted by a mind avid for the worst.

Edwin was struggling for speech. Releasing the knot of his tie seemed to help and he burst out with, ''You completely misunderstood! When I said 'fathered' I did not mean giving them my *name,* I meant *giving them to her.* I insisted on her having those children to take her mind off that wretched brother of hers. I thought that motherhood would bring her to her senses. She didn't want them! And she took her revenge on me by dumping them on me when she ran away.''

Does he know what a bastard he sounds? thought Bone, watching Mrs. Mallard put her hands to her mouth with a look of dismay. Poor Lionel, poor Clovis, even more helpless pawns in the power game of marriage than many children are. It's surprising Lionel lasted as long as he did; and remarkable that Clovis has come out of it with the humor and resilience that evidently attracts Easter. She'll be the saving of him.

With this optimistic thought, he was able to step forward, take Mrs. Mallard's arm as she stood, shocked and beginning to gibber protests and excuses, and lead her past Dr. Clare and his wife-to-be into the hall. There, she seized her opportunity and sank, weeping, onto Bone's chest.

When they finally got away, leaving Mrs. Mallard climbing the stairs to pack her bags to a running accompaniment of hiccups, and Dr. Clare's fiancée busy clearing up the kitchen thus resigned to her use, they walked toward the main road and a possible taxi to carry them back the short distance to the conference. As they went, Sergeant Shay said, "You ever read *Alice in Wonderland,* sir? I kept thinking of it back there. All they were short of was a pig and someone sneezing in that kitchen. And I wonder if that Mrs. Mallard has thought of all the misery she's caused."

Bone was of the opinion that, if she did, she would consider the people who suffered the misery to have deserved it richly. Then he wondered how much of the world's misery was caused by those who made vital decisions about what was right for others.

By the end of the conference, Bone was beginning to wish he had eaten more than one hot dog in the taxi going to Easter Lennox's flat. His stomach muttered comments on the guidelines that were set out for future investigations; in other words, Bone thought, when the next poor victim turns up. He watched Blane, writing, fill page after page with notes, knowing he would have to read them. The tragi-comic lunch interlude had not lasted long enough to make him late for the delayed afternoon session, but his mind had reached the stage it often did after the solving of a case, of a weariness that made him realize how much energy went into thinking. At least the statements that would have to be got and read over and signed were not his pigeon.

Only now when he was beginning to relax did he recall with a lift of spirits that Grizel was coming to dinner tonight. He glanced at his watch under cover of the table and cursed the speaker, a little man with a low, droning voice and a habit of pausing and then repeating himself. Mrs. Ames had left some chicken salad from Marks and Spencer in the fridge for his supper: "There's enough for two! I keep forgetting your daughter isn't here." He could get an appropriate bottle from the off-license on the corner; there might be time to chill it before she arrived. *Get on with it, man.*

He fell asleep in the car taking them back to Tunbridge Wells, and woke with a stiff neck and dry mouth as they were coming down the Pembury Road. Blane was pointing out the improvement in general visibility caused by the October gale of '87 to an unconvinced-looking Shay. It was muggy again, after the air-conditioned chill of the conference room, and his clothes felt sticky. He was glad he had not been wearing his best suit . . . there should be time to shower and change before Grizel came. First, though, he must call at the station and collect Locker's promised report on the interview with Dr. Michelle Morrison.

He was still reading this, in a fresh shirt and summer slacks, when the doorbell went and he ran down to let Grizel in. She was wearing a black slinky dress that startled him, as she usually appeared in teeshirts and trousers. Black should have made him feel cool, but it didn't.

"Nice earrings." They were hoops of silver set with little glittering stones, he supposed not diamonds.

"Glad you like them, Robert. I'll let you know when you've got to jump through them. What's for dinner?"

"What a practical woman you are. It would be wrong to lead you to suppose we are going to have smoked salmon and champagne—there wasn't a shop with smoked salmon for sale at this time." He put Locker's transcript aside on the table and went to the fridge.

"Robert! There *is* champagne! Have you caught your villain?"

"The poor devil's dead and buried, I'm afraid. Well out of it." He wrestled with the cork and scored a shot on the ceiling. Grizel swiftly advanced her glass and watched the foam froth over the edge and subside.

"Are you always sorry for the villains, Robert? Do I see one of these modern coppers who think everyone's a victim of society?" She raised her glass and clinked it to his. "I drink to your success, now and future."

"And I'll just drink to you," said Bone gallantly, with a wish that he had something clever to say. He should have remembered people's fondness for drinking toasts with champagne. It fizzed and tingled in his mouth and made him want to laugh, more from relief than anything. Not till then had he known how the case had been riding him, an Old Man of the Sea heavier and heavier on his back.

Grizel was prowling about the kitchen, the skirts of her black dress showing an understandable inclination to cling to her legs as she moved. She bent to stroke the cat, who having finished his meal was lounging on his beanbag and licking his wrists. She spoke over her shoulder.

"You've not answered my question, Robert: about the villains."

Bone was busy putting bread to toast for the salmon mousse. Mrs. Ames had thoughtfully provided the mousse for the weekend, knowing it was a favorite of his, and it was coming in very handy for starters. He arranged bread on the grill and thought before replying. He could hear, above the noise of the cooker, Ziggy purring.

"I don't think I am by any means always sorry for villains. Nor do I think society is responsible for them. Mind you, *somebody* is. My poor villain this time was the product of what had happened to him, all right. Neither his father nor his mother wanted him and in the end, he took it out on her."

Grizel twirled round by the window and her skirt affectionately followed. "You mean that the woman at Summerdown was killed by her son?"

Bone juggled the toast over. "That's what I mean. Not pretty, is it?"

Grizel was standing behind him now, drinking her champagne. He could smell her scent. "Odd. I was going to say: we're more used to parents killing their children these days. It's as you were saying this morning, Robert, very Ancient Greek. But what a horrible thing."

Bone brought the toast to the table, and Grizel lifted the folder to make room. "Still more homework? Not the next case already?"

Bone put one of the ramekins before her on a saucer;

on its surface perched a battered little sprig of parsley. He had failed to keep some fresh, as Cha did always in a mug; he felt incompetent. He put the folder on the trolley by the door.

"No, still this one. The statement taken this morning by Steve at the Austin Clinic. Your ex-pupil Michelle Morrison, the house-dog there."

Grizel, buttering toast, looked up. "Hadn't she made a statement already? And at the inquest? When I last saw her, she was very upset about that consultant's suicide; she thought a lot of him."

"Enough to lie about him, anyway," said Bone, starting on the mousse. It did not distract him from watching the elegance of her wrist as she ate.

"Lie about him? To protect him in some way?"

"Rather the opposite, if anything."

Grizel leant sideways and rapped Bone on the knuckles with her spoon. "Spit it out, Blabbermouth."

He wiped the salmon mousse from his hand with mock-elaborate care before he replied. The action reminded him of Lionel Clare's horror of pollution. Witnesses had testified to his invariably wearing gloves out of doors, where contact with unclean objects must constantly threaten. He had worn gloves in the car, silk-backed kid, and he must have been wearing gloves even on that hot evening when he visited his mother for the second and last time.

"Your young friend gave him a false alibi, the night he killed his mother."

"Why? Did she know what he'd done?"

Bone collected the ramekins, dumped them on the draining-board and set about arranging the chicken salad on a large blue dish. "Not a clue. It seems he'd been fretting about the place all day, and seemed suddenly to make up his mind, she said. He asked her to cover for him—he was on night call and sleeping at the Clinic—and said something private and urgent had come up and he'd be back in an hour or so." Bone put a plate before Grizel and offered her the salad. "Damn, I forgot to heat the rolls."

"Never mind that, just give me one." She looked up, with her quick lively smile. "A cool roll. Thank you . . . He had private and urgent business? Would that be murdering his mother?"

"Private and urgent enough. I don't suppose he went to Summerdown meaning to kill. He needed to confront her, I believe, with something that had been driving him wild to think about, and when he got the wrong answers it was her bad luck—or his—that there was a weapon to hand. No, Dr. Morrison thought he was off to see a woman. He'd broken up with his secretary the week before and she fancied it was some new young woman he was going to see, the reason, in fact, for the break-up. No one pleased him for long; they made the mistake of being human."

"Celia, Celia, Celia shits," said Grizel, eating salad.

"I beg your pardon?" Amused but startled, Bone regarded her demure bent head.

"The refrain to a poem, to a girl called Celia, by Dean Swift. He had the same problem with women: they were all dismayingly human." She sent a peanut coated in salad dressing skittering across the table, tried to field it, and heard it hit the floor. Immediately there were sounds of Ziggy doing his best to eat it. She said, "I thought the papers said Dr. Clare had taken his life because a patient had died?"

Bone buttered his cool roll and nodded. "But a mistake was made. She made it while he was out—pretended to go and consult him as she was supposed to do, and came back with a dosage apparently on his authority."

"I see." She had put down her fork and looked at him. She should, he thought, always wear black to set off her eyes and hair. "That was why she didn't talk when he was dead."

"Oh, he'd taken responsibility already, that morning when he came on the wards. A farewell act of generosity, I suppose; he told her that, as he'd been away when he should have been there, he was in fact responsible. After all, he knew he wasn't going to be around for it to make a difference to him, and he also knew that Morrison couldn't afford another mistake."

"Another?"

"Last year before she came to the Clinic she'd been in trouble over a man brought into Casualty at the hospital where she was then. Smelling of drink and staggering. She'd just come from stitching up a knife wound, and diagnosed him as drunk." Bone poured champagne. "He was sent home with what turned out later to be a fractured skull and serious internal injuries. His family sued."

Grizel picked up the glass and held it, thinking.

"Poor Michelle. She'll be in a terrible state now. I must try to see her tomorrow if she's off duty at any time. She told me she doesn't usually stop till midnight, when she stands with her feet in a bowl of cold water and hopes she won't be called in the night."

"Doctors, air traffic controllers, police, Cabinet ministers; all having to make decisions of importance when they're in deep fatigue. Steve says she was in a state of semi-collapse when he spoke to her. She may have been relieved to get it off her mind. Guilt is intensely exhausting."

Grizel sat thinking, and then roused herself to drink champagne. "The day's getting cooler at last, Robert. I don't know how you manage."

Bone knew she was not referring to heat. It was also getting dark and he fetched matches to light the candles he had put on the table which, together with linen napkins, raised supper to a higher level more worthy of Grizel. They sat and watched the flames waver and catch hold, and Bone did not tell her what he was thinking.

17

Michelle went methodically about the flat, tidying. There was at last time for it. She wouldn't want people to think she lived in a mess like this, even though she did. Her grandmother had told her, quite seriously, that you should always wear clean underwear in case you got knocked over in the street and taken to hospital. Working in one, she had seen the sort of little things people did worry about: old Mrs. Shulman racked with misery because the moustache she usually plucked was growing and her hand, paralyzed by her stroke, couldn't manage any more to present a decent image to the world. The problem was, Michelle had empathized too much with her patients; Dr. Clare had warned her about it. He himself never seemed to feel a thing but it had got at him in the end. He was at peace now.

The idea was seductive, like a hot bath at the close of an exhausting day. She put the last cushion straight and went to find the pills. She drank the water and got them down in the bathroom, looking at her face in the mirror with curiosity, at the face of herself doing this thing, but it seemed to belong to another person. She rinsed the tumbler and put it back, and then went to lie on the bed, to wait. There was no regret, only relief; you didn't have to live with your mistakes, after all.

*   *   *

The phone broke into Bone's dreams as a giant hornet trying to get into his ear. Reaching out, he knocked a cassette of Rossini's *Petite Messe* to the floor and spilt water from the bedside tumbler. His voice was blurred and his eyes still shut when he said, "Hallo?"

"Daddy! You weren't asleep? It's half past nine!"

He woke instantly. "Cha! Anything wrong?"

"Well, just a bit. Oh, *I'm* all right, it's Mrs. Grant who isn't. She slipped on the wet duckboard outside the tent last night and cracked her wrist. Mr. Grant took her to hospital and they put it in plaster and everything but this morning she says she's sorry but she really feels too awful to go on. She's shaken and it hurts and she feels sick. So we're coming back today, Mr. Grant's loading the car now, and Grue."

"What rotten luck. Tell her how sorry I am; and sorry about your holiday, pet. You've had quite a bit of it, though; and it'll be nice to see you again. When do you think you'll get here?"

"Oh, some time this evening. Mr. Grant isn't sure when, as he means to take it easy for her sake; and she spelled him on the way here and he's driving all the way now. But don't worry, I've got my key if you're not in . . . You're not *ill,* are you?"

"No, of course not. Why?"

"Well, not being awake at this time. I just hoped I'd catch you before you went off, I don't like ringing the station, they're so official."

"I simply overslept." Bone tried not to think about why; in conjunction with Charlotte it was out of place. "I can hear Ziggy shrieking for his breakfast. I dare say he can hear me talking."

"Darling Ziggy! How is he? There was a lovely cat just like a pirate with a patch over one eye at one of the farms we got eggs from and he made me absolutely long for Ziggy. Has he missed me?"

"I can't say he's gone off his food."

"Oh, I must go, Grue's making faces and I think Mr. Grant wants to get going, see you, Daddy, kiss, kiss."

Bone heard the click and buzz.

He got up, discovered his dressing gown was, for some reason, under the bed; picked up the cassette, mopped the water with the hem of his dressing gown and went to feed Ziggy. The house still seemed full of Grizel's presence; very likely her scent hung on the air. He remembered going slowly down the stairs with her, and watching her drive away, very late last night, or very early this morning. As he was opening a tin and Ziggy was walking on his feet, he thought about a number of things: if there would be enough food for the weekend, whether he was glad or disappointed that Cha was coming home a week early. Seeing Grizel would be more difficult. No more tête-à-têtes here at his flat . . . He remembered the blond cropped head, and smiled involuntarily as he bent to put Ziggy's dish down on the lino.

Grizel had already told him that she didn't particularly care for the villagers at Adlingsden monitoring her visitors. "You are grateful for Neighborhood Watch when you're living alone and frightened of burglars, but not so keen when they're timing how long it takes the milkman to deliver." He himself had seen Mrs. Parton on more than one occasion manicuring the leaves on her side of the perfectly kept box hedge. She had greeted him civilly each time but with a scanning glance that had made him feel she'd shape well as a witness. Unfortunate that both school teachers and police were in the public eye, expected to lead lives of unparalleled regularity. Of course, marriage would act like Persil on anything that had gone before, but marriage was something he was not sure either he or Grizel really wanted yet.

He grimaced at himself in the bathroom mirror as he shaved. Pulling flesh taut made one realize that age had pulled it slack a little already: gravity at work until it finally dragged you into the ground. Age battered you, took away your confidence, that wonderful confidence of youth that will try anything once. Grizel had tried marriage once with Lewis Shaw; the experience had not left her eager for more commitment. As for his own feelings, he was perhaps unwilling to examine them; the raw wound of Petra's death was now a scar sensitive to touch. He had the illogical impression that having an affair with Grizel was less unfaithful to Petra's memory than marriage would be. And there was Cha. He hadn't the faintest idea of how she would take to a stepmother, even one she liked as much as she liked Grizel. A favorite teacher at school is one thing. A stepmother in your home is quite another. You can like your biology teacher enormously, but not care for her to marry your father, whose attention until now you have exclusively enjoyed.

Bone splashed cold water on his face and reached for the towel. Once more the phone rang while he had his eyes shut.

"Steve—I'm on my way—"

"Bad news, I'm afraid, sir. Dr. Morrison has taken an overdose. Cleaner found her this morning in her flat. D.O.A."

Those bleak initials. Bone remembered a pleasant-faced, rather thin girl with soft brown hair, glasses and tired eyes, worried and tense as she answered the coroner's questions. Doctors had the highest rate for suicide and were usually efficient at it.

"Hell."

"She was upset when I talked to her," said Locker.

"I know damn well you didn't harass her. Look, Steve, she was over-worked and over-anxious. She couldn't stand having made another mistake."

"Having to admit perjury—"

"And for Lionel Clare of all people. Don't blame yourself, Steve. That's a luxury well beyond our means. I'll be over in half an hour."

Mrs. Mallard's score had gone up. A murder and three suicides from her burst of spite and injured pride. The stone cast into the water sent ripples spreading far out of sight.

Clovis came through the hall at Summerdown, out of the sunlight at the back. He wore a green knitted silk shirt Bone had last seen on a dummy in the gallery.

"Oh, hallo. Is it warrant time for somebody?"

"Time for a bit more truth, Mr. Shelley."

Clovis looked at him, paused, then said, "Better come through to the morning-room." His voice was strained. The prospect of truth might always be a daunting one to him.

Following him, Bone wondered if it was a good idea for Clovis to live here, in this house of tragedy; would he stay here? It was to be hoped he didn't intend to mimic Miranda's escape, her creation of a world of her own here. Of course Easter was no Kay; she wouldn't collaborate in withdrawals and fantasies.

"Earl Whitewick's here. In the gallery with Easter. He's come up with a great scheme for this place . . ."

Bone noticed the absence of lay-figures in the morning-room, and wondered where they had gone. Not, he hoped, cleared from the house for good. Clovis saw his glance round and looked enquiring.

"The dressed-up companions," Bone said.

"All in the gallery for the moment." Clovis sat on the end of the inglenook settle, and Bone went to the window and turned. Sun gilded the creamy panelling, flared on Clovis's head.

"I heard yesterday," Bone said, "from your father and Mrs. Mallard, what it was that she told your brother Lionel. She was wrong. She misunderstood something your father said to her."

Clovis leant back and shut his eyes. In the quiet, a wood-pigeon burred its double note, a spade rang rhythmically somewhere in the garden, and voices upstairs discussed idly.

Bone said reasonably, "You might as well come out with it all. We shall need a proper statement later and the truth will have to be told, in some decorously covered form perhaps, at the inquest. What we know is that Lionel had time to come here that night, and that he had been here before. Your mother would have let him in."

Clovis, without opening his eyes, said in a flat voice, "That's what I think happened. Well, I know it did."

He sat up, came to his feet and walked away across the room, clasping his hands behind his neck to pull his head down.

"He didn't tell me he'd done it. He didn't say what he'd done. At the Clinic he told me what that obscene old busybody said; and at the time I nearly laughed—it sounded so over-the-top; theatrical: *Dr. Clare is not your father. I had it from his own lips that you are that woman's children by her own brother. Children of incest!*"

He turned and flung out his hands, shrugging. "I said *Don't be a fool.* I meant it's no big deal. Even if it's true it hasn't done us any harm. But Lio was past listening, and—well—when I got here I knew why."

He gazed out of the window. "It was like the stop of everything. I'd just found them only a year or so ago and they were so happy here . . . and I'd been starved of her all my life. It was all gone. Only Easter; she kept the world going until I could sort of get back into it again.

"I knew it was Lionel had done it. I knew he'd been here because he said *Our mother admitted it too.*" Clovis looked at Bone, not seeing him. "I sat in the Clinic car park for a bit and then he came out and flung into his car and drove off like some bat out of hell. He drove so badly I thought he would hit something before long, and I went after him. I think I felt he needed keeping an eye on; or I could talk to him again. I tried to. It was stupid, going up like that after the carwash. His car came out all gleaming, and he saw me."

The whites showed almost all round Clovis's eyes as if he mirrored that glance; or saw, here and now, what had followed.

"I tried to open the door, but my hand slipped, it only half opened and the car was still moving. And Lionel, his arm moved and, well, his head fell back."

"And you ran."

Clovis gave a brief quick nod. "When I was driving

210

I felt wet on my ankle, and his blood was on my shoes. . . ."

From upstairs came a cheerful ringing call. "Hi there! How about coffee for the workers?" To Bone's surprise Clovis called back "Yeah!" and began to move toward the door. Easter had got him very well trained indeed. The interruption, too, was obviously welcome. It might be that Clovis had come out with all the truth he could handle.

"Is it all right if I make coffee? Will you have some, Super? Do you want to know any more?"

To solve his hesitation between obliging Bone and obeying Easter, Bone came with him to the small kitchen, a room lined with cupboards, its tall window made dark by pyracanthus crowding outside. Bone sat on the cushioned Windsor chair before the fireplace, as Clovis got the Primus going and put the kettle on.

"If I can live here," Clovis said, setting out china and reaching the Gold Blend jar from the cupboard, "we'll need electricity in this room at least. Earl is full of generous ideas and bogus arguments about proper security alarms being in his own interest; he wants to make the place into a sort of Whitewick exhibition house, and I'm trying to be realistic." He leant back on the cupboard and said, "I'd like this place to be mine as they wanted. To be alive. So a compromise with Earl's ideas seems as good a way as any. He doesn't think it would demand much of us: groups of architecture buffs by appointment. The figures, the companions you call them, I like that—in proper clothes in the rooms; hope Mrs. Perceval can take it. And the Whitewick Foundation would keep the fabric in repair, which I can't do on the income that they left."

The kettle began to hum.

"Superintendent—"

"Mr. Shelley?"

"Is that true? Are you sure old Mallard was wrong?"

"Your father left no doubt about it."

Abruptly, Clovis swung out of the room. Bone heard him fling up a window and whistle. A distant shout answered, and Clovis returned. He checked on the kettle and said, "Adam has a different story. I think I can get him to tell you."

He picked a small brown teapot from the shelf. "He doesn't like coffee."

"If you're making tea," Bone hinted. Giving a preoccupied grin, Clovis emptied coffee granules from one cup into the jar, and dusted it out with a teacloth.

"It's bitterly ironic if Lio believed a story that wasn't true. But anyway you must hear—hallo, Adam."

At the doorway, panting from his run, Adam peered between the swathes of his hair, a red setter to the life. "My God, you're fast," said Clovis, impressed.

"I ran."

"You remember Mr. Bone . . . Adam has a house down the garden, away in the trees there. It was derelict when he came back, and he mended it. He helped Kay with all sorts of jobs around the place, and with the garden."

"Mr. Whitewick wants to reinstate the garden," Adam said.

"And you're the only person who remembers how it was."

Adam shifted his feet modestly. He was nervous of Bone, glancing under his brows, and Clovis put out a hand, reassuring but almost proprietorial.

"Can't do without Adam. And I need your help now over something."

Throw the stick, Adam's face said, I'll fetch it.

Clovis took coffee and biscuits up to the planners in the gallery. He told Bone that Earl wanted Easter to help him with the definitive life of his grandfather.

They sat in the morning-room, Adam on the floor near to Clovis, nursing his large cup of tea. Clovis took hold of his shoulder and moved it to and fro. Adam did not look up, but Bone could see him relax.

"Adam wants to mend the tower door. Your lot told us to leave it alone, though. When will it be all right to mend it?"

"I'll let you know. I dare say it'd be all right today, but I don't want to tread on any administrative toes."

"Adam's a carpenter—gardener—bit of a smith—nothing he can't do." Clovis and Adam exchanged glances of pride and confidence. Bone thought that this first glimpse of Clovis with someone to look after was encouraging. Genuine red head ducked toward dyed one, and Clovis said in a private voice, "Could you do something hard? Could you say again for Mr. Bone what you said to me about my brother and Miranda?"

Adam bit his lips. He put down his cup and pressed his hands together. Clovis's grip did not lessen; the supple thumb massaged Adam's shoulder.

Taking breath, Adam glanced at Bone but he spoke to Clovis, hurried but hesitant, in pell-mell bursts.

"I was in the conservatory. I heard the doorbell and the knocker. Mr. Kay was in the garden. Riddling soil for the carrot-bed. I thought the person would go away when no one answered. They always do. But she opened the door. I thought it was you. I was going out to Mr. Kay but she came into the drawing-room, see, so I stopped still behind the creeper for they'd have seen me. He was the one that came before. That looked like her. I don't want to talk about this, Mr. Clovis."

"Please. Just tell us what you told me before."

"He said, *I came because I have to know,* and Miss Miranda said, *What is it? Ask me and go.* And he said, *I've been told something appalling. Vile. Unspeakable.* And Miss Miranda, she said, *Ah me, what act that thunders in the index?* And he said, but I thought he would choke, *That you and he, that your brother is my father.* Miss Miranda said nothing, a minute, then she said very loud, *You should be glad to have such a father!*"

"And then," Clovis said, as Adam rocked forward over his hands, "then it happened. It's all right, Adam. It's over."

"Never be over," said Adam to his knees.

"It will. It will. Just time. Things get better with time. It takes a long time," said Clovis, "but they do."

The swathes of hair went to and fro. "I let her die. I ran for Mr. Kay and I should've helped her." The voice was rising into that moan.

"No," Bone said decisively. "You couldn't have helped her. You did the right thing. If you'd tried to help, it might have hurt her."

Adam's head came up. Bone, with little idea whether or not it was true, spoke with authority. "Nothing you could do would have helped her, except bringing her brother. You did that."

Checking anxiously with Clovis, Adam saw him nod. "I told you; and now the policeman says so. You did the right thing. You did what she wanted." As Adam sighed, Clovis sat back and in an ordinary voice said, "I meant to ask you. We're going to need more lettuce."

"I'll get it." Adam climbed to his feet; pleased, distracted from the memory. "I'll get some and wash it. How many? Will two do?"

"Two, I should think. Thanks."

Adam set off for the door at a trot. Clovis said to Bone, "We couldn't do without Adam," and the long face turned to him and beamed. The dog had a new master.

They heard him go away through the conservatory.

"That's what he told me, word for word, yesterday."

Bone thought that Adam probably had an excellent aural memory, the memory of someone who for choice did not read but who could remember things heard.

"You say definitely that old Ma Mallard was wrong; and what Miranda said is ambiguous. Do you know, I'm quite sorry; I'd sooner have been Kay's son than Dad's. Still, it's obvious really. There are far too many of Dad's nasty little traits in me."

Bone did not say, *I'd noticed*. He had noticed, in Clovis today, a change from his former masterly passivity, in assuming responsibility for the house, even to a limited extent; and for Adam.

Clovis had assumed, of a sudden, a self-conscious air. "It's very likely better not to have double helps of

Shelley," he said. "Easter tells me the vasectomy I talked of is too late."

"Indeed?"

"Indeed. I've every reason now for wanting to keep Summerdown going—keep it in the family."

"Congratulations," said Bone.

He hoped Miranda would have liked there to be a child again, her own grandchild, happy at Summerdown.